CW01498681

The Three Wives
OF
CHARLIE MELLON

IN SEARCH OF LOST SOLES

The Three Wives

OF

CHARLIE MELLON

IN SEARCH OF LOST SOLES

IAN SIRAGHER

The
Book
Guild

First published in Great Britain in 2025 by
The Book Guild Ltd
Unit E2 Airfield Business Park,
Harrison Road, Market Harborough,
Leicestershire. LE16 7UL
Tel: 0116 2792299
www.bookguild.co.uk
Email: info@bookguild.co.uk
X: @bookguild

The manufacturer's authorised representative in the EU
for product safety is Authorised Rep Compliance Ltd,
71 Lower Baggot Street, Dublin D02 P593 Ireland
(www.arccompliance.com)

This work is entirely fictitious and bears no resemblance to any persons living or dead.

Typeset in 11pt Minion Pro

Printed and bound in Great Britain by 4edge Limited

ISBN 978 1835741 931

British Library Cataloguing in Publication Data.
A catalogue record for this book is available from the British Library.

To Claudine, without whom Charlie would never have been born, let alone give a story of his own.

ONE

Today was always going to be… 'challenging'; that might have been a good word for it, but it turns out that 'catastrophic' and 'calamitous' are earlier in the dictionary for a reason.

If you need a starting date, then I'd say it was the 5th of October when life flicked a small stone of causation sliding down the hill of fate. And just forty-two days later, I'm buried somewhere inside a snowball of consequences and about to cannon through the hallowed halls of Ipswich Crown Court.

If you think that sounds bad, all I can tell you is, actually, I should be somewhere else. I should be facing down my nemesis in a Ragnarök battle that will decide if I lose my house and maybe even my wife.

Yet here I am, stuck between the dock and a hard place.

But, already, you're probably feeling a bit overwhelmed, so let's take a step back. I'm going to rewind the clock to a simpler time when all I had to worry about was where were the missing one thousand right-footed Adidas trainers, and what was I going to do with fifty tubs of liquid silicone? Oh, and whether the kitchen had renovated itself in my absence.

It was my unexpected meeting with a deer on the evening of the 5th of October that led to this particular Den Newman.

I'm not talking Bambi; I'm talking a Jaws of a beast, probably called Donner *and* Blitzen.

On 'the night in question', as PC Sewell is undoubtedly going to call it, I was proceeding southerly, down from Cretingham, where my field of Xmas trees is growing. I'm moving at a speed *'consistent with the time of day and road conditions'*. Then, this Prancer comes bounding out of the tree line like Elmer Fudd is chasing him.

So, I gun the engine of my van.

For why did I speed up? Because if I brake, old Comet is going to leap, catch on the middle of the road barrier, and join me in the cab. Now, I already have a half-finished Pot Noodle and a scribbled list of kitchen parts sitting on the passenger seat; I do not have room for Prancer.

So, yes, bizzies off a spade time. I put my foot to the floor, and zip past Dancer quicker than a dose of salts through a fasting guru.

Which was all fine and dandy, there should have been just the tiniest smell of burnt rubber to mark my dodge with death. Then I see PC Sewell standing by the side of the road and pointing the business end of a radar gun in my general direction, and the threads in that part of my story start to unravel.

No, I didn't bother to stop. I either was or wasn't going to get a ticket, and stopping to chat wasn't going to change anything. Of course, I sort of knew I was picking up speed on the tricky slopes of 'whatever next?' but instead of worrying, my thoughts turned, as they always do in times of crisis, to my wife, Eileen.

There's something Baby Spice about Eileen, if at twenty-nine you can still make that comparison. Also, Eileen has dark shoulder-length hair and isn't quite so skinny, and she prefers jeans to a miniskirt. However, one thing they have in common is they can't sing and are crap at dancing. Which is two things.

Ah, but where they overlap perfectly, where the old Venn diagram is just a single circle, is that infectious *joie de vivre*. Like Emma Bunton, Eileen has a laugh that starts as a chuckle, then builds, and ends up taking over her whole body. You can just see the sun shining out of her when that happens.

Oh, I love her, did I mention that? She's the best thing that's happened to me in my thirty-five years of life on this planet.

Actually, I need to jump back a bit, to a couple of weeks before the deer incident.

Picture it. I'm sitting on a kitchen stool, coffee in hand and an Eileen signature bacon and egg breakfast sandwich on the fold-up table in front of me. It's amazing what she can do with a two-ring gas stove and an air fryer.

My lovely wife and I are talking about two things: the kitchen and The Letter.

"So," she says, looking at the kitchen, or at least the space where the kitchen will eventually be. "A good day to pull out the rest of the old worktops, do you think?"

My focus isn't with her, it's on The Letter.

I can tell, by the fact that the envelope is brown, that this missive is one of the universe's causal forces. That conviction is reinforced by the letters JCSB and the black crown, printed on the front. JCSB stands for Jury Central Summoning Bureau, and I'm not going to mansplain what *that* means. I show it to Eileen, who stops going on about the kitchen long enough to read it.

"Maybe I can get a deferral. What do you think?" I ask.

Eileen gives me a look, which somehow takes in the kitchen as well.

"You know what Ben Franklin said, about never putting off until tomorrow—"

"Yes, right," I reply, "that's the same Ben Franklin who nearly got electrocuted by being in a thunderstorm at just the wrong time."

We pause for a coffee-slurping impasse. But I'm thinking, calculating.

Me, you see, you wouldn't guess, but I'm a believer in the old wu-wei. I know, not much of a call for Daoism in Stowmarket, but 'little of' does not mean 'none'. Wu-wei, as my dad used to say, is about knowing when to act, and when not to.

So, right now, I'm trying to figure out not simply what to do, but when not to do it.

It's not that I have any problem with doing my civic duty and sitting on a jury. At this particular moment, though, I can't spare the time.

For why? For because, as I mentioned earlier, I'm looking for one thousand Adidas sports trainers. Right-foot trainers, to be more precise.

There, look, there it is again. I put my best foot forwards and walk straight into the newly poured cement of detail. I have to explain.

Vietnam is not Germany. That might seem obvious and unrelated, but I promise, the sludgy tracks of exposition will reach the dry path of understanding.

Back at the end of 2010, nearly half of all Adidas trainers were made in Germany. Then, some senior purchasing director discovered Vietnam. Already you are running ahead of me, already you can see the humanitarian decision of the Adidas management team to bring work to the poor people of Hanoi.

So, quite quickly, a good deal of the manufacturing equipment once sitting in expensive factories in the Ruhr is shipped out to less expensive ones in Hanoi. That is capitalism in action and there's nothing we can do about it. Someone's Xmas bonus relied on those factories moving, and we can't stand in the way of bonus, can we?

Of course, when you set something new up, things go wrong before they go right. And that's exactly what happened. For a short while things did not go right at all. Someone pushed a wrong button, or wasn't able to translate German to Vietnamese, I don't know. The outcome was five hundred pairs of trainers that weren't; pairs, that is.

When I said things didn't go right, I meant it. All one thousand trainers of a particular batch were for the left foot.

Now, the last eclair of detail in this cream-tea of reportage.

You know where Stowmarket is, right? Stowmarket is approximately thirty miles from Felixstowe. Felixstowe is where fifty percent of all the containers that come into the UK arrive. That is a big number.

And, yes, you guessed. After a ten thousand sea mile journey, a certain Maurice P Elsworthy, importer extraordinaire, found himself with a load of trainers that, until we really become serious about Paralympics, aren't much good to him. He decided to cut his losses, claim a refund from Adidas, and sell the trainers at a dockside auction.

And that is how I became the owner of one thousand left-foot Adidas trainers; at the princely price of fifty pence each.

I know what you're thinking. I know exactly what you're thinking because Eileen thought the same, and she's not backwards in coming forwards when it comes to letting me know her thoughts.

Wu-wei, always the wu-wei.

You see, I'm betting that that factory didn't just make one thousand left-foot trainers. I'm betting that they packed them wrong. Someone pushed the incorrect sorting button, a fancy metal gate got stuck, they don't have left and right in Vietnam, I don't know. But I'm betting that sometime, hopefully sometime soon, five hundred pairs of right-foot Adidas trainers are going to appear on the dock at Felixstowe, and that's when I'll strike.

I'm sure, it's almost certain, probable at least. Otherwise, I'll think of something else. There must be a use for one thousand perfect condition left-foot trainers. Surely.

Now you understand why I can't just rush off for jury service. Because every day, every hour, I need to be watching the Felixstowe Dock 'Unclaimed and Damaged Stock' auction website. I need to see if my ship has come in, whether the boot is on the other foot, whether things have turned out *all right*. You get my drift.

If you're a nine-to-fiver, then this probably all sounds a bit left-field. Me though, I'm what you would call a serial entrepreneur. I've got my Christmas trees up at Cretingham; I do markets where I sell classic (for which, read expensive) LPs and CDs; that sort of thing. And, yes, I wheel and deal, buy a little something here, sell it there. No nine-to-five for me. These trainers, they are going to be what *makes my year*. You wait and see.

The trainers, then, they are mostly what is on my mind this morning, and of course, when I am going to get on with the kitchen. Okay, get *started* on the kitchen.

Eileen, looking as beautiful as ever with her tousled hair and measuring stare, passes me a second coffee as I click on the auction website on my laptop. I start scrolling down the short-hand codes and letters that might point to my trainers.

From the heavy silence emanating in waves from Eileen, I realise I'd better pick up the point about the kitchen.

"Yes, maybe. Though I have to…" I say, definitely not committing.

The thing is, I do have other projects on. I'm going to have to plant my garlic bulbs soon, and there is an interesting-looking house clearance in Claydon I want to sniff around.

I'm trying to keep my head down as I talk, but I can't. Our fingertips touch as Eileen gives me the mug, and I lean over and steal a kiss. She doesn't mind; she never does.

Then there's a change on my phone: the little email counter number increases. Like all of us, I get a lot of emails. Unlike many people, I love it. I'm always drawn to them. You never know what they are going to bring. I like that in life, not knowing what is going to happen next. Which, overall, is just as well, as I seem to have quite a few 'whatever nexts' and 'who would have thunked its' in my life.

Eileen wriggles around one of the unopened boxes to get to the dishwasher. Checking the two rubber pipes are still leak-free is so much easier now that I've pulled the machine away from the wall.

I click on the email icon and up it pops. The first thing I notice is the name, her maiden name, Claire Faye. The next surprise is the subject:

"Can we meet?"

For the vaguest half a second, I think about not telling Eileen, but only for that fraction of a moment.

"Hmm?" I say, a 'you might not like this but at least I'm telling you' sort of hmm.

Eileen knows my noises, she knows *all* my noises, if you get my drift. "Hmm?" she says, eyebrows going up in the way that just makes me want to go over and kiss her again. Five years married, and it feels like five days.

"Hmm, as in Claire... Faye," I say, angling the phone towards her.

"Claire?" Now her eyebrows come down. "Your ex? What does she want?"

That, as they say, is the sixty-four-thousand-dollars question.

Claire and I have an *interesting* history, which also involves Snow Patrol. But that part of my past isn't for discussing now, it's more of a third pint in the pub, that-was-a-good-evening-that-was, type of story.

Eileen is looking at me. She can tell I've tumbled down a set of memories, good and bad. If she weren't Eileen, she might worry about what I can hear and see in that cinematic flash-back.

"Well," I say, scratching the back of my head, "usually—"

"Usually," Eileen interrupts, "whatever she wants to talk about gets complicated."

That's not entirely fair, but I don't say anything. I'm not *that* stupid.

Claire and I are similar spirits in many ways; we both surf our own way over the great waves of life. This can be seen in her business, a dress shop with a difference.

As a general principle, in terms of being good ideas, privately owned dress shops are right up there with leaving the bonfire to go skinny-dipping at the start of the horror movie.

This isn't me being sexist or bigoted. This is from the

horse's mouth. The Black Horse actually, as I've been told this by my friend, Rob, who is a bank manager.

Typically, high-class, upmarket dress shops are opened by someone who knows of just such a shop closing down, and where the stock is going at a 'ridiculous price'.

The one thing all these shops have in common is that, rather than being gold mines, they are money pits. The problem, you see, is that places like Stowmarket, Claydon, Copdock, Coddenham, they just can't support even one high-class dress shop.

Claire, you remember Claire? She had a different idea. Yes, still dresses, but not to sell them, but to hire them out. Her shop, 'The Big Night Out', doesn't rely on a few of the wives of the Ipswich Mafia to keep in business. Her shop is aimed at the wannabees, and, as far as I know, is doing all right. In fact, she was able to help me out a little while ago with a cash-flow issue.

So, her asking to meet, it sets distant warning bells ringing in my head. I read the email again, but there are no clues.

"When will you go see her?" Eileen asks. See, she doesn't ask, will I go?

"Oh, like I said, I want to pop over to Claydon, and I might swing by the Slubber's, to chat to Van. I could see Claire first."

"Van?" Eileen asks. "Is he still up to his old tricks?"

Van, from Van Diesel, because whenever a crate of coats or jeans broke open at the docks, he'd be the first one scooping up the damages and saying, "Deesal fit our John."

"No, he doesn't operate the crane anymore—"

"Not since he found out those metal containers don't break open, even if you could drop them?" Eileen asks, all sweetness, light, and suspicion.

I ignore her cast aspersions, and she continues with a follow-up question.

"This new job, any risk he'll meet some nice lady who'll take care of him?"

This is typical Eileen; she's always trying to sort out Van's love life. He's never had a great deal of success with the fairer sex, though not for want of trying.

"Maybe." Certainly, he'll meet more people in the office than he did sitting in a crane. It's his new job I want to chat to him about. He tracks containers and shipments. "You never know," I say. "This stuff" – I wave at the computer – "is not always right up to date."

"Hmm?" She would make a great police interrogator. I keep talking.

"It's not that I've got much cash tied up in those trainers, but one thousand pairs at, well, they've got to go for fifteen to twenty pounds a pair. That's—" I pause, then, "Well that's a finished kitchen right there."

Eileen shakes her head, then smiles; she knows I'm doing it, chasing this deal, because that's what I do.

That's me. If you really want to know me, that's me. I carve my own way, make my own luck. No nine-to-five, no boss, no one to tie me down. Always, it's my target, my dart, my game, and my bullseye. It's not money, houses and cars I'm chasing though, just my own life.

'Chasing Cars'. Can't imagine how hearing from Claire brought *that* song to mind.

"That," I say, "was a wonderful breakfast, and now I must get going. What are your plans?"

"Oh, same old, same old, at the school," she replies.

My wife is the Administration Manager at the Stowmarket Sixth Form College. The Head's 'right-hand man', with her eyes everywhere and her finger on all the pulses.

"New term has started well, the kinks have been ironed out, but we're still short on a delivery of A-level Mathematics-Algebra books. Mostly today I will be reminding people just who pays their bills, and what they need to do to keep that happening."

"And, at the end of the telling-off, they'll be thanking you and asking what else can they do for you? I'm sure. Lovely breakfast darling," I say, pecking her a kiss and making for the door.

A short while later, I'm outside. It's September cool this morning, but a good day seems promised, and for a moment I just soak it up.

We, Eileen and I, live in a row of three tiny cottages, knocked together to make a single house. These three used to be part of the estate whose woods I can see from my back door. The cottage, as I now think of it, is low, like they always used to be, wooden beams and old red bricks that glow in the sunset. Small windows too – the Lord of the Manor didn't like his peasants being able to see out. Maybe it doesn't look much, but it's already a place of magic, my place of magic.

Over the last four years, I and various friends and associates have been turning the three cottages into one, as time and money allows. Upstairs we're all done: three big bedrooms, one with an en-suite, and a second bathroom. Downstairs, well, a little more to do, like the kitchen, but there's already a big living room, and dining room, and a place where the utility will be.

Outside, the three gardens are now one big area where we grow fruit and vegetables, which we share with the deer that come in from the woods. One area Eileen has kept for flowers. This place has got bucolic running through it like a stream through a mountain glen, and I know just how lucky I am to have it.

Of course, it's not all sunshine and blue tits hanging out the washing. The Wi-Fi is shaky, the track leading up to the main Ipswich Road is rutted and full of muddy potholes in the winter; and every now and then the local hunt corners some 'wee timorous cowering beasty' and rips it apart in my driveway.

Last time that happened, I had a bit of a run-in with the Master of the Hounds.

It's the letter from the JCSB that brings back that memory. I must ring them today; but I was thinking about Arthur Pulbright.

Pulbright owns the woods; his land stops at the bridlepath between the trees and my garden. Well, he also owns the big house over the hill, several farms and half of bloody Stowmarket. You see, that's what a good education, hard work, and a family history going back to the Normans can get you.

His connection with the JCSB is only what you might call tangential, but that's how my mind works best, sliding off one thought into another until it plops into the little slot on the roulette wheel. Pulbright is a magistrate, see: courts, jury service, same building as it happens, magistrates and Crown Court.

That's why the monkey wrench incident came to mind.

That never went to court. Not with all Pulbright's threats and bluster, because why? Because I had his hunt bang to rights.

Look, I'm born and bred Suffolk, maybe not a man of the soil, but I know where my roots are. If you get your jollies chasing a poor harmless fox over miles of countryside with a pack of bloodthirsty hounds, well, that tells me something about you. And don't tell me it's all about tradition. Time was, people used to drop defenceless old women in the river claiming they were witches and hang kids for stealing handkerchiefs, and I don't see many asking for *that* to come back.

So, the hunt story.

I was looking after Marty Taylor's two Jack Russells while he was out with Chrissy in the Algarve. Energetic little things those dogs, so I set up a run for them on the patio.

That afternoon, I'm working on the van: routine maintenance, new suspension or something like that. At some point I hear the horns blowing. Off in the distance, along the bridleway back to Needham, so I don't take much notice.

Then the noise is getting louder and, all of a sudden, the two Jacks are snapping away and setting off a racket. So, I climb out from under the van, cracking my shin as I do, and walk round to the garden.

It's bedlam. The Hunt are careering down the track, bloody trumpets going, ground shaking and horses shying and whinnying. The hunt dogs are swirling around like the rats from Hamelin, and Eileen is standing holding a Jack Russell in each arm, trying to make for our door.

I'm a hero, me, like hell am I. Never been in a fight, not a real one, just the odd 'look out for your mates' dust-up on a Saturday in Ipswich. But I don't stop. Or don't think, depending how you look at it.

I have a monkey wrench in my hand, and I go running forwards. The hunt dogs are keeping up at Eileen, who's trying to kick them away and nearly at the door. All I can see is red, red-coated twats shouting at the dogs and the possibility of much more. I wade in there, swinging the wrench, and clout one of the dogs as it jumps up at Eileen.

It screams, as you'd expect, and whines. For a second, I think it is going to come at me, but I've caught its leg, and as it comes down all it can do is yelp. Then I'm in there, shouting and kicking, and making far more noise than I'm doing damage. The dogs turn towards me, and I shout something stupid, like "Get down". Well, what do you expect? The 'there may come a time' speech from *The Lord of The Rings*?

So, I'm swinging the wrench around, and Eileen has nearly reached the door to put the Jacks inside. Me, I'm surrounded by a whirlpool of dogs, frothed with a scum of hunt members on the edges.

Pulbright is there, shouting at me for savaging his pack leader and waving his whip in the air. Then the hound master catches up, pulls the dogs to order and out of my garden, my land. For a moment we have a stand-off. Pulbright looks like he wants to step back two hundred years and have me transported. All he can do though is spit and go redder than his jacket, because I'm in the right of it.

Now, for why did I suddenly think of this? It was three years ago.

Well, as I say, the JCSB letter reminded me of the courts, and Pulbright is the local magistrate, of course. That usually wouldn't matter, and on that September morning, it didn't.

However, if, just suppose, if, sometime in the future I'm going to have to go to Pulbright's court to defend myself against a speeding ticket, then, things might be a bit more sticky.

TWO

I get to Stowmarket around ten-thirty. Which is because I didn't leave until ten-fifteen, despite my best intentions. To be honest, when my best intentions and what actually happens *do* coincide, I am as surprised as everyone else. That's just how life is, and it's a situation the universe and I have come to accept.

The tissue in the washing machine of my plans is the JCSB, or the JCB as I'm now thinking of them.

My call asking for deferral starts well. I begin with cheerful yet slightly apologetic tones, confident I'm conjuring 'honest and sincere'. After a long tumbleweed of silence, I realise I'm actually evoking 'suspicion with a touch of disdain'.

The young lady on the phone asks, "And what is your reason for non-attendance?"

"What have you got?" I ask, slipping towards 'dodgy and devious'.

The cold wind blowing down the phone gets chillier. I rewind before I sink any further. Sometimes it helps to throw yourself on the mercy of the court.

"I'm sorry. My, my boss asked me to enquire. I'm a bit nervous."

Everybody has a boss, and mostly people who answer the phones know what it's like to have an unreasonable one.

So, soon we're into something that might sound like discussion but feels to me as if I'm stamping on a minefield while holding my hands to my ears. Then she asks a question that I can work with.

"Is your employer unable to give you time off?" Maybe there is a tiny hint in her voice. I don't know, but I'm optimistic that way.

"Me? Naaaooow." What started as a proud statement about self-employment morphed from a dodgy, doomed caterpillar of despair into a beautiful butterfly of opportunity.

"Now, that's a good point," I say, looking around the kitchen and knowing exactly what 'my boss' would prefer me to be doing. "She has said there are urgent tasks, which, if unfinished, would cause a great deal of…" I glance at the notes scribbled on the back of the JCSB envelope "… financial hardship."

Emily on the phone, we're on first-name terms now, seems pleased, like I am a student who has passed a test.

"Okay, right, good, well, look, Mr Mellon."

"Charlie," I say, automatically.

"Mr Mellon. I'm going to send you a deferral letter, but it is only that, a deferral, you understand?"

I say I do, while dancing a small jig, and nearly oversetting the plates drying in the rack.

Her final words interrupt my dance.

"You do appreciate, don't you, Mr Mellon, that you must offer alternative dates within seven days?"

I nod, say I do, and put the phone down with a cheery goodbye, and make for the door. I'm late.

*

Claire's shop, 'The Big Night Out', is on Stowmarket High Street.

Stowmarket is a quiet Suffolk town. If you have visions of quaint nineteenth-century buildings, white-fronted, three-storied, and looming over the pavement, you're about right.

Somehow, though, while it has all the modern cons, the estate agent and mobile telephone companies, you get the sense that most of the buildings are merely waiting for when their occupier is going to be replaced by a muffin seller and a sweet shop offering bullseyes and ginger beer.

The shop window of 'The Big Night Out' is impressive. It has a floor of silver balloons, and five of those headless mannequins, which I find a little bit creepy.

Each dummy is wearing a dress that puts the jaw-drop of 'you've got to be kidding me', into the tearful exclamation of 'how much!' That was the point, though; these dresses aren't there to be sold, but to be hired out.

Claire, is, as I have said, my first wife. We met when we were both twenty-one and I had no idea about finding the right time for the right action. She is short, slim except where she doesn't need to be, and has more energy than a basket full of kittens. We fell head-over-heels in love, and after that, things went downhill.

Now we have both matured. Her blonde hair is still bobbed in a Betty Boop sort of style, and her smile still opens a lot of wallets. There is, though, a slight tiredness around her pale blue eyes, and every now and then she sits down when before she would have been setting something to rights in the shop.

She sees me as I walk in, and checks her watch. I know I'm late.

"Charlie," she says, "you're early. I have quarter to eleven in the sweepstake!" There's a smile on her face, though, and this is more a reference to our earliest days. I toy with saying something about at least not being eighteen months late, but decide I'll wait until I know why I'm here.

"And you're looking as ready to go out as ever," I say. She was never ready to go out when she was supposed to be, and we settle on this as a score draw.

She comes over and greets me with a peck on the cheek. As always, she smells wonderful, lilacs or something.

The shop looks good too, lots of stock, I mean lots. She must have been reinvesting the profits.

The place is fairly small, but they've sectioned off areas by decade and event. So, if you fancy the 1970s (and who doesn't?) and you're going to a nightclub, there is a rail section for that. Four rows, four decades, and each row divided into event types. Pretty good really.

There's always great music playing, and the lighting

is upbeat and enthusiastic. Everything is style and sophistication. Walk through the door and you think you've stepped into a London boutique. There is even a new assistant out at the front. She's affecting that snooty look that suggests you've trodden in something and tells you she's forgotten that she's only a shop assistant.

Even this early in the morning it seems busy enough. Two women I vaguely recognise from the Conservative Club are in one corner, squealing in the way women do when they jointly find an item of clothing they both 'simply adore'.

Claire takes me through the shop, and offers me coffee, nodding to the woman at the counter to attend to the Conservative Club ladies.

We go into the small back room and sit down.

"It's looking really good out there," I say. "Coming on well."

"Yes." She smiles again, but this time it seems like a bit of an effort. "Giselle, my, well, my assistant, she came up with some great ideas."

"An assistant?" I say. "When did that happen?"

"Oh, about six months ago. She had experience. Worked for a Cambridge shop doing similar to me, only it had to close."

We fall silent for a second; we both know what it is like to see business ideas fail. It hurts.

"Well, your gain." I'm dragging this out a bit, I know that, but little alarm bells are ringing, and if I don't open the box, the cat isn't dead, right?

"Oh yes!" Again, she brightens, but it is as if she

is forcing a blancmange of hope through a keyhole of optimism. "Giselle's put in a barcode system for the dresses, we can track them all in and out, and the payments go right to the bank account."

"Well, impressive." It sounds a bit like overkill to me, but what do I know?

"I've got over three hundred outfits, Charlie. Do you have any idea how hard they are to keep track of?"

I think about it for a second, scratch my head, trying to imagine it. Yeah, I can see keeping on top of all that stock must be tough.

"Made a big difference, only, just at the wrong time," continues Claire.

"Oh?" That comes out easily enough, but really it is 'oh-oh', as in here comes the bad part.

"Yes, now things have slowed down, really slowed. I'm sorry, Charlie. I've got to ask for the loan back. Things aren't going well at the shop, and— it's all getting a bit tight."

Shit.

As I said, Claire and I both understood that we should never have got married; she especially understands that *I* shouldn't have. That, though, was fourteen years ago, nearly twelve since the divorce, and Stowmarket is a small place. Put all those variables into the equation and the fact that she lent me ten thousand pounds should not be too surprising.

The van had died, and the house had soaked up more cash than expected, and the taxman had come knocking. I've helped Claire out in the past, and she had always promised to do the same. But I hadn't planned on her needing it back this side of the Adidas trainers turning up.

I make a face that I hope suggests a willingness to repay, if I can. It's all right for Robert Browning and his 'a man's reach should exceed his grasp', but he doesn't have to pay the VAT man.

She looks at me for a few more seconds, then continues, shaking her head slightly and looking older than I've ever seen. That is weird. Claire is one of those women whose appearance is 'ageless', with occasional bursts of 'in her prime'. How she looks today, though, it suddenly makes me feel *my* age as well.

Again, shit.

"I don't know," Claire continues. "Things have gone weirdly quiet over the last three months or so." She glances back into the shop where the doorbell is ringing as the two Conservative Club women leave.

"Sales have dropped off. I mean, September is usually quiet, but soon I'd expect people to be getting ready for Christmas, booking gowns, and paying deposits, but—"

She shakes her head again. I nod, sigh, and begin to wonder how much I can get for one thousand left-footed Adidas trainers.

"How bad is it?" I ask, which really means, 'How much time do I have?'

"Well," she says, raising a small smile. "If you're counting like you just jumped off the top of a high building." She screws up her face, then continues. "And so far, things are going okay. Well, you're about halfway, and the concrete is rushing up to meet you. I can last four weeks or so. Rob is chasing me, gave me until the 10th of October to get the overdraft down. He has inspectors coming in, or something."

Rob, I have already sketched a little about him, but now, despite the rapidly approaching pavement, we need to take a detour.

Rob Simmonds is the manager of the Ipswich Lloyds TSB Bank.

I introduced him to Claire as I've always found him to be okay as a bank manager. Now, I know that is like saying, 'He's okay for someone in a profession right up there with child social services and estate agent in the popularity stakes,' but I'll give him his due, he tries.

You can often see him rushing around Suffolk in his company-issue BMW 3 Series. He has grey hair, which he keeps cut short, showing off a rounded head. The head itself always seems a little small for a body that answers the question 'Who ate all the pies?' As a bank manager, he, of course, wears a suit, most of the time charcoal grey with a white shirt and a surprising flash of colour of a tie, orange, or red.

Now I think about it, the way he bustles from place to place, then leaps out and slowly wanders around, sticking his beak into everything, reminds me of a wood pigeon.

"Well. You know Rob," I say. "He'll try, but when his boss in Cambridge says 'jump', he's as frog-like as all of them."

There's a moment's silence between us. A problem shared, as they say, is a problem doubled. Now I'm holding the hot potato, and I know I'm going to have to do something. I'm just not sure what.

"How, how much, do you need?" I ask, though inside I know that it doesn't really matter; five hundred or five thousand, they are both more than I can manage right now.

Claire drops her eyes for a second, then she looks at me, swallows, and says, "I really need it all, Charlie. You gave me three back, but I need the other seven, as soon as you can. I'm sorry."

Shit. Shit, and, for want of anything better, shitty shit shit.

Right. Triumph and Disaster aren't just the names of two solicitors to be treated with equal disdain. There is always a way forwards. I've been in much worse situations, and every time, things got better, then worse, then better.

"Well," I say, pushing my hands on my thighs and standing up. "I'd better get off my arse and see how I'm going to get you the money."

The look on her face, a mix of relief tinged with surprise, is a bit disappointing; what had she expected?

We get up and start through to the shop. Claire puts her hand on my arm, and for a second, I get that jolt of electricity I always got from her.

"Thank you, Charlie."

"Hey," I say, "we might be divorced, but we're not separated." It sounds good, and I put my best smile on. Inside, though, the panicked swan of terror is swimming furiously against the river of 'how the fuck do I get out of this?'

She sees me towards the door. The shop is empty now. 'Giselle', the assistant, is typing something into the computer; she looks up nervously and smiles. It crosses my mind to suggest that she may have to go soon, but that's not my place.

As we get to the entrance, the doorbell chimes and a woman walks in.

A 'woman walks in'? I can hear Eileen with one of her best 'hmms?' when I say that.

How do I describe my first sight of Marianne Tilsley?

Look. It's half-ten on a reasonably chilly September morning. We're on the high street of a dull Suffolk town, and Marianne walks in as though she was walking onto a yacht, as Carly Simon put it.

Marianne is about my age. I'd guess five feet ten, slim, with long dark hair, and made up in a way that looks like it took five minutes, and probably took the best part of the day so far.

She's wearing a slinky jumpsuit, which emphasises her legs at one end and, by the almost midriff slit, her breasts at the other. Said breasts are jiggling either side of a décolletage in a way that it would be rude *not* to stare.

I pull my eyes up to hers; she has one of those smiles that says she guesses what I'm thinking, and if I'm not, she'll want to know why.

There is a moment of awkward silence as Claire watches the little tableau, then she coughs. Before I can react, at least before I can react in an appropriate way, Marianne says, "Oh, Claire, hello, so glad I found you in. And who is this?"

She has a voice that puts the smog into smoky, and although she's talking to Claire, her eyes are on me. For a second, I feel like I'm fifteen again and am asking Mary Turner to come for a walk down the footpath, and we both know what that means.

"Ah, hello, Marianne." Claire breaks my confused reverie. "This is Charlie, my ex." She says the last in a tone of voice that is either a claim or a disclaim, I'm not sure. "And," she says to me, "this is Marianne Tilsley, a customer, and friend."

Marianne smiles; her vaguely extravagant lipstick brings my focus to her full lips and bright white teeth.

I'm not stupid. This woman is the female equivalent of Lord Byron. Well, she might not be mad, but she's definitely bad and dangerous to know. I have no intention of doing anything other than slide around her, avoiding that interesting scent, and getting out to my van.

She, on the other hand, seems to have other ideas.

"Oh yes, the famous Charlie. How nice. I've heard so much about you, and thankfully, none of it was good." She laughs, but there is a hard sort of invitation in her eyes; one that I do not plan to RSVP.

"Oh really?" My eyebrows raise, and I can't avoid the hint of pleasure. Alarm bells are ringing in my brain, but some part of me is barking away like a Pavlov dog.

"Noooo," she says, laughing again and putting her hand out, then gripping my arm for slightly longer than necessary. Well, actually it wasn't necessary at all. "I'm only kidding. Claire has always said such good things about you. Especially your... musical talents."

She makes that hesitation sound like she was referring to something else, but I try to ignore it.

"Well," I say, "I must be going." I move to get past her, and for a second her grip on my arm increases. Then she lets me by, but fails to move quite far enough out of the way. I swerve past her, still a hand's-breadth distant, but warm enough, way too warm.

I step outside, breathe in deeply and shake my head. I need to focus on money and finding it.

It's not that I would even consider cheating on Eileen, but I've known a couple of women, and men, like Marianne Tilsley. They float around the Ipswich scene as cool as cucumber, but are more like icebergs, just waiting for their next *Titanic*.

THREE

"I'm a multi-tasker, twisted multi-tasker."

Prodigy is playing on the CD, but the words are my own. I like singing in the van; it helps me focus. The high roof of the Ford Transit makes for good acoustics. While I sing, part of my brain is putting things in some sort of order, ready for me to deal with them. Perhaps I should pick a better song, maybe 'Money' from Pink Floyd.

For a moment I drift off into distant days, nine years ago. The stage, the crowds, and me, standing there with my guitar. No. Now I must focus.

Keith Flint screams again about starting fires, and at the traffic lights, I grab my phone and flick through to Rob's number. Of course, I only get his bank manager voicemail; that's fine, he *should* be with customers. I leave him a message.

For just a moment I think about the weird idea of a 'voicemail'. Stephen Fry wittered on about that on *QI* a few days ago, how mail comes from the French for a box or something, and— my phone rings. Amazingly, it's Rob.

"Mr Mellon," he says, formal, but in a cheery way that means he's not being too serious. We tread a fine line; we might be good friends, but he's *married* to the bank.

"To what," he continues, "do I owe the pleasure? Have those trainers turned up yet? Going to need a bigger box to put the money in?"

"And good morning to you, Mr Simmonds, sir," I reply. Never hurts to get your crawling in first.

"Sir, is it? I see, then maybe we should meet. Look, Charlie, I'm just on my way to a customer." Rob is always just on his way to something. "Can we catch up later?"

Keeping one eye on the lorry in the outside lane, which is doing a piss-poor job of overtaking, I imagine the water snake of my plans wriggling across the river of the day, and we agree to meet up in Felixstowe that afternoon.

That gives me enough time to drop into Claydon and look at the house clearance.

*

You never know what you're going to get with a house clearance. The strangest one I went to was where every room had been turned into a shrine.

Warren Heath way, that was. It was sad and touching at the same time. Five-bed place, and each room had a name on the door, hand-painted on a piece of wood. Inside, those rooms were just full of stuff, clothes, pictures, books, toys, knick-knacks, old CDs and records, presumably from the person whose name was on the door.

It was the pink room that got me, though, the one with 'Maisie' on the door, with a few little flowers added. There was a cot in the middle of the room, and toys, cuddly ones, mostly animals, lots of elephants. It was like you could feel a small, sad history written in the dust and debris.

Anyway, thankfully the Claydon house isn't like that. It is full of old furniture, of course, though one room is cluttered with bits and pieces of arms and legs, from shop dummies; that shifts it a bit up the weird ladder.

The young guy, Dave, trying to clear the house, looks uncomfortable. He has a couple of red spots on his neck, and one on the back of his hand, which he scratches at absently as we talk.

"My dad, God rest his soul, he worked up at Mendlesham, the BT research site, where they did lots of inventing. When he retired, he started on prosthetics."

Again, he scratches, and I edge him out of the bedroom we're in, and he yawns.

"Scuse me, I slept here last night. Anyway, what was I saying? Oh yes, the models and things. Gave my poor mum the creeps, but I always thought it was kind of fascinating. He did a few things for a couple of films, but mostly he was interested in really helping people, only—"

He shrugs and the echoes of unfinished dreams seem to rumble through the place.

Most of the house contents aren't really my sort of thing, but I can see he is desperate; he has driven up from

Fleet or somewhere. Then, I see one of those little bonuses I keep my eye open for.

A big collection of vinyl records, a long shelf of them, no classical, but I recognise a few from the thin spines alone. Dave's watching, like I'm a trout and he's just flicked a fly at me, but I try not to rise to his bait.

I clock the records with barely a glance, and we continue to wander around. My heart's going a bit, not big time, but stock is stock. I run a stall at a few markets. The stalls are my bread-and-butter income between errant trainers, Christmas trees and any other bonus I come across.

We wander round into the garden to a lock-up garage. He opens up the door, which screeches like a cat with its tail on fire.

The garage is full of tubs of silicone, unopened, and a few more shop dummies. I am only looking out of courtesy really, and I guess he can see.

"If I could clear *this*," he says, "at least Emmaus might take the rest. Dad's workshop, well, maybe I'll keep that stuff." I can hear defeat in his voice.

Again, we both study the garage. There must be fifty or so tubs of the silicone; God knows what his dad wanted that much for. That stuff sells for around fifteen pounds a tub. I study it, a pained look on my face.

"Maybe, for two hundred pounds," I say. It wasn't hard to make that look a stretch, though I always keep a chunk of cash in my wallet – for emergencies.

Now he looks at me, scratches the inside of his neck, and I almost feel sorry for him.

"How about," he says, "one hundred and fifty, and you clear everything?"

That takes a few seconds. He is offering *me* money.

I make a face that I hope tells him I'm a good guy really, shit, I am a good guy really, and rub the back of my head. He is getting his wallet out.

Sometimes I let myself down.

I reach into my pocket and pull out my wallet.

"How about," I say, "I look through those LPs in the living room, we work out a price for whatever I fancy, and I'll clear the shed, free of charge?"

He scratches a red spot by his lip, then nods.

"Sure, that could work."

Payday, possibly two.

I'm a wheeler-dealer, switched-on wheeler-dealer.

We wander back into the living room, and I drift towards the record collection like it was of little interest. Dave is still chatting, and scratching.

"Yes, it's been a bit tough. We have a new baby, so getting up here, well, it all takes time. It's not like he was ill, my dad."

"Oh, new baby? Boy or girl?" I ask. I let my fingers run across the albums, random like.

"A boy, Jack, six months old, bit of a handful, well, usually."

There's something in his voice that tells a story I don't want to hear, but I'm not thinking quite straight.

"Yes, he's well, you know, kids get things. We're waiting on some tests." He flicks a glance at his phone, almost without thinking.

I pull an album out, The Beatles' *Please Please Me*. My hands shake a little. Dave's turned to the window, gazing out there like he's trying to see all the way back to Fleet, I reckon.

It's always the same, isn't it? You start to chat to people, and suddenly they open a door into your head, and you forget that you're doing business.

I pull out the LP. It's a stereo, third pressing, 1963, pretty good condition. I let out a sigh.

"What? Is it scratched? Sorry about that." He turns back to look at me.

"No, no," I say. "So, you selling this place?"

"Wish I was, that would be good. No, this is just rented, stuck with three months on the lease yet. No, if I'm lucky we'll have enough for a beer and sandwich. Such is life."

Ah fuck.

"Look," I continue, "there's a few good ones here, this" – I hold up *Please Please Me* – "you could get three–four hundred for this."

He steps forwards, and for the first time I see him almost smile.

"What, really?"

"Yeah, and there's a couple of other possibilities."

I'm trying to shut myself up, but the words just tumble out. Why couldn't he be some smug git on the make?

"I'll tell you what." In for a penny. "I'll have a look through. Any that are really valuable, I'll put to one side for you. The rest, the rest I get to keep. What do you say?"

He blows out his cheeks.

"I say you're a bit crap at the making money house-clearing racket, Charlie."

He's probably right, but sometimes the universe just wants to test you.

It takes an hour to go through the records. I did all right, and so did he. At least I go away feeling I can look myself in the mirror.

Then I spend another half hour loading up the van with the dummies and tubs of silicone. There is also some of the green setting catalyst that turns the silicone from a white sticky thick paint into a soft rubber foam. It's fun stuff if you want to make a weird *Mission Impossible* mask or some such.

By the time I've stored it all, I have a few ideas where I could move it. I know a wholesaler up Norwich way who might take it.

Anyway, I'm soon on my way up the A14, around Ipswich and out to Felixstowe.

*

Nice, Felixstowe, if you like shingle beaches and a thousand container lorries an hour. Nah, it's okay, but not a holiday spot. Thing is, it's stuck out at the very arse end of Suffolk, and to the north you've got places like Aldeburgh and Orford Ness. Shit, even Sizewell is on a nicer piece of coast than Felixstowe.

The people, well, people are just people, but I've got some great friends in Felixstowe. Today, though, I'll only have time for Rob and Van.

My main office in Felixstowe is the Slubber's Arms. Great pub run by Fazil, a cheery Asian guy from Bradford. He's always a bit difficult to understand, though, with his strong Yorkshire accent. His being from way up there in the frozen North is why it has that name. Slubbering, I eventually understood, was something they had to do in the dark satanic mills when most of the world map was painted red and the buildings were stained black with coal soot.

Anyway, the Slubber's; I know what you're thinking. Dark wood, horse brasses, ringing fruit machines and small wooden tables with rheumy-eyed men staring into half-full, or half-empty, glasses of bitter. Maybe on a wet Wednesday in February, it might be like that. Today, Friday afternoon with the dawn of the weekend already throwing its welcoming brightness across the craggy ruins of the week, it's a bit more lively.

One side of the bar there's a group of dockworkers, hi-vis jackets, dirty jeans, and a few of them taking surreptitious sucks on those bloody vape things. Beyond them, in a corner, five girls from the local Tesco are plotting to take over the world. Here and there, business-suited men and women are tucking into the plain but tasty food Fazil serves up during the day.

I order the chilli and chunks of brown bread I always get. He's had that same pot going as long as I've been coming here. I pick up my pint of Old Speckled Hen and find a table, near the back but with an eye-line to the front door.

It's not long before Van arrives.

I'm in two minds about Van. He has the sort of nervous attitude that puts 'landslide' into 'shifty', but he's always been straight with me. I think he's watched too many of those TV programmes where there's a ferrety grass-cum-dealer-in-stolen-goods guy, and he's taken the character as a role model.

Whatever, he sits down in front of me, eyeing my beer and chilli, and, fair enough, I go order his.

By the time I get back, he's dumped his grubby anorak to reveal an almost clean suit, whitish shirt, and dark tie. The clerical effect is marred by his top button being undone and there's a vaguely dull yellow tidemark around the collar.

He really needs a woman to look after him, Van, but he's never been lucky like that. Well, good luck starts with being a bit cleaner and tidier than he usually manages. Eileen and I have set him up a couple of times, but it's never got anywhere.

He nods thanks to me for the beer and takes a spoon to the chilli. For a second, we just enjoy the moment. See, that's Daoism for you, it's all about seeking balance. For a time you can't measure I forget money, and fifty tubs of silicone and the unfinished kitchen, and just absorb a sense of calm.

Then, I'm back.

"Well?" I ask.

He knows what I mean. His eyebrows twitch as though they're made of two dozen starlings sitting on a telephone line, and I assume he's thinking.

"Maybe." His voice makes me think his tonsils have spent a week in a shed used for smoking fish.

"Maybe?" Hope rising, I hadn't expected that.

"Just maybe. There's an LCL come out of Qui which has stuff from that same manufacturer."

LCL, I know that is a shared container. Loads of different products in one container. Qui, I guess, is a port in Vietnam. Van goes on.

"Haven't got all the papers yet, their stuff is always late. But, you know, the last lot was on a mixed container as well, and it's got the same loading path. Here." He pulls a printout from his inside jacket pocket, and points at a string of numbers, which might as well be in Vietnamese.

"And when," I ask, "will we know? When's it due?"

He peers at the sheet again, mutters, moves his head back and forth, and looks up into the air like there is a map there.

"First week of October, maybe later."

Shit, I think.

Van continues, "Depends on Rotterdam, how long they hold them up, load of lazy shysters the Dutch." Rotterdam shifts about four times as much stuff compared to Felixstowe, so I ignore that and let him play the expert.

"The bottom line is, they won't arrive until mid-October, at best, if you're lucky. That horse ain't riding to your rescue, even assuming it's the right one." He chuckles for no reason I can see.

We chat a little more and I buy him a second drink, only a half this time.

"All right for youse who don't have a boss watching you," he says. I wonder for a moment if I would trade a boss for the regular salary, then shake my head. Never in a million years.

We talk about this and that, his attempts to find a girlfriend, how Ipswich Town Football Club are doing. Both he and the club have been scoreless for a while, him probably a lot longer than them.

"Anything good coming up?"

"Oh, I'm on a new site at the moment," he says, and I look confused. "Dating site," he clarifies.

"Oh right, they any good, then?" Maybe Van not actually being in the same room as his potential date is a good thing.

"Not really, one day though, it will happen, I'm sure."

I nod, then I try again.

"Any stuff coming in I should try for?"

Again, he does the eyebrow-twitching thing, with a rub with his forefinger for good measure.

"Well, five hundred socket sets. The importer went broke, but a few London guys sniffing around there." He knows I don't have the cash to compete, so he shakes his head, then continues. "Couple of thousand Rubik's Cubes, but again, they're pretty hot. Oh, and several thousand bandages, which were supposed to be T-shirts, but somebody ripped somebody else off. Probably get incinerated."

Nothing much, then. Bandages could be good, but NHS procurement being what it is, even free, they're not worth the effort.

He glances at his watch, shakes his head, slurps the last of his beer, and, after a quick handshake and a promise he'll keep his eyes open for the running shoes, makes for the door.

I turn back to my own beer and start thinking about Rob.

If I'm going to repay Claire, it's going to be with Lloyds Bank money, and Rob is going to take some convincing.

It's still a good hour before he will get here, and he'll probably be running a little late anyway, so I think about my options.

The Slubber's is just my Felixstowe office, not my local, so I don't really want to hang around drinking. I decide on a walk, clear my head, and think about Claire, about how I'm going to get her money.

Me, my problem, is always the same. I'm pretty asset-rich, the house and stuff, but cash, cash is a bit harder to come by. Sure, I might be able to rustle up a couple of thousand, but that's going to leave me really tight for new deals, and emergencies, and the kitchen. I wave goodbye to Fazil and leave.

Outside, the wind is blowing a mix of dock stink, North Sea salt, and seagull screams. For a second, I consider going back into the pub. But instead, I take a walk towards town. It's not far. Nowhere is far in Felixstowe.

There is nothing wrong with Felixstowe that a few wrecking balls and several hundred million pounds couldn't cure. Give it its due though, it never pretends to be what it's not. It has an honest, smart enough and nicely pedestrianised, town centre, and all the normal shops. It even has a little covered stand thing, where once a week in the summer, the local youth group belts out traditional brass band music.

Turns out, it also has a library. I'd not noticed that before.

Low 1960s gruesome style, but big glass windows through which I can see a few people milling around. It has steep steps up one side and a long sloping walkway up the other.

'Internet available here' says a sign in the window, and that pulls me to a halt. Maybe, it's worth a look.

Sure enough, I'm soon directed to a little booth with an old PC. The battered keyboard has a little stub where there should be an 'e', and what I work out are the 'i' and 'l' keys are just white blobs, but overall, the PC does what it says on the box.

I spend an hour hunting around, researching and thinking. I get a few ideas, then, just as the nice young lady librarian tells me my time is up, I realise that I should be getting back to meet Rob.

*

Impressively, Rob is waiting for *me*. He's picked a table over in a far corner, nobody nearby.

As I get halfway across the pub, another guy joins him, younger, eager looking, bright white shirt, dark tie, and a suit that he might have got married in. He has 'junior assistant manager' written all over him. The youngster passes Rob a tonic water and puts down a similar glass in front of himself. They notice me, and both get up.

It's then that I see the sling.

Rob's right arm is tucked awkwardly against his body, a blue sling scrunching up his otherwise perfect grey suit. He comes forwards grinning slightly and after a quick greeting to 'Danny, my assistant', explains about the arm.

"Broke the ulna," he says. "Getting too old for five-a-side, even playing in goal." He waves the arm vaguely at me and I try to imagine him, red-faced and shouting in an echoing sports hall. It's not easy.

Danny is obviously well trained; he offers me a drink. After a moment I decide I'll let the bank buy me an Old Speckled Hen, yes, a pint, and a packet of dry-roasted peanuts.

As the drinks are fetched, Rob continues.

"Actually, it's been pretty good." He lifts the arm. "Danny has to chauffeur me around, and I was given first-class treatment on the flight to Prague last week, what with 'needing help to board.'" He laughs that genuine laugh that reminds me that even bank managers are human.

Danny gets back with my drink and peanuts. I open the pack entirely, flattening out the foil, and leave a pile in the middle. Rob pecks at them as we talk.

It's only as we start that I realise just how nervous I am. Usually, you know, life throws me lemons and twenty seconds later I have a lemon stand outside and have sold half the stock. Today though, instead of confidence, I feel an emptiness, a realisation that things aren't going as I expect them to and might not improve.

It's weird, and why I hate having a boss; I don't like my future being in someone else's hands. Yeah, I know, I will get over this, things will get sorted, but for a moment I feel a little too old for ducking and diving; when do *I* get the chauffeur?

"So, I spoke to Claire." Rob heads me off a little at the

pass. "She said you were going to sort out the money you owe her?" He turns the statement into a question, and it's obvious that he thinks this is about as likely as Ipswich winning the Championship.

"Yes, that's my plan, why I suggested we get together." I agree – nice words, 'suggested' and 'get together', casual, could be applied to a summer BBQ. But I can tell by the way he takes a tiny sip of his tonic water, and glances at Danny with a flashing eyebrow raise, it's me that's going to get roasted.

"Right, and you have the seven k you owe? Or coming in soon. The trainers are arriving?" That could sound cutting and hard-faced, but to Rob it's just business, just his job. I remind myself it's not personal, but that's not easy.

"Er, not quite, I was hoping, maybe, you could give me an overdraft increase for, six months, even three would help, up to Christmas." I'm talking myself down even as I start; I'm off my game.

Rob shakes his head.

"I don't think so, Charlie. We're, The Bank, is tightening up a bit at the moment. You've been up against your limit a while now. We've..."

I let him talk, nodding sometimes, but I'm not really listening. It's all about policy and procedure, why he can't do things. I sort of get it; it's what I should have expected. It's all crap really – not Rob so much, he's telling me straight. It's those TV ads, black horses galloping across the sand, running for their lives away from where they need to be.

We debate back and forth, but I can see he's not going to help. I change tack, really for both of us to not have to hear his 'no way' again.

"What do you think is going on? How come Claire's business has slowed down?"

"I don't know," he says. "I mean, you know Claire, she's got it together, and customers come a long way to see her, but trade is dropping off. I can't say a lot."

"Yeah, yeah," I say. He's pretty good at not sharing my stuff with Claire or hers with me. "But in general, is there a slowdown?"

He thinks for a moment and looks at Danny, who shakes his head.

"No, generally, things seem okay, not booming, but ticking over pretty well."

"Maybe, maybe Mrs Faye needs to have an internet presence?" Danny asks, a little nervous. This is the first time he's decided to leap in. He's got a point; it was one of the things I looked at in the library. There's at least one competitor hiring gowns out that way.

"Danny's doing an MBA. Going to be a high-flyer," Rob says, and Danny flushes slightly, but keeps going.

"You know, it's the Ps: product, price, promotion, and," he hesitates, ruining the effect, "place," he finishes.

We kick that around, and I can see that Rob's just glad that he's killed the overdraft request, without really having to dig into it. I don't see any point fighting when he's just going to say that it's not down to him. Maybe it's the broken arm; somehow it makes me feel he should get some sympathy.

An idea is niggling at me, but then another thought comes to mind, and whatever was bubbling to the surface evaporates. If it was important, it will find its way back.

"Hey, Rob, do you know…" I hesitate, to make it seem unimportant "…Marianne Tilsley?"

Rob laughs and again glances at Danny.

"Oh, the famous Marianne Tilsley, how do you know her?" There's a smile on his face that implies far more than he says. "She's a little out of your league, Charlie, like Man U and Donnington FC distance. Why do you ask?" As always with Rob, when he's not actually turning you down for an overdraft, he just sounds like a mate in the pub.

"Oh," I say, and really, I'm not sure. Maybe I can hear the French horns that open Beethoven's fifth, sounding in my head. "I bumped into her today, at Claire's."

Rob nods, then says, "Marianne, soon-to-be not Tilsley, in the same way she stopped being—"

Rob clicks his fingers, thinking, then Danny says, "Hurst."

Rob nods. "Yes. Right now she's in the middle of a divorce from Terry Tilsley. The property developer?" He makes the last bit a question, like I should know the name. I mull it for a second, and it comes to me.

"Ah, TT Housing, doing that development out Martlesham way?"

I've seen the houses, not quite Mac Mansions, but sort of. Not my style at all.

"Yes, that's right." He sighs and I get the sense that Terry Tilsley is one of the much bigger fish that Rob has to batter every now and then. I don't ask; he wouldn't tell.

"Ah right," I say, easing him on.

"She's a smart one, Marianne. She used to be his assistant, but more than that, in a business sense, I mean. She put together some really good deals, has a nose for finding plots of land to build on. I think you'd need a much larger overdraft to be interesting to her though, Charlie."

I put my hands up in protest. But, if the thought hadn't crossed my mind, why had I asked?

In the end, peanuts finished, and a second tonic water declined, they stand.

"Portman Road tonight," he says. "Charity boxing event. This" – he raises the cast – "should get me a few sympathy drinks."

I look at it again. It's not that big. Just his forearm. It looks impressive, though.

"Does it hurt, or get in the way?" I ask, and I'm not entirely sure why I care.

"No," he answers quickly, shrugging. "It's just to protect the arm. To be honest I reckon I could still drive, but" – he drops to a deeper tone – "The Bank say their insurance doesn't cover it."

I look again. It's plaster, and a bandage wrapping, fits neatly around his forearm and half the pudgy palm of his hand, leaving all his fingers free to flex. Again, that something is niggling me. Something interesting. It's like one of those magic eye pictures is coming into focus, but I can't see it yet. It will get there.

They leave, and I sit down again. I've had three pints, but over quite a few hours. I'll have one more, and a packet of crisps, let the A14 traffic die down.

I need to think on a few things; amongst them, how do I find seven thousand pounds when there is nowhere left to look?

The Slubber's morphs a bit, the day crowd drifting away and the early evening ones taking over.

I like pubs, not the ones that have become restaurants pretending to be pubs, but the proper ones. Not a big royalist me, but Prince Charles, who I've never told anyone I'm named after, he got it right: a good pub is a hub of the community.

For The Slubber's, 'the community' right now means students and the kids from as far away as Trimley, which is a good two miles. Two miles is a long drag for a student to walk.

They're coming for the music. There's always some local band in the big room off to one side on a Friday night. I can hear them tuning up the guitars, calling to each other and banging the amps in a way that has me cringing.

Takes me back so far, like I'm looking down a kaleidoscope and can see my younger self. Christ, I'm getting old. Thirty-five, and I can't even find a lousy seven thousand pounds.

It's just all tied up right now. Some I sunk into the kitchen units, and all the other work on the house. A chunk is in my Christmas trees, growing away up on land in Breckland. More is in the record stock.

I make a living, I do all right, just right now cash is tight. But if that fucking boat would turn up, I'd be laughing.

"One, one, two, two," breaks into my thoughts. Sounds

like some nineteen-year-old wannabee roadie whose voice only just cracked, and I can't help but feel better. Stuff happens, things will turn out all right. I don't know how, but they will.

So, I know what else will help. I get up and make for the exit, stopping for a piss first. It's a long way back to Stowmarket; that sounds like a good title for a song.

It's just edging to sunset as I get out of Felixstowe, red streaks across blue-grey skies and silhouettes of cranes. I'm soon out on the A14 though, and speed dial Eileen to chat before I get home, where we can talk more.

"Hey, lover boy," she says, picking up on the first ring, and again I get that sweep of energy I have whenever I even think of her. "You'll have to hurry," she continues, "my old man is out drinking in the pub, so we've got time." I leave it a second, then she continues in mock surprise, "Oh no, is that you, Charlie? I thought it was the window cleaner!"

"Way my day is going, I might be starting a window-cleaning round," I say. "Not that I could afford all the expensive gear."

"Bad day, darling?" she asks.

"Nah, not really." And it hasn't been. "Just, you know, I can't make out if it's a light or a train at the end of the tunnel."

"You'll work it out, I'm sure you will. Come home, get some rest, go to bed, later get some sleep. Tomorrow will be a new day, you'll see," she replies.

We chat about this and that, how her day has gone. As we do, I see another call coming in: Private Number.

Usually I'd take it, always answer the phone, always follow up an idea, that's me. Most times it's worked out really well, and even the dodgy ones I get a laugh from. Today, though, in that little cocoon of the dark, the lights from the cars on the A14 sweeping across me, and the darkening sky fading the world, I can't be bothered. I let it go to voicemail.

Eileen tells me about her day, keeping the school in check, and as she does, I can hear the banging of pots and pans as she prepares dinner. I've food on the table and a solid roof, and her, what else do I need?

Well, seven thousand pounds would be nice. But that problem will still be there tomorrow, so I don't need to chase it today. Maybe I could sell the Xmas trees as they are? I know a couple of possible buyers. Enough, see? That's how my brain works, even when I push the problem out the front door, it scuttles in through the back.

Eileen says she has to finish with the window cleaner, oh, she means prepare the veg. I say goodbye, knowing I'll be home in fifteen minutes.

The little 'message waiting' sign has come up on my phone, but again, I can't really be fussed. I'll pick it up tomorrow. Then I think, what if it's Van? About the trainers.

So, I click on the voicemail button, and skip through the crap to the message.

"Hello," a female voice says, and it's like she's there in the car, leaning on my shoulder. I know instantly who it is. It's Mrs 'my middle and first names are trouble', Marianne Tilsley.

"I hope you don't mind me calling, Charlie." There's a tiny pause, like she's tasting my name or something. "I took the liberty of asking Claire for your number, after we met today." Again, she pauses.

"Claire was very… complimentary about you, at least for an ex-husband. I'd never talk about *my* ex-husbands that way." She gives a little laugh. The whole femme fatale thing is a bit overdone, but, hey, it's nice to be *fataled*.

"Anyway," she says, after a husky breath. "I have a business proposition for you, something that you might find very… attractive." She seems to love those little pauses, and I can imagine her smiling and looking directly into my eyes as she waits to see what I think she is going to say.

"So, if you're… interested, give me a call, anytime. The number is…" She reels off a series of digits, which I can't catch, and the message ends.

My mobile phone says that's the end of the messages and offers me the opportunity to delete this one. After two minutes of wondering and re-listening, I leave it there.

I'll think about calling her tomorrow.

FOUR

In principle, there is nothing wrong with four o'clock in the morning, nothing that adding at least three more hours to it won't fix.

The kitchen is cold. It should be cold at this time of day. The sun hasn't crawled over the horizon and the only sounds I can hear are the creaking of the house, the barking of a fox somewhere out in the woods, and the gurgling of the coffee percolator.

The weekend has come and gone. Entrepreneurs like me, we don't work Monday to Friday nine to five. Our ever-sharp business minds are out making deals and kicking the tyres on the wheels of commerce all the time. So, my mind has been working over the weekend, sifting ideas to separate the wheat and chaff.

To be honest, all I had to show for it was a big pile of chaff.

Until an hour and a half ago.

It's five-thirty. I've got a coffee in front of me, and a blue notepad full of scribbled drawings, underlined words and exclamation marks. The coffee is my second, or third; it would be a shame to waste a full filter load.

On reflection, making coffee was as sensible as Washington saying, 'looks like a good day for a paddle'. I was already wired enough. My notes have gone from careful details to what looks like Leonardo da Vinci channelling a four-year-old.

Hmm, I've done it again. Let's back up a bit, maybe I should give a little explanation.

Three cups of coffee ago I was in bed, Eileen snoring softly next to me. I had been tumbling back and forth, awake at times I thought I was asleep and dreaming I was awake when I was sleeping.

Mainly my dreams involved finding seven thousand pounds and whether I could get left-legged hopping added to the list of Olympic sports. Throughout the dreams, Rob Simmonds and his smart sidekick Danny stood on the sidelines urging me on, saying that as soon as I didn't need the money, The Bank would be happy to lend it to me.

I'm not a jealous man; my mate Spinoza has something to say about that and, in general, I agree with him. Fortune passes everywhere, and someday it will pass to me. But at four o'clock I felt I could have done with some of Rob's luck. Hell, even breaking his arm had simply got him five-star treatment.

That's when I got it. The idea of the century.

I, I am unstoppable, I am a god of ideas. In this mood, I can get anything done.

Okay, there are some details to work out. Little bits of 'how?' which are rapidly becoming 'how the fuck?', but if I am anything, I am a problem solver.

I mean, how many people can wake up in a trailer park in the US, visa expiring, deserted by everyone they had thought were friends, and still get home without a problem? Right, true it was via Guatemala and on a banana boat, but if I can do that, I can manage anything.

Now all I have to do is work out the details of this idea, get the old grey cells working as that detective – Pierrepoint? – used to say.

Details, schmeetails, this idea cannot fail. Actually, that's true from two points of view: it won't, and I can't afford it to.

I reach for another coffee. The percolator has stopped perking and is only dripping, and maybe I should not drink the rest. Maybe I need a walk, let things settle down a bit.

So, good idea, quick constitutional at quarter to six in the morning, then back for Eileen, breakfast, and The Idea.

It's still coursing through me, The Idea, but as I step into the cold and not yet light, everything calms.

I fucking love the woods at the bottom of the garden. It doesn't matter how I feel. If I go in there alone, it's like this great calm blanket of something different and important has dropped on me.

Everything that's running around inside me just stops and breathes in the scent of the trees. The silence. I know it's a contradiction, but it's like that silence is saying, 'I don't know what you're fussing about, we'll still be here long after whatever crap is bothering you is forgotten.'

There's a dew down, and I get my wellington boots, pulling on their tops. As they tug back, another thought forms. I let that swirl back and forth in my head and step out onto the track proper.

So, I walk out into the woods. Shouldn't really. There are a couple of footpaths through it, but not here. Here the track is only for The Right Horrible Arthur Pulbright JP and magistrate, but I don't imagine he'll be up and about.

I said it was silent, but it isn't.

I can hear the clack-clack chirp of an angry bird. A rook maybe, or perhaps a magpie. It's pissed about something. Too early for a kite to be out there, and not many around here anyway. Perhaps a fox or cat?

It's got my attention now, and as I walk, I allow its call to pull me on. There's two of them, I reckon, having a good old chat, or more agitated than that. Angry, and a touch of fear. You don't usually get that with magpies; they'll put up a good show, or make a run for it, but never really frightened as such.

There's a small track to the left, goes down to a clearing where, every now and then, Pulbright and his friends blast away at the pheasants and pigeons. Don't get me wrong. I've got my own licence, have been known to knock down a few for the pot. I don't know though, just lining up and shooting whatever gets driven out of the woods seems, let's say, unnecessary.

So, I take that left turn, and sure enough, the clack-clack and angry caws are getting louder. Up ahead, I see what it is.

There are two magpies, one is hopping around and

fluttering back and forth; the other isn't. That one is stuck inside a wire and wood trap.

I know straight away what it is. Pulbright's gamekeeper, Terry Deck, has set it up, to keep those 'egg stealing bastards' away. I've heard him in the Red Bull enough times.

The trap might, just possibly, be legal. If he has a licence and if he's been down to inspect it in the last twenty-four hours. Only, Terry is away at a wedding this weekend, so I'll bet the seven thousand I don't have that he hasn't checked this trap.

It pisses me off anyway. We've made things tough enough for the wildlife without this as well.

"Hello, Mr and Mrs Magpie," I say, shooing at the one that's outside the trap. It jumps up to a branch, then looks down at me, clacking away.

The other fixes me with its big black eyes, pointing a beak that could punch a hole in your hand, and showing off the gorgeous rainbow colours in its tail feathers.

I lift up the trap lid and step back.

The daft bird cocks its head at me, and I step back further. After a few moments it hops up to the edge. Now Mrs Magpie in the tree is down, clucking and clacking, and a few moments later, they're away.

I look at the trap, then accidentally tread on it half a dozen times and throw it into the undergrowth.

That was a good start to the morning, so I begin to wander back home, more coffee and more plans to work out. I walk back down along the path, my boots getting a good clean as I drag through the high, dewy, grass.

When I get to the rutted bridlepath across from the

cottages, I turn left and wander that way, kicking a few stones as I go. The bridlepath comes out to cross the main road about three hundred yards up from the cottages. When I get there, I take the right, and walk back down. Not much traffic that time of day.

I can see Eileen's shadow in the bedroom window as I pass the house, and carry on as far as the broken tarmac road that leads down to ours, and I take that. By the time I've completed this circle, Eileen has the coffee on.

Eileen looks up as I take my boots off in the porch, waving a plate at me to ask if I want breakfast. I give her 'that' grin and she shakes her head at me.

"So," she asks, raising her eyebrows, "a four in the morning rising. You have a plan for Claire?"

"Ah, not exactly, not quite, yet." Claire is right up there on my list to be dealt with but had been tumbled away by my brilliant idea. Perhaps not the best moment to share that though; Eileen likes to keep me focused, if she can.

"Don't let it slide, Charlie. I never did like you owing her. Could you, you know – maybe get a buyer for the trees?"

It's no surprise she's thought of that. I might be able to, they will be ready soon, but that last growth spurt is where all the profit is. I sit down to the breakfast, cut up a mushroom.

"That's got to be plan Z, I think."

"And plans A to Y, how they looking?" She's not going to let it go, and fair enough, but sometimes I'd like her to give me a break.

"Whoa!" I leap up, dropping the fork, which now

has sausage on, and run across to her. I kiss her hard on the lips and reach for my notepad, then scribble a phrase down. It's perfect, absolutely brilliantly fucking perfect.

Eileen is sort of used to my sudden switches of emotion, but I can see that this has confused even her.

"Just what was all that about?"

I don't want to tell her yet. I mean, I do, but I want to work it out a little more, see exactly how I can do it. I'm jigging up and down now like I've got a pair of ferrets in my trousers.

"Oh, just an idea I've got. I'll tell you soon."

"Charlie?" There is exasperation, amusement, and resignation in her voice, which is a mix probably only I could cause and recognise.

"Look," she says, pulling me back. "Just why is The Big Night Out having problems? Christmas is coming, Halloween events, business parties – she should be booming."

These are good points. I nod, thinking.

"I'm not sure. There is a new competitor. But Claire's shop seemed pretty busy."

"Could you, maybe, help her a bit on that side?" Eileen asks, squinting a little as she thinks.

"What? Getting customers to take her stuff? Don't think that's quite me. Though maybe…"

"No, Charlie, I didn't mean like that."

My visions of helping in the changing room vanish.

"But, you know, her website isn't up to much, and perhaps you could look at what's happening in the shop."

That's how much Eileen trusts me, or rather knows

me. She's putting me back in the lioness's den. But maybe it makes sense; just why have sales dropped off?

"You," I say to her, standing up and moving a little closer, "not only have an amazing body, but a pretty good head on your shoulders."

"Well, of course," she says. "Now, your turn to do the washing up. I must be going." With that, she kisses me, and makes for the door.

And I still haven't told her about my brilliant idea. That, I can surprise her with tonight. I finish up my coffee and breakfast, pick up the plates and give them a quick wash, and leave them to drain.

As I finish, the back door letter-box rattles and Kevin, the postman, waves as he walks past.

I wave back and pick up the letters, gas and electricity bills on top, and a handy bank statement. I know the state of all three of these, and 'state' sums it up. It's the kitchen that's caused the drain, and those bloody trainers. I had been sure they would come good before the Christmas tree harvest.

Don't worry, something will come up. It always does. There is a fourth letter, from the jury service. Instructions to offer three dates, or else. The 'or else' seems to include fines with a lot of zeroes in them. I look at it for a while, thinking.

See, I don't really like being tied down, me and calendars are chalk and geese, as the saying doesn't go. I pin the letter to the cork noticeboard so that I won't forget it – can't say fairer than that.

Now, I want to do a bit of research on the computer,

size up the competition for what will almost certainly be the biggest business idea I have ever had. Then, I'd also better call Claire, pop over and have a sniff around the shop. I think she'll be okay with that, and it will show willing.

I pick up my phone and see the little voicemail icon from Friday is still flashing. I ignored it over the weekend.

Marianne. What does she want? And do I want to get involved? There is something about her.

If I were a private detective then she would be the dark-haired beauty who asks for my help to find her lost earrings, while all the time trying to make me the patsy for the murder of her husband. The thing is, though, those dark-haired beauties are often the ones with money. What had Rob said, something about her getting divorced?

No. I shake my head. I've got plenty going on.

I reach for the phone to call Claire. As I do, it rings, and I answer without thinking.

"Ah, the elusive Charlie Mellon, I've tracked you down at last."

Of course, I recognise the voice. If it had been the electricity company chasing payment, which I didn't have, things would have worked out far better.

"Ah, Marianne," I say, cringing.

"Yes, Marianne." Suddenly she's more businesslike.

"Look, Charlie, I'm not going to beat about the bush. I need some help, and I think you're the man to… give it to me." Again, the deliberate hesitation.

"Ah, I don't know, I'm… pretty busy at the moment." It's the best I can manage, and not very convincing.

"Oh, I'm sure you are, Charlie, so let me start from a place which might help free you up a bit. How does ten thousand pounds sound?"

She knows exactly how to get my attention.

"Well," I say, "I might be able to free something up in my diary. How does fifteen minutes ago sound?" I was going for 'eager and interested' but realised it came out closer to 'desperate and man-whore'. Still – ten thousand pounds.

"Good, good. I thought that might... pique... your interest. I'm living out in Hadleigh at the moment, we could meet at... the Golden Lion, there. For coffee and a chat, say eleven, that would give us plenty of time."

I mull that for a moment. I need to see Claire. Of course, I could see her *after* Marianne, but something in me is waving hands back and forth and mouthing '*no*'. I'd like to make it a bit more under my control.

"I need to—" What, what can I say? "I need to go out to Cretingham – my trees." I shake my head – I need to check they haven't what? Gone for a walk?

I stammer, "Could we make it, Claydon, the Crown, there, on the High Street?"

Marianne gives a little laugh, as though she's not used to having to negotiate where to have a date, not that this is a date.

After a second, she says, "Okay then, Charlie, as you like, it's a... plan. See you at eleven, looking forward to it." The phone clicks at her end, and for a moment I just stare, then shake my head. Life, eh?

*

As I drain the last dregs of the coffee, I catch a movement on the footpath leading up to the kitchen door. A second glance tells me who it is.

The man is wearing a tweed jacket and brown trousers, tucked into green wellington boots, which are glistening with the dew from the calf-high grass in the woods. He's carrying what looks like the remains of a chicken coop, or maybe a bird trap.

He doesn't look happy, but Terry Deck, gamekeeper and general pain in the arse for Arthur Pulbright, never looks happy. He has made a career of being obnoxious ever since I fought him at school.

What can I say about Terry? Well, he's not the world's brightest. He's the sort of man who, if he was going to have a house built, would choose the first of the three pigs to be his architect. I swear, I once gave him a Xmas card with 'read the other side' printed on the inside and outside, and it kept him occupied for an entire evening.

He's also a bully, and a nosey, gossip-spreading little turd, who has the hots for Eileen. That last doesn't surprise me.

I stand up and get to the door just before he can knock on it. Still, his hand is raised as if ready to bang, and for a moment he looks confused as he tries to recompute what he needs to do.

"Good morning, Terry," I say in my best 'piss off and go away' voice. "To what do I owe this… honour? Selling modern art installations now, are you?"

I glance at the ruined bird trap hanging in one of his over large hands. I can see that a piece of wire has just snagged his trouser leg, and I don't think he's realised.

"Mr Mellon," he says without preamble, or like he was already stuck in one gear, and can't easily change.

"Mr Mellon," he repeats. "Did you see anyone coming out of the woods today? Earlier, vandal-looking sort of person maybe."

I pull my ear out of habit, trying to look casual and keep the smile off my face.

"Oh no, I don't think so, no Huns or Goths either." That whips past him like a greyhound after the electric rabbit, and I see him blink as he tries to process it.

"This," he says, lifting the bird trap remains, and finding the wire caught in his leg. He tugs at it for a moment, then it comes free with a rattle and smear of blood.

"Shit." He rubs at the place on his leg, then turns back to me.

"I found this, in the woods, broken. Someone," he says, attempting portentous, but it comes out with a slight squeak, "destroyed it."

He continues. "And I followed their tracks, through the woods to there." He points at where I came out of the woods an hour ago.

"They—" He looks up the bridlepath, which leads eventually to the road. "They went that way, I reckon, but I wondered…"

I know what he's wondering, and he should know I know, though I wouldn't wonder if he didn't. That will take Mr Pulbright to explain to him.

"Wondered, if you…" He pauses. Maybe he's been taking lessons from Marianne.

"If I?" I ask, imagining a pat of butter remaining frozen in my mouth.

'If you,' he wants to say, 'kicked the hell out of my trap, you slimy little shit.' For a moment I want to look down at my own wellington boots in the porch. Are they still wet? Do they perhaps have a piece of chicken coop wire stuck to them?

I step out onto the path, easing him backwards, and look up the track, the direction he had pointed out, and I had walked earlier.

"Oh, right," I say, "Well, no one there now."

"I know that, I'm not stupid," he says, wiping his hand. The blood he has transferred from his leg leaves a slight stain on the pocket of the shirt. I raise my eyebrows but keep quiet.

"So, I have to tell Mr Pulbright you saw nothing?"

"Tell him what you like, Terry, I really don't give a shit." There is something about Terry that always gets my goat. "Now, get off my land, please." I don't know why I stuck the 'please' in at the end. Force of habit.

"No need to be like that," he says, "unless you know something." It's a remarkable intellectual leap for Terry, and I'm surprised he doesn't go pale with the effort.

"Oh, just piss off," I say, stepping forwards again. He hobbles back, turns round, and starts down the path.

"Wouldn't surprise me if it were you what did this," he says, holding up the broken remains.

I shrug. He can't prove anything, and I really don't care. What can he do? Of course, this was all before the speeding ticket, and having to face the magistrate, Mr Pulbright.

That little encounter sets me up for the day, and I soon find myself whistling 'Who's Afraid of the Big Bad Wolf?' as I get on with more important things.

Ten thousand pounds? Just what does Marianne Tilsley have in mind for that? Still, stranger things have happened. When you've woken up, deserted, in the middle of America, with twenty-five thousand dollars in your pocket, nothing seems too surprising.

First, I grab my notebook, take a new page, and scribble a headline: '*Give Me a Break*'. Perfect, absolutely fucking perfect.

Next, the practicalities. The stuff I got from the Claydon house, that will be a good start. But how to make them? That is the challenge. Well, I know sort of how to do it, but then they have to be removable, there is the trick. Being removeable is, after all, the whole point.

It is half-ten before I surface, and to be honest, I wasn't much further forwards. Yes, I could make what I wanted, even had the model, but that was as far as I could get. It was like my first time, with Nicola Nightingale: she was willing, but no way could I get that bloody bra-strap undone.

Eventually I had to give up; time to go see the femme fatale.

It didn't take long to get to the Crown in Claydon, and I was a little early.

Nice enough place. Last decorated fifteen years ago in mock village pub style – black leather straps with horse brasses, old pub mirror over a gas-fired grate made to look like a real fire, some tables and chairs, benches along the wall, and a few bar stools.

For a moment I hesitated between the bar, which is where the magnet of habit was dragging me, or the lounge.

The bar had only one customer, Peter Clegg, who, I had to laugh, had two crutches to support what, by the plaster, I guessed was a broken ankle or similar. Petey was, and might someday again in the future be, a window cleaner.

The Crown is the habitual starting point for his round, and probably there was a direct link between that and his injury. I could hardly ignore him, so went to have a chat, call it product development research.

I only ordered a coffee, which caused John behind the bar to raise his eyebrows, and chatted to Pete while looking at his plaster.

"How they get that off?" I asked.

"This?" he said, tapping the plaster as if I meant his leg. "Oh, big metal grinder thing, with a blade. Makes a helluv a racket."

I nodded, keeping one eye on the door.

Marianne Tilsley turned up about eleven-fifteen; I had been just about ready to give her up and go see Claire. Marianne nodded at me from the entrance and wandered into the lounge.

By then there were a couple of pensioners having a cup of coffee and arguing over who was to pay for the toasted sandwich they were sharing. Fuck me, when did pubs become cafes? Still, a man's got to make a living, I guess.

Marianne got a much bigger eyebrow raise from John than my coffee order had. She was dressed in the tightest fitting sports jogging gear I had ever seen, black with pink stripes, which outlined her cheeks like the contour lines on an Ordnance Survey map. A fleecy pink top, zip half undone, and a very tight sports top, outlining two more mountains, finished the outfit. She looked a little flushed but had lipstick and some other fairly subtle make-up.

"Sorry I'm late, Charlie," she said, air-kissing me in a way I had not expected. "Pilates this morning, ran over a bit." She opened her arms slightly, as if to prove she had been exercising, and I stammered, asking her what she'd like to drink.

"Oh, a water please, sparkling, Perrier by preference, ice, lemon, and…" She hesitates, looking around, then shakes her head. "Probably no point asking for a sprig of mint, is there?"

I catch John's eye and give the slightest shake of my head as I relay the order. I have the horrible feeling her drink is going to come back with a piece of celery or similar sticking out of it. But thankfully, no.

Meanwhile, Marianne sits herself down in one of the big, brown leather lounge chairs. I say sits, but really she curls herself into it, almost like a cat, feet tucked under and relaxed like we'd known each other a thousand years.

"I always feel so good after Pilates, like I've just had a good—" She does what I now know is her trademark pause, gives a small giggle, and says, "Well, something else that gets the blood pumping, like a run."

John calls me back to the bar for my second coffee, and I scoot over there. This time he hardly looks at me, like he doesn't want me to see what he thinks he saw.

I sit down and look at Marianne, trying to ask the ten-thousand-pound question. She watches me for a while. Way too long; she is just loving this.

"Well," she says. "Thank you so much for agreeing to meet. Claire told me how busy you are." I didn't think Claire would have shared too much, but who knows?

"What it is Charlie, what I need your help with, is…" She unfolds her legs and leans forwards, placing her hand on mine for a moment.

"I'd like you to buy a house for us, Charlie," she says, looking deep into my eyes.

*

"Marianne said what?" Claire looks at me like either she'd misheard or I've gone mad, both of which could have been possible. I tell her almost as soon as I get to The Big Night Out. She would have guessed that something had suddenly shifted anyway, I admit it, I am to a poker face what The Rolling Stones are to ballroom dancing.

"It's all pretty weird, and to do with her husband, or soon-to-be ex," I explain.

Claire's face clouded. "What, Terry Tinsley? You don't want to get tangled up there, Charlie. Surely you know about Terry?"

Well, sure, I know some of the stories, about how he started, but I'd never got close to him. Property developers, they might look like businessmen, but most of them started as bricklayers and built their way up. I admire that, but it's the survival of the fistiest sometimes.

"Well, yes, but he can't be *that* bad?"

"Charlie!" Her voice rises. "He walks around with two minders most of the time. He came in here once with Marianne, then left when he found out we didn't sell the dresses. 'No wife of mine is going out in second-hand gear.'" Claire's voice deepens and her shoulders go up like she is a rugby forward.

I laugh; no matter how she tries, she isn't going to look like a fifteen-stone builder turned property magnate.

"It's not funny. He's not funny. He had that thing, the road rage case a few years back, you know, threatened someone with a tyre iron."

I vaguely remember that, but Claire is missing the point.

"The thing is," I say, my smile coming back, "all she wants me to do is buy a house, in my name, then sell it to her, and she'll pay me five thousand pounds." No need to tell Claire *everything*.

"But why, Charlie? It doesn't make sense."

The back door opens, and Giselle sticks her head through. We both shut up, and Claire looks around.

"Oh, sorry to interrupt, I was wondering if you'd like a coffee?" Giselle is watching me, in a way that suggests Claire has only told her the bad stories. The shop doorbell rings, and Giselle looks over her shoulder, a flash of annoyance on her face.

"No, thank you," says Claire. "You'd better see to that." She nods back to the shop.

"Look, the point is," I continue, "if she pays me, I can pay you, at least some of what I owe."

Claire shakes her head for a moment, then shrugs. She

was always like that, not really seeing the big picture, you might say.

"Well, that would be good, of course, only, just tell me again what she wants."

I sigh; women always want details, like where are you? and where the hell is that?

"Okay. She wants to buy one of the houses up on Terry's new development, Martlesham. Only…" Now I am saying it, it sounds maybe not quite right. "Only Terry won't sell to her, because it's her, or he'll rip her off. So, she wants me to buy it, and do a deal to sell it to her straight away. She'll pay the cash for the purchase, and everything, and I get a little surplus."

See, simple, what can go wrong?

Again, Claire shakes her head; she always sees the problems, never the opportunities. I shift direction.

"Look, I was thinking, about the shop."

"Yes?" She looks pleased to be off the Marianne story.

"Right, things have been going well, and you've got plenty of stock, so what's changed?" I ask.

Now she nods, in an 'I don't know' sort of way.

"It was going great, I even needed Giselle. Now I'm almost at the point of having to get rid of her, missed her salary last week. Sales have dropped right off."

"Anybody new on the market, competition?"

"No, not that I've seen, and I'd know, I'm sure."

"Well, I was thinking, you know," I say. "It's all about the four Ps. Product, you've got; price, I don't think you're out on that; place, the shop looks good; and production, erm, I mean, promotion."

She studies me, and I can't tell if she's impressed or suspicious.

"Okay?" she says, looking at me as though she wants to ask who I am and what have I done with Charlie.

"So," I push on. "I was thinking I could help with that a bit. I visited your website."

Now she looks embarrassed. "I know, Charlie, I know, but I haven't had the time, or money, to get it looking better."

I put my hands up, then open them.

"Whereas I, I might be able to help with that. What if I could get your site spruced up? Do the SCO and stuff." I bite my lip; it's SEO, not SCO, but maybe Claire doesn't know.

"You can do that?" She manages to put a stress on the beginning and ending of the sentence, which would be disheartening if I were not such a positive person.

"Certainly, or I know a man who can. Up in Cambridge, owes me a favour and just been made redundant. Big marketing guy, I'm sure he'd help." I believe it. David Barrington is the sort of man who loves taking on projects like this, and he does owe me.

"Whatever, Charlie," Claire says. I can see she is underwhelmed. "But I really need cash, as quickly as you can, you know?"

"I know," I say. "And with Marianne, I might be able to get an advance."

For a second, she seems to flinch, then gives me a sigh which sort of has the sound of 'it's your funeral' wrapped up in it, but I ignore that.

"I'll have a chat to Marianne, I promise," I say. Then,

"And could I have a look around the shop? So I can do a…" The words are on the edge of my memory, then come. "A design brief, for David."

Claire shakes her head, resignation rather than saying no.

"Whatever, Charlie, and thanks, but I need that money, ok?"

I nod my head. Strange, as I do, I get the feeling that what I'm really doing is putting it on the chopping block.

I wander back into the shop; this time it is empty. It still *seems* busy though, the music, Mungo Jerry, 'In the Summertime', filling up the place.

There is a load of stock. I mean, there would be no point shaking a stick at this lot, you'd need a bloody forest. Every rack seems to be full. I guess that is part of the problem, though. If more of it was lent out, the racks would be a bit more empty. Those full lines of dresses are also where some of Claire's cash has gone.

Of course, I have no idea how a women's dress shop should look. I'm more used to sitting in the pub singing 'Come On Eileen' or nodding enthusiastically at everything I'm shown. So, what do I know?

I stride around, studying the labels and trying to get a sense of the place. Giselle is watching me; I get my first proper look at her. Previously she's sort of hovered in the background or hung at the door. In her twenties I'd guess, thin, dark-haired. She has me thinking of a jackdaw, on the lookout; a bit of a loner.

I get that feeling again, the one that says Claire has told her about me, our history, disappearing for eighteen months. She is doing a great job of putting her disapproval into her stare. I try my number one smile and walk over.

"Hey, nice to meet you, Giselle, isn't it? I'm Charlie, Claire's ex." I offer her my handshake.

I have a great greeting; I like people and like meeting them. Okay, my winning smile has got me into some trouble, but grumpy and sullen, that's for losers.

Giselle is clearly Charlie-proof.

"Yeah, I know," she replies, putting into it the sort of enthusiasm normally reserved for root canal work. She looks at my hand as though I've just walked out of the gents, and she suspects I hadn't washed. She picks it up and gives it back to me with the vaguest of shakes. Okay.

"How you enjoying working here?" I have to try something, only now I feel a little like the Duke of Edinburgh, and have the weirdest desire to put one hand into the small of my back.

"It's sallright," she replies, the words blending into each other as though they are running through a stick of rock.

She comes out from behind the counter, and starts towards one of the racks of clothes, easing me towards the front door as if by accident.

Well, if that's how she wants it to be.

"You don't seem pleased to see me?" I make it a comment and a question, but more the latter than the former, no bush-beater, me.

Now she turns to face me, glances over my shoulder at the door to Claire's office, and says, "Look, Charlie Mellon, I've met lots of dead-beats like you. Wannabees who promise the world then just piss off. Claire told me, about you. And Snow Patrol. And pissing off to America when you were supposed to be married." She drops each sentence like she's hammering nails into the lid of my coffin.

Honestly, I'm surprised, and I guess it shows.

"And now," she continues, quiet but with the weight of a lava flow. "Now you're out to borrow money Claire hasn't got, and screw up the first decent job I've had in a long while."

There is real venom here, and for a second, I think I can hear a tremble or maybe anger in her voice. My mate Spinoza, he says to look out for that sort of thing, that the bodily state reflects the mind. No shit, Sherlock. I can tell well enough, though, that she sees me as to blame for her not getting paid.

"Whoa. Okay..." I stop. Wu-wei, wu-wei, this is not the time for that argument.

"Well." I pause; I am obviously learning from Marianne. "Giselle." What sort of name is that? "It's lovely chatting to you, but I must go con some other vulnerable woman out of her savings."

I make for the door, push when I should pull, and rather ruin the effect of my snappy exit.

FIVE

"Pinch, punch, first of the month and no returns, my darling." Eileen hands me a coffee, and peers over my shoulder, having delivered the punch.

I turn, give her a kiss, and nod thanks.

"Damn, never a white rabbit around when you need one." I smile, can't help but smile when Eileen's there. Then I turn back to the mould. It won't come off the shop model's arm, and I really thought it would this time.

Nearly two weeks since I had the idea, and 'Give Me a Break' has hit an operational roadblock.

But the idea. Oh, every time I think of it, I just get this smile of anticipation and certainty; it's going to be massive.

See, it all started with Rob Simmonds, when he came in waving that plaster cast on his arm, talking about how he'd been helped by everyone. Then, next morning, I was up and drawing the plans. Only, it still won't quite work.

It is worth the effort, though. It will make millions, or at least a few thousand or so a year, I'm sure.

Look, picture the scene. You're at the airport. Crowds of people all lined up to get on the plane. You can just feel the space in the overhead cabin reducing as every parent has loaded every child up with the two bags they can bring on. And anyway, there's that horrible tension of having to wait while the Gold Card Holders, Frequent Flyers, Parents with Children, and those needing assistance are called up.

Only, this time, this time you're there. You're the one 'needing assistance'. You're right at the front of the queue, and the smiling air steward looks at you with sympathy and guides you on. Perhaps even offers you a free glass of the business cabin champagne.

For why? For because you have a broken arm.

No doubt it was shattered in some brave accident where you saved a dog from a steamroller or stopped a speeding horse that was about to trample a cluster of old ladies.

But, and here I have the urge to tap my nose, what you have is not a broken arm, as such, but a plaster cast!

Yes, ladies and gentlemen, boys and girls, mayor and mayoresses. I present to you the fabulous, tailor-made, plaster arm cast that you can slip on and off with ease, and which, while you are wearing it, gives you super-human queue-jumping powers!

And what, you ask, is the name for your business, Charlie?

Drum roll, maestro, please, it's called: 'Give Me a Break', of course!

Charlie! You exclaim, that is fucking genius; how

much did you pay Saatchi and Saatchi for that piece of marketing magic?

Nil, zip, nada, is my reply. It's all my idea, and you will bow down in awe at my magnificence!

At least, eventually you will.

I glance around the shed. I had three models; that's six arms, right?

I now have two, arms that is.

One arm has a chisel still sticking in it, said chisel having first pierced two inches of plaster. Another arm, or half of it, is in the dustbin. Apparently twisting a stick-on plaster cast creates a lot of torque, and definitely a lot of shouting.

The third arm I don't really like to look at. It's in the corner of the shed, smeared in an unattractive mix of Vaseline, silicone and plaster, looking like something out of *The Mummy*.

You've been counting, haven't you? That's three arms. Start with six, destroy three, I should have three left.

The fourth arm? Well, it's somewhere in the woods, and I know I should retrieve it. Only, well, I think I set a new plaster-covered-shop-dummy-arm throwing record, and I'm waiting for the *Guinness Book* people to turn up to ratify it.

"How's it going?" Eileen asks. She does it in a way full of sympathy and hope.

"Bloody undercuts, bloody plaster, bloody hell," I say, succinctly, laying out the problem.

"Don't give up, darling," she says, "you'll find the solution. Eddison tried sixteen hundred different materials for light bulbs before he got the right one." The thought of sixteen hundred arms sends a shiver through me, but I nod.

"And he'd borrowed the whole idea from someone else in the first place," I say.

I push the face mask off my head, where I'd rested it to kiss Eileen.

Then I take another look at the model's arm and silicone I got from that house in Claydon. They were the other part of the jig-saw puzzle that made up my idea, like the universe was shouting at me to give it a go.

Of course, cause or effect? Did I think of the idea because I have them, or did I have them because the idea was going to come to me? That way lies madness; we can only deal with what we have in front of us.

But really, with the silicone I should be able to make one that *looks* like a plaster one. Few bits of bandage, wrap them around the arm of the model, slap on some silicone, and Robert's your father's brother. Only, no. It didn't look right, and anyway, trying to wrap the arm in bandages and silicone was as easy as trying to fill up a sack with snakes, when the sack has a hole in the bottom.

"It's the plaster, is it?" Eileen asks. "Could you go back to the other approach? Where you just used the silicone from Claydon?"

I shake my head.

"Well, I know you, Charlie, you don't know the meaning of the word 'daunt', so I'm sure you'll find it. Tell me again, see if that shakes an idea loose."

"It's the bloody bumps on the arm, and the arm itself.

I can never get the plaster actually off the dummy's arm. I mean, they're meant to be sawn off."

"But if you do that…"

"Then the customer can't put it back on!"

"So?"

"So, I need an arm that I can use as a mould, and which I can get the sod-damming plaster off afterwards, which right now—" I point at the detritus around the shed, and vaguely out into the woods.

"It won't do."

Eileen looks at me.

I know what she's thinking, because she's been saying it.

Do I really think this is a good idea?

Shouldn't I be finding the money for Claire?

Why does that Marianne woman keep calling me up for meetings?

And when am I going to restart on my kitchen?

I get it, I really do. These are good questions, but right now I need to answer that other tricky one. How do I make a great stiff plaster cast, which comes away from whatever arm-shaped thing I've made it around?

When I have the answer to that, then I can focus my attention on the others. Not that I'm ignoring those other little issues, but right now, I've got to solve this one.

Eileen can see it's bugging me; my stubble beard, plaster in the hair and a wild look around for a bottle of whisky probably give it away. She goes to sit down, lifting my rubber gloves that I've dropped on the wooden stool, and pats her lap.

"Sit down for a moment, let's have a chat."

Now, what can I do?

A chat. Eileen's chats are famous; they always end in decisions and new directions. I nod. She's right. I perch on her lap, my foot on the floor, both shoes covered in plaster, and feel the fight drop out of me.

An hour later I am back in 'the bomb site', as Eileen, in an approach which is as subtle as the stage make-up of Kiss, has taken to calling the kitchen.

I'm no further forwards on the plastered-arm front, but I'm showered, I've had breakfast, and I shut the shed door. Overall, I feel a bit better.

"Leave it for a day. Step back. If there's an answer, it will come." That had been Eileen's advice, wise words, but not altogether inspiring.

She manoeuvred me back into the kitchen and got me to change the gas bottle for the hob, and fix the temporary pipe to the washing machine. I even shifted a few of the boxed kitchen units to a more satisfactory corner, stacking them carefully one on top of the other.

I thought that helped a lot, but it hardly got a grunt of thanks from Eileen, who left for work with just a glance at the improvement. Sometimes I don't understand her.

The plaster is pulling at me, but I know I should ignore it. Get on with some other project, be constructive, that's what Eileen said, and I will be.

Studying the bomb site, kitchen, my eyes fall on the noticeboard. I can put that straight; it is always lopsided.

I look around for my spirit level, which is handily in the corner with a long metal ruler and pencil. Eileen must have just dumped them there without thinking. That's unlike her, but she's under stress at work at the moment. As I get the noticeboard straight, I see it. The bloody JCSB letter.

It is buried, under the electricity and credit card bills, which are *both* under the kitchen unit layout plans that Eileen must have pinned there for safety.

The bloody JCSB. It's fine, I'm sure it's fine. I checked the date I got the letter. The 21st of September. Now it is – pinch, punch – the 1st of October. That was, 'thirty days has September', ten days ago. Ten days, and I had to get back to them within – seven days. Ah, but working days, surely?

I grab my phone, which is on the workbench I hadn't realised I'd left out, dial, and as soon as they answer, "Jury Central Summoning Board—"

"Can I—"

"Please listen carefully to the following options, which have recently changed."

After pushing three, two, three and one, I eventually get through to a human.

"Ah, great, hi. I, I had a deferral and rang a few days ago to give you new dates, but ah, I haven't had any confirmation. Thought I should check, you know? Just in case it got… not put into the system."

"Okay," says a not entirely convinced voice. It's sad to be so suspicious all the time. "Could you give me your deferral reference number?"

"Right, that's four-seven-three-six, A for Alpha, C for Charlie. Which is my name, Charlie, sorry, I didn't catch yours."

There is a slight hesitation, then, "Cheryl, Cheryl Baker, I'm the clerk to the court's booking admin assistant."

"Lovely name, Cheryl, nearly like a female version of Charlie."

"Hmm."

"Ah, well, as I say, I want to check—"

"Yes, you said. What was the new reference number you were given?"

Shit.

"Oh, erm, well, that is… I, we, had a leak in the kitchen, all my paperwork got soaked. Been up to my arms in rubber gloves and water all weekend."

Hey! Holy shit – yes!

"Oh, I'm sorry to hear that. But you managed to save the first notice details?"

"Yes."

Now I'm leaping up and down. Holy shit shit shit, yes, I have an idea for the moulds.

But Ms I'm-far-from-convinced Cheryl Baker draws in a breath, and it's all I can do not to put the phone down, but I guess the jury stuff is important.

"We don't seem to have any record of your call. Perhaps that too got lost in your flood?"

I ignore the sarcasm.

"Oh really? Just as well I checked then."

"Right. What starting date did you offer?" Her voice is as flat and cold as a frozen pond.

"Erm." Damm – shit, pick a date. "November 15th, yes, that's right."

"Really?" Suspicion in one so young is disappointing.

I flip through the wall calendar on the noticeboard. Oh, fuck.

"No, sorry, did I say 15th? I meant 16th, Monday the 16th. Your jury services dates start on a Monday, don't they, Cheryl?"

"Hmm. Well, we don't have you down for that, but, given the extraordinary situation of your house flood, I can log that in for you." I think she means extenuating, but I don't push it.

Big sigh, see, it was all right. And, holy shit, I might have found a solution, a solid solution to my mould problem.

Cheryl is going on about numbers and references and the penalties for not turning up. I jot the number down, rush a goodbye. I think I might have blown her a kiss.

Then I run to the shed.

*

The shed is a bit of a mess. It is suffering from two intensive weeks of failure, but now I'm on the track to success. I can smell it.

First, I have to search through the shelves for the one box I need. Obviously that entails finding quite a few boxes I don't want, but by a process of deduction and shouting, I track it down.

They are there, I knew they were. Long, blue, and gorgeous, if you like rubber.

My phone rings. I sooo want to ignore it, but right now that's not an option. I look at the screen, relax a little and also feel my curiosity piquing. It's David Barrington.

David. The company that he worked for as their marketing and product design guru has just gone belly up, and we've shared a few beers as he makes his new plans. Over the last couple of weeks he's been looking into The Big Night Out for me.

"Davey, Davey, Davey," I answer the phone, channelling the Kaiser Chiefs.

"Charlie. You sound pretty upbeat for a man who, yesterday, wanted to give it all up and find a desert island." David sounds cheerful as well.

"Oh, that was yesterday, and I don't believe in yesterday. I've got a belter of a plan, David; this is going to work." I talk to him with the phone in the crook of my neck, while hanging one of the blue rubber gloves on the washing line.

"Glad to hear it. Look, I'm ringing about the shop."

"Right, thought you might be, how's it going?" The glove drops off the pegs and I scoop it up, slopping water all over myself. That was a stupid idea.

"Good, yes. It's fun to be at the front-end again, after the remote-control debacle." He uses words like debacle, strategy and integrated product design processes, does David. But otherwise he's okay, and a true friend.

Maybe if I put a hole in both sides of the glove near the top? They're pretty strong. I walk back into the shed, looking for my drill.

"Sorry, Dave, I didn't catch that," I admit.

"I said, there's something a bit weird about the stock control system."

"You mean, other than she doesn't seem to have one?" I ask, but actually I thought there was – like a tag on every dress.

I find the drill, and it's still got a bit in it, should be the right size. I go back out, firing the drill as I do, and, miracles, the battery still has juice.

"No, well, yes. It's just that I'm not sure about the underlying reconciliation and product code attribution Al Gore rhythms." He says, or something like that. I'm a bit distracted as an industrial-strength blue rubber glove spins around, pinned by my drill.

"Right, right, that was my thought," I say. That's marginally better than saying nothing, but not a lot.

"You a bit distracted, Charlie? This a bad time?" David asks.

I'm just trying to untie the washing line, but it won't come. I wander to the kitchen to pick up the scissors, still talking.

"No, well, yes, sorry, just, I'm right on track now. Nearly cracked it." I stop at the washing line, snip it, and thread the glove through.

"I get it, Charlie. But look, I think we should meet up. There's definitely something iffy going on, and, well, she's *your* ex-wife."

I tie the washing line together again, and it looks like the glove should stay on there. Can it take the weight, though? That's the question.

"Really?" David was a top man at the design agency, Mr number two or three. If he thinks there's something weird going on, then, as Bill and Ted would say, the Circle

K is definitely in trouble.

I tug at the glove, seems pretty good, and go to get the water jug.

"Right, of course. Look," I say, thinking fast, "I've got to see Marianne today, at the solicitors. We're using some guy in Cambridge, which she says is because she doesn't trust anyone round here, they've all worked with Terry. We could meet in the Baron, or I'll drop by yours."

See, I'm a multi-tasker, sexy multi-tasker. I start pouring water into the glove, which swells, and the line sags, but so far...

I can hear David working things out.

"Sure, come by here. The boys would love to see you. Jenny's out with the dog training thing – what time?"

The washing line sags further, the holes in the rubber glove look okay though, and now, the glove is nearly full. I give a fist bump and a jump, nearly, nearly.

"Erm, I'm at Hewitson's at two. Shall we say three-thirtyish?"

"Sounds good, see you then."

The phone clicks off, and I stand back, hardly daring to breathe. The glove hangs there, a few tiny drips of water coming from it where I didn't pour straight, but it looks okay. Now, all I need to do is tie the top off.

Later, after I changed my T-shirt and trousers, I sat thinking, imagining those Greek gods, Necessity and So-close-but-no-banana, making urgent love. At last, Invention comes struggling into the world.

First – fill your glove with silicone and leave it to set on the line.

Then – get a move on up to Cambridge leaving what looks like a cannibal's butchery hanging in your garden.

*

Speed limits are more like recommendations really. I drive safely given the road conditions and how late I am.

Which is pretty late, but I will make it. The phone rings and I slip it under my chin while pulling past a removals van that is fighting its way up the only slope on the A14 between Stowmarket and Cambridge.

"Marianne," I say, trying to inject cheer into my voice. "All okay?"

"Oh yes, Charlie, I always enjoy calling you, you have such wonderful… energy."

I go past the van and slip in behind a Porsche, getting ready for my exit into Cambridge, about four miles ahead.

"I'm just coming into Cambridge now," I say. "Should be fifteen minutes or so, though you know what that last drag down Newmarket Road is like."

"Ah, good, wonderful. Erm…" This time the hesitation seemed, well, still not fully genuine, but almost. I say nothing. I've found it best that way.

"I had to see my lawyers today, about Terry and… the divorce."

I make a very non-committal grunt sound.

"Anyway." She sighs. "Whilst I was there, I popped in on Lance."

"Okay." Lance Tyler – I keep imagining that if he'd been

a she, her name might have been Ruth. He is handling the purchase, and sale, of the Martlesham house.

"Well, it seems that, oh, it's all a bit difficult to explain."

Shit. This is another of those half step forwards, half step back, trip over the hidden block in the road, days.

"Oh?" I try not to sound like I can see ten thousand pounds vanishing out of the window.

"Yes, well, I mean, it should still be okay. It's some tax issue or something. Look, can we meet to talk?" The idea seems to come to her suddenly.

"I thought we *were* meeting?"

"Yes, but you see, that's what I want to chat about, some of those little… details. I'd like to meet alone, without having to pay solicitors' fees. I mean, we're friends now Charlie, we could have a little lunch together. Get to know each other… better."

Ten thousand pounds, ten thousand pounds, eyes on the prize, Charlie. Eyes on the prize. I let the mantra run through my head a few times, then blow out my cheeks.

"Well, if you think we need to."

"Oh, I do, I definitely do."

"How about the Wetherspoons in the centre?" I like the beer there and their curry is… interesting.

"Oh, I think we can do better than that," Marianne says. "I've… I'll book a table at the Ivy – my little treat."

The Ivy, nice place, I've walked past it a few times. They don't have a 'please wait to be served' sign. They have two or three very attractive young ladies who look like their day, week, or even their year would be made if you just crossed the threshold.

The turn off the A14 is coming up, so I slip into the inside lane, gunning past the Porsche on my outside. The driver sticks his middle finger up at me.

"Shall we say quarter to two?"

I glance at the clock, half past one.

"Yes, of course, see you there."

"Wonderful. I'll be waiting, but not too long, I hope. You wouldn't keep a lady waiting would you, Charlie?"

The line goes dead as I start the half-hour fight through the traffic into Cambridge.

*

Twenty minutes later I am at the Ivy, and that is good going, I can tell you. As I said, it's a nice place. Has a sort of 1920s mixed with 1950s elegance.

The walls are a riot of colour and confusion, entirely covered in apparently mismatched pictures, ranging from line drawings of fossils to reproductions of Toulouse-Lautrec theatre posters. But it works. Low ceilings, but bright lighting, together with a spread of elegant tables and chairs, which go back much further than you expect, complete a feeling of sophistication.

The waiting staff are all smartly dressed, with well-trained corporate smiles and an elegant way of gliding around the place as though they are on roller skates.

Me, I'm in jeans, T-shirt and my second-best hoodie. Okay for the Slubber's or at a push the Wetherspoons, but I feel as out of place as a lamb chop at a vegetarian picnic.

I am guided to the table in a quiet little corner where Marianne is waiting. She has a glass of champagne in front of her and a bottle cooling in an ice-bucket.

She, of course, is perfectly dressed in a tight-fitting black trouser suit and vaguely filmy black silk top, which cuts the line above her breasts at the border between fashionable and 'come back to my place for coffee'.

She remains seated when I arrive, leaning forwards in a bob of greeting, which lets the top fall forwards, and I sit down quickly.

"Glad you could make it, Charlie – I'm not used to being kept waiting. Still, I had good company." She raises the champagne glass, and the waiter who brought me over takes the bottle, tops up her glass, and begins to fill a second for me.

We chink glasses and she looks into my eyes. I pick up the menu.

"Yes – sorry, traffic was a disaster." The champagne is good, and though I'm more a beer man, I don't mind slumming it sometimes.

"I, I've got to meet up with someone later," I say. "Are the burgers good here?"

We fall into the expected pattern, reviewing the menu and comparing orders. I shake my head at the idea of a starter, but end up having one anyway, to keep Marianne company.

Eventually, after a top-up or two of champagne, I ask, "So, you said, there might be some… issues?"

"Oh, nothing too drastic, but you know. If there is interest to pay on the bridging loan."

"Which you said you'd pay." I need to be clear about this; Eileen had pushed that point home.

"Which I will pay, Charlie. But, you know, Rob and Lloyds lent you the money for the deposit, then after you complete, I can buy from you. But, if there's any delay, there'll be interest to pay."

Rob Simmonds had been far from comfortable when Marianne and I had talked about this deal. But she clearly has more clout than me, and he'd agreed, with her guarantee, to fund my deposit on the plot she wanted.

Delay? The champagne has dulled my fear of disaster, but where this is going is cutting through my complacency like a combine harvester through a field of cow pats. Bad stuff everywhere.

Marianne reaches out and lays her hand on my arm.

"Oh, don't worry. I'm just saying, if. You know what lawyers are like. Well, if." Her hand is still on my arm and she is looking into my face, leaning forwards. I am unsure where to look.

"Then, what?" I ask, swallowing.

"Well, I pay you the money you need for the monthly bridging loan interest. But—"

"But what?" I ask.

"Well," she said. "It's a tax thing. Any payments I make to you, they count as income for you, or something, so you might have to pay tax. Interest on property deals is not tax deductible, Lance reminded me. I should have known."

Tax, next year's tax? *That* was the issue? Right now, today's cash flow was way more important.

"Oh, I have a good accountant. I'll work something

out," I say. If that was what this was about, then we hardly needed to have met. Again, my imagination runs through a scenario that ends in disaster and no Eileen. No, *that* is never going to happen.

Marianne smiles. She has a great smile, not as good as Eileen's, I remind myself, but nice.

"Oh really? So… a delay wouldn't be a problem?" She pushes.

The champagne is having its effect on me, and now I have the urge to be somewhere else. Marianne's hand is still on my arm, and I shift clumsily.

"You think there might be… delays?" She'd paid me a couple of thousand to get started, but the rest was on exchange and completion. I need completion sooner rather than later. The crocodile of Claire's VATman is lying in wait for the wildebeest of my hopes, and things do not look good. I need this to happen fast.

"Because," I continue, "I was wondering if, perhaps, you could advance me a little more."

"Oh, I'm not sure, Charlie. It's a little bit soon for an advance." She tilted her head and smiled a tiny smile. "We hardly know each other."

I try again. "You see, Claire asked me to help her out."

"Well," Marianne replies. "This isn't really the place to discuss personal loans, is it? Maybe, though. We'd have to talk it through a bit, security and such. How do I know what you're good for?"

Again, that arch look. I know, I know, I'm a man. I can't help how my brain works. How far would I go for the money?

As if prompted by some sudden thought, she stands.

"Well, I need to… powder my nose… freshen up a bit. Be right back."

She takes the path behind my chair, her hands lying on my shoulders momentarily, as she breezes past in a cloud of something that smells enticing.

Once she's gone from view, I slip out my phone and send a text.

It takes Marianne a while, so I finish off the champagne, I and the waiter fighting over whose job it is to pour the last glass.

The timing works well, though. As she arrives, smelling even better, my phone rings.

"Hello, David," I say, "chasing me up?" I look at Marianne and make a 'sorry about this' face. I hold the phone away from Marianne, but can see her listening to my side of the conversation.

"Hi, Charlie, you texted?" David Barrington says.

"Right yes, I'll be there, sheesh man, no need to get difficult."

"What?" he asks.

"Look, I'll be there," I say with a little more strength, getting into the role. "I'm just a bit… busy at the moment."

"Ah," says David.

"Right, now, you just make sure everything's set, right?"

David laughs. "Yes, massah, sure, massah, lift that barge, tote that bale."

I try not to laugh.

"Good, see you when I get there." Then I click the phone off.

Marianne looks at me, eyebrows raised.

"I'm sorry," I say. "I need to get going, need to see a man about a website, or maybe two."

"Oh, must you?" There is surprise and, I reckon, disappointment, honest. "I was hoping we could chat more. I'd love to find out about you and Snow Patrol. Is it true," she leans forwards, hand on my arm again, "about all the groupies, on tour?"

It's not easy to strip Charlie Mellon of words, and now she even has me thinking in the third person. I stand up, maybe a little too quickly.

"Perhaps another time," I say. "I really must get going. Thank you for lunch, and the champagne."

"Oh, thank *you*, Charlie. I look forward to hearing about *everything* you got up to in America, next time." Somehow, she manages to make that sound far more than it should have done.

*

I can't remember a time when I didn't know David. He's a friend who I can rely on, and he can look to me anytime too.

Sitting in his office room in his house on the corner of Holland Street and Carlyle Road in Cambridge, I feel relaxed for the first time in three or four hours. We both have coffees, and Snoozette, his mum's Pekingese dog, is snuffling around for biscuit crumbs.

After the surreal lunch, this is so much better. Give him his due, David didn't ask me about the text, which, of course, meant I had to tell him.

"And will you?" he asks. "Tell her how you and—" He hesitated. Then, "Gary… met up? How that all started?"

I shrug. Really, I wanted to have as little to do with Marianne as I could, at least as required for the other eight thousand she is going to pay me.

"I don't know. That whole scene, I can hardly remember those days."

"What? They were your crowning glory."

He was right in a way. I had loved that time, but that was the past. I would never don my Tina Turner wig and strut my stuff to 'Nutbush City Limits' again, ever. I mean, look what happened last time.

"No. That's over. Now, what do you want to tell me about The Big Night Out?"

"Right," he says. Suddenly he's all businessman and smart marketing man. I still don't understand what happened with the company he'd been with, but – shit happens. He seems to be enjoying being between jobs, though.

"So," he said, "I went over to Stowmarket. Claire's smart, and I think she's onto something. It's a good business model."

"In that case, why is she so short of sales?"

"Yes, it's strange. I mean, people who go in there, they have a reason to go in, you know, they go there expecting to hire. And when I was there, quite a few did, say eighty percent or so, but—" He shakes his head. "Dresses booked out, they've dropped off. Claire has a computerised booking in and out system, little laser-scanned tag for every dress, really impressive."

I remember her saying about that, how it meant she could track all the dresses, make sure they were cleaned, ironed, re-racked.

"So?" I say, confusion obvious.

Jenny stuck her head around the door.

"Oh, hello, Charlie, have you got Snooze in here? Ah there you are, come on, you." Snoozette looked up from her place under David's desk and scampered off.

David was scratching the back of his head.

"Charlie, you ever heard of GIGO?" he asked.

Gigo, means nothing to me. "Some Japanese monster, like Godzilla?"

"No. It's Garbage In, Garbage Out. Means if you tell a computer system something that's wrong, then the answer it gives you is wrong."

"What, you mean, somebody is stealing money from Claire? Cooking the books?" I can't really see that.

"No, not quite. She let me have a little ferret around, everything looks okay. But—"

"What?"

"I'm not sure yet. Let me ask you something. What do you know about Giselle?"

"Giselle? The assistant? Not a lot, she's not a fan of me, that's sure."

"Yes, she didn't think much of me wandering around either."

"So, you think she's got her hand in the till?" I ask. That might make sense, I suppose.

"No, no. Not exactly. I mean, it's all electronic, I tracked every dress hire to a collected payment, so, no."

"What then?" David doesn't usually play games like this.

"Honestly, I'm not sure. But I have a plan to find out. Now, tell me about this idea of yours."

The sudden change caught me out, but I didn't need a second opportunity.

Give him his due. David doesn't just pat my 'Give Me a Break' idea on the head and tell me what a clever boy I am. It is like talking to Rob, but ten times more so.

"And you got the production side sorted, then – you can make this thing?"

I have a flash of a vision of a silicone-filled arm hanging on my washing line.

"Yes, probably, almost definitely."

"Right." He draws the '*right*' out, his way of starting a new thought, which is probably going to finish with '*that might be difficult*'. "Tell me about it."

*

"Are you staying for dinner, Charlie?"

I look up from the scribbled papers and drawings that we produced in the last – snow drops and fuchsias – three hours. Estelle, David's wife, is looking at me, not even mildly surprised by the bomb site I've turned David's office into.

"Ah, we're nearly there, I think, don't you, Charlie?" says David. He is smiling the smile of a man who has wrestled a problem to the floor and beaten the hell out of it.

"I reckon, well, I'll give it a try," I say. "I think it might work, this time."

And I really do. This time, surely.

"Well, celebration time, then. Will you join us?"

I look at my watch; it is half seven.

"Erm, I'd love to, Eileen, but no, I really think I'd better get going," I say.

David looks at Estelle, that smile on his face; she nods.

"I think you'd better, no doubt your wife is on your mind."

*

These things I will one day learn. One swallow does not a summer make, count not your chickens before you've chopped their heads off, and a cold takeaway curry isn't a substitute for having a working kitchen.

Eileen is at home when I get there, looking lovely and wonderful and sexy and beautiful and the very epitome of being loved. All of this I make abundantly clear, while handing her the slightly leaking plastic bag the Chennai provides.

"I come bearing dinner," I said.

Eileen raises her eyebrows and doesn't step forwards to greet me, despite my open arms.

The bottom of the bag is dribbling a few drops of pale-yellow curry sauce onto the kitchen floor. Luckily that doesn't matter too much, those floorboards are going to be covered – eventually.

"It might need microwaving, though, I—"

She looks at me again, one eyebrow raising further,

and her lips compress into a line so sharp it cuts me off. My eyes flitter around the kitchen, not because I don't know what is in there, or rather what wasn't in there.

It, the kitchen, looks pretty much how it had been this morning. She can't blame me for that. The workbench, plans, ruler, toolbox, hammer on top, exactly as Eileen, Eileen, not me I stress, had left them. Her mess, not mine.

Actually, something *is* different. The area around the bottom of the washing machine has been cleaned, quite a big area. It is still wet. I'm not stupid; I can put two and two together and know what for.

"Ah," I say, not my most eloquent, but I'd had a beer at the Crown while waiting for the Indian. Or had the beer come first?

"Ah." Eileen nods, saying it slowly, the way I imagine a guillotine blade being drawn up sounds. "You fixed the pipe this morning?"

I had; give me a task and I get on with it, though something more urgent might take precedence, sometimes, such as mould-making.

"It came loose?" I ask. Shutting up, or throwing myself on the mercy of the court might have been better.

"Yes," she says, in a tone that sits right next to 'deathly silence'.

I put the curry on top of a couple of the cupboard unit boxes. Getting the food had been Van's idea, and like most of his ideas, one that would have been better ignored.

"Charlie," Eileen says. This time her voice is softer, and that is much worse. "I'm..." She falters. Eileen does not falter. For a moment I am distracted as I see the takeaway sauce is beginning to congeal on the cardboard box, but the units should be all right.

She comes forwards to me, looking beautiful, but tired. For a moment I want to blame her job. I take her in my arms, and she buries her head under my chin. She is warm, and soft, and suddenly seems fragile.

"What?" I ask.

She takes in a breath. "Charlie, you know I love you." That sentence pretty much always precedes a 'but'.

"But sometimes it's just bloody hard." I want to joke, but even I know that would not be a good idea. She continues, "I had hoped that, just maybe, something would get done here. Anything to show, I don't know, that things won't always be like this."

She pulls away from me slightly. My eyes run over the kitchen, which looks like it has for the last six months, really.

"I get it," I say. "I do, only—"

"Only what, Charlie?" Now she steps back, flushed. "It's always only something, Charlie. Always other things take place ahead of us, of how we live. Where were you today? What deals were you chasing? How has it taken you six hours to get home from David's?"

Six hours? Well, an hour or so from Cambridge, but I hadn't left exactly when I'd said. The boys had come in and I'd been chatting to them. Then Van had called, asked to meet, which reminded me.

"The trainers, the trainers," I say, "are on their way." Then I had to add, "Probably." No one would know for sure until the batch was opened.

"Oh, well, that's all right, then. We can finish the kitchen, can we? Stop living in this tip."

"Well, no, not yet, I mean, I don't know for certain, and then I'll have to sell them, and it will be Christmas coming, and the trees will need pulling. That's always a big job, and of course I've got to see Claire right." Eileen doesn't always see the big picture. She starts talking again, and – mercifully – I shut up.

"And, you forgot, there's 'Give Me a Break' and just why on earth is there a rubber glove congealed in a pile of what looks like green foam in the middle of what you laughingly call the lawn? When will you be giving me a break, Charlie? Just a little one, just something that's not, not so…" She stopped to take another breath. "So, chaotic."

Chaotic?

Flexible, nimble, entrepreneurial. Those were the words that best describe me, not chaotic. It is all under control, I'm a multi-tasker, sexy multi-tasker.

"And you know what the worst thing was?"

I shake my head.

"Knowing you'd been out having a nice meal in a fancy restaurant, whilst I have to put up with a shit load of crap at school. When do I get the nice meals out, Charlie? All I get is cold Chinese."

"Indian," I say, again a sub-par response, then, catching, up, "Me, nice meal?"

"Oh that little slimeball Terry Dreck dropped by, said it was to warn me there's a hunt in three weeks' time, or something else that made no sense. 'Oh, by the way,' he said, 'did Charlie enjoy his meal at the Ivy today? Lovely company,' he said. I assume he meant Marianne man-eater Tilsley. Well, did you, Charlie?"

Now I am reduced to silence. Me, Charlie Mellon, speechless.

SIX

The next morning is very frosty. Outside it is fine, lovely bright autumn start to the day, vague hint of mist rising from the trees, two little does wander along the track, beautiful.

That is outside. Inside is where the temperature is reaching freezing.

Marriage is tricky, and Spinoza doesn't say much to help; advice to master one's emotions to achieve a more stable and joyful life is all very well until your wife asks why you never mentioned having an expensive meal in a smart restaurant when you can't pay the electricity bill.

We never go to bed on a quarrel, but Terry Deck's little play on the roulette wheel of my life did have us in a spin for a few hours. After a quick canter around the background to my meeting with Marianne, we got on to the kitchen, and the washing machine, and the mess the garden was becoming with what Eileen called my experiments and I insisted were trials.

Eventually, I made some promises, which I have every intention of keeping, starting with getting some work done on the kitchen that very morning.

Only.

Only, Francis Greenham called me, early. Francis is a gamekeeper turned poacher, yes I know how that sounds, from up Cretingham way. Cretingham is where my Christmas trees are happily growing into a small bundle of cash just when I need it.

It's hard to take a call like that, when your wife is giving you a 'when are you going to start on those cabinets?' look.

"Francis, my man, how are you?" I smile down the phone while trying to pretend that it was usual for him to call me at seven-fifteen in the morning.

"Right, right." I nod, laughing for effect and pushing the phone closer to my ear, just in case any of what he is saying might disturb Eileen getting dressed.

I move towards the bedroom door.

"Oh, so, it's not where I left it then?" Best I could do, make it sound like he was looking for a tool or shovel, not fifty yards of fence.

"Yes, sure I can." Again, cool, casual, perhaps not the response he was anticipating to his urgent demand to get my arse over there if I wanted to have any trees left.

See, mastering one's emotions, that's all it takes to have a stable and more joyful life.

"Right, that shouldn't be a problem," I say, swallowing hard and wishing it were possible to be in two places at once.

I click the phone off just as Francis was asking if I

could hear properly and reiterating that if I wanted any Christmas trees left that I could actually sell, I'd better get over there and put the deer fence back up, pronto quickly.

"Everything okay?" Eileen asks, as she comes out of the bedroom, clipping an earring in.

"Oh yes, fine," I confirm in my best 'can't wait to get started on the kitchen' voice.

My phone rang again; I glance at it and click it off, but probably a little late.

"Who was that?" Eileen asks, in a casually cooling voice, which had just a touch of 'and why is *she* calling you?' in it. Be honest, be truthful, but…

"Oh, just Van, reminding me, giving me an update on when the container with the trainers in will arrive." I cringe, remembering how I'd answered the phone.

"Ah," she says, in a tone that only vaguely made me wonder if my pants were busily burning. "So, they're definitely in that one, are they?"

"Oh well. No, that is, not for certain, but he reckons, by the tracking numbers and everything, you see they have a Manufacturer's Sequential Global Shipping code…"

"Don't," says Eileen, the temperature dropping. I thought I'd been doing pretty well.

"What?" I ask, the phone vibrating in my hand until I found the off switch without looking down.

"Just don't, Charlie. Least said, soonest mended." She leans forwards, gives me a goodbye kiss that is more of a vague breathing in through her nose. "I have an early meeting at school," she continues. "You can fix your own breakfast, can't you?"

It isn't really a question, but we both pretend it could have been.

Now this is a point where a few dots join up, not all of them, but some, because, really, this is when, and really why, I got my speeding ticket, the one that has ended up with me delivering the story of my life.

You will recall my close encounter of very nearly the turd kind, with a certain large deer? Which I started to explain a short while ago.

You will also recall my hurry, my death-defying foot to the floor acceleration. Then, PC Sewell, standing there with the radar gun.

As I said, I didn't hit the brakes, not trusting them entirely, especially the one on the right front wheel, but also I reckoned, if they did work, there was a good chance I'd slip-slide straight off the road.

Thirty seconds after passing the speed-trap, the blue-lights of 'gotcha' had lit up my mirror and I knew that it wasn't an ice-cream van.

Even at that moment, police behind and the last bits of my life flashing away before my eyes, I had been thinking of Eileen.

That all happened today, the end of today. I had been speeding because Eileen would be home soon, expecting kitchen movement. I already knew that my rearranging the boxes in a *Titanic*-deckchair-like attempt at seeming to have done something would not suffice, and that there would be a tabernacle choir of music to face. That thought almost tinged this policeman-orchestrated delay with a tiny gold ring of relief, almost.

I had pulled over at the next lay-by, the police car drifting in behind me, parking up with a sarcastic sort of brake squeal that sounded like 'you're nicked'.

It was Sewell who got out. He was tall and thin; the headlights from his car shone between his legs, making me think of the aliens who were supposed to have landed over at Rendlesham. He walked like he had all night to cover the thirty odd yards between us. As he did, he pulled a note pad from his top outside pocket with a practised flourish that suggested he was going to slap my face with it and challenge me to a duel.

I started to open the door.

"Stay in the car please, sir," he shouted. It started as a threat and finished as an accusation.

I sat back, put the interior light on, and wound down the window, which jammed a quarter of the way.

The rest, as they say, is history, and to get to the next point in this particular strand of it, we need to weave our way through a few other bits and pieces. Pieces which involve David and, perhaps surprisingly, the stuck-up little madam from Claire's shop, Giselle.

*

The Crown at Claydon has a different feel at five twenty-five in the evening, compared to my last visit with Marianne. In the saloon there are neat tables occupied by couples debating what to eat, probably deep-fried whitebait starters followed by recently microwaved lasagne, and chips.

In the bar, well, it's almost a pub. A dice throw of locals, I guess a builder, a carpet-layer, and two young lads who seem to get by with no particular jobs, but lots of skills, are arguing about everything and nothing. Each of two opposite corners is occupied by an older man with a newspaper and a pint of beer.

I'm sitting with David Barrington at a table for four. He looks like the cat that not only got the cream but rustled an entire herd of Jersey cows. My back is to the front door, and David keeps looking over my shoulder and glancing at his watch, while occasionally laughing.

"Davey, Davey, Davey, Davey." I try, but the discovery that three of the kitchen-cupboard units have doors that are much closer to terrified than *distressed* has sent my *joie de vivre* on a one-way ticket to somewhere dark and foreboding, like Norwich, this afternoon.

"Hey, cheer up, Charlie." David tries. "It might never happen."

That, of course, is exactly the problem.

Not only is the kitchen taking giant strides backwards, but I'm only three days away from needing to find Claire her money, and in that particular egg and spoon race, I have no egg, nor spoon.

His eyes raise as I hear the pub door open, then drop again to me.

"So, how's the great house deal going?"

I shake my head.

"Well, to be honest, I'm not sure."

His focus shifts more completely to me.

"What do you mean?"

"Well, you know, in *Jaws*, the scene where the student at the beginning decides to go night-time skinny-dipping?"

David nods.

"Well, in that scene, at the start, everything is all hunky-dory, nice bonfire, guitar playing, laughter. But you just know, as the camera pans to the absolutely flat water, that there is *something out there.*"

David takes a sip of his beer and nods again. Good listener, David.

"Well, we should exchange on Friday, two days' time. I exchange to buy—"

"And sell?"

"Yes, I exchange to buy from Tilsley construction, and sell to Marianne, and…"

"You get paid and can pay off Claire?" David finishes for me. Then, "Only?" His eyebrows raise in question.

"Only, why do I have this feeling that a bloody great shark is waiting under the water?"

He studies me for a moment, then shakes his head.

"Yes, that's not like you, Charlie; perhaps you're getting old?"

"Well thanks, mate, but I'm still younger than you." Now I take a pull on my beer. It tastes good but sloshes up against the dam of my worries, rather than washing them away.

"Anyway, why did you ask me to meet you here?" I ask. "You been at The Big Night Out again?"

His smile comes back; suddenly he's like Poirot, Sherlock Holmes and some TV show where they reunite two long-lost school-days lovers.

"I have. A few times actually, and it's been very… interesting."

David is no poker player. I can see he's bursting to tell me, but he'll do it in his own time.

"Did you ever think," he asks, "that Claire has a lot of stock?"

"Well, yes." I had thought that. "But she has some whizzy computer system to track everything, doesn't she?"

"Oh yes, very good. All the clothes have their own bar-codes, she can track what is going well, when they are back, when washed, everything, very impressive. You know," he is warming to his description now, "she could track every payment for every dress, right to her bank account."

"Sounds like Claire, she always did like to keep a track on things," I said, and we both fell silent for a second. David, of course, knows my history there.

"Quite. You see," he continues, "I wondered if Giselle was somehow involved. The slowdown is obvious from the end of June, about three months after she started."

Giselle? Snotty salesgirl who looked at me like I was a dog-turd. That would be good.

"And was she, but how could she?" This conversation is beginning to resemble the kitchen, not really getting anywhere.

"Ah, good questions, and you're right. And no, she couldn't. Every one of Claire's outfits that got hired out, the money went into Claire's bank account."

Oh, well, that had been short-lived.

"Only…" David continues, and again almost laughs, then stops. I feel the door open behind me.

"Ah, the very person." He stands and waves, not that we are hard to spot. The Crown is not that big.

I turn. Giselle is staring at us and there is something about the look on her face. Sure, she doesn't like me, but, unless I am wrong, she is frightened. She comes over and David sits down in a new chair, leaving her the place next to him and opposite me.

"Giselle, glad you could make it. You got my little message then, I assume?" says David.

He is really enjoying this, maybe a tad too much, but even I am getting into the swing of it.

"Charlie," David continues, "let me introduce you to Giselle Bingham. Giselle runs a small business, hiring out party dresses, don't you, Giselle?"

She just looks at him, her eyes close for a second, then she sighs and says, "Oh, just say what you've got to say, let's get this crap over with."

She had always seemed tough before, but now there is something else, a hardness like cold flint maybe.

"Very successful business it is too," continues David, "mainly because it has so few overheads, and even the wages are paid by someone else. Isn't that right, Giselle?"

"You can't prove anything. Anyway, what do you want, a cut or something?"

Even I can see that that is a denial and an admission in a single sentence.

David turns to me.

"You see, what Giselle did is, I admit, quite clever. She is running her own sales, through Claire's shop. I don't know when, but she brought in" – he looks into the air, as though thinking – "about fifty of her own dresses."

"Sorry, what?" I am having trouble keeping up.

"Not sure when, probably over a couple of weekends, or maybe, ohhh, of course, as if they were returned items." Again, he laughs.

Giselle claps her hands slowly. Never seen someone quite so smug when getting caught out.

David looks at her, his face paling, and for a moment he seems less sure of himself.

Giselle leans back into her chair.

"Go on, let's hear it, this should be good," she says. She is giving a good impression of ice, when David was expecting jelly.

He shifts over to a rucksack by his feet and pulls out a brown folder. It might have looked dramatic, but he catches the top of his glass with it, and slops beer on the table. Giselle doesn't even bother to hide her laugh.

"Okay," says David, sort of regaining some calm. "Here is a Companies House listing of The Big N.O. Limited, set up and owned by you. A few months ago." He goes to hand the papers to Giselle, who ignores him. He passes them to me, all official-looking, her name, some address in Needham.

"That, of course, was after your business 'Dress to Impress (Cambridge) Ltd' went into liquidation last year."

Giselle's business? Claire had said Giselle had experience, but as an owner? More papers, again ignored, but I see maybe a look of pain on Giselle's face.

"And finally, a little transaction record, for a dress…"

"Oh, don't bother, this is all so boring." Giselle

interrupts him. "So you really think I care? What, let me guess? You…" She studies David for a moment.

"You got someone to hire out one of my dresses, and you tracked that the payment never made it to Claire?"

"Yes. Your dresses have a slightly different code sequence, don't they?" I can tell David had wanted to say this as though unmasking a killer, but it comes out like he is agreeing he wants sugar in his tea. Then he recovers a bit.

"It was clever, the computer system. Anything that was one of your dresses, from the old shop I guess, any of those, the payment went to you."

It dawns on me what she's been doing. Just for a moment, I'm impressed. Running her business through Claire's, I've got to admit, that takes some balls.

David, though, is building to his big finale, and I don't want to ruin it. I almost expect him to stand up and say, *'Lewis, book her, I'm going to listen to opera.'* Then, though, it starts to unravel.

"Yeah, yeah, so you're the big detective, but tell me, Mr smart-arse, what law have I broken?"

Everything goes quiet. I can hear the fish being fried in the kitchen and the old man in the corner turning his paper's page over.

"I've not stolen anything, have I?" She continues, "So, what's the point of this cosy little meeting? Especially with him." She points at me.

David suddenly looks like he is floundering; I'm still getting my head around it.

"So, Claire's sales didn't really drop?" I ask, playing catch-up, and for time – together. "Only some chunk of the sales, they, they went to her?" I pointed at Giselle.

"Yes," says David, "about twenty percent, I calculate."

Giselle shakes her head – disdain or dismissal, I wasn't sure.

"As I said," she says again. "What's the point of us meeting? Ooh…" Now she laughed.

"You thought, what? Let me guess? Big reveal, big threats and—"

She looks again at David, and almost laughs.

"You thought you could get that money back? Thought you were going to ride in like some knight on a horse and pull *his*" – again she waves at me – "pull his balls out of the fire?"

I wince; she continues, "Well, no way. You try going to the police, and what are they going to say? Just what have I stolen?"

David doesn't nod, but I can see he is thinking, then he speaks quietly, "I guess that might be true. I had hoped you might show some… contrition. Well, at least Claire now knows why her sales are falling, and she can get rid of you, so she can put a stop to that."

Giselle shrugs a 'who-gives-a-fuck?' sort of shrug, though something else flitters behind her eyes. She stands up, the chair scraping across the wooden floor.

"You think you're so clever. And him." She looks at David, then down at me. "I bet you." She stares at me for a moment. "I bet you've done far worse. Claire's told me about your deals. That stuff with Marianne Tilsley sounds dodgy as hell, and what other crap are you stealing from the docks?"

Now it is my turn to pale slightly; Claire always liked to gossip.

"Well, we'll see," she says again, then she turns and makes for the door. As she reaches it, it opens, and she has to step back to allow three students in. It blunted her dramatic exit, but not by much.

We watch the door shut and I take another pull on my beer.

"You, have you told Claire, about all this?"

David is quiet for a moment, then nods.

"Yes, she's changing the shop keys and alarm code as we speak. Giselle has both."

"How did she take it – what did she say?" She is strong, Claire, but betrayal – she finds it hard enough to trust people.

"I'm not sure, I said I'd—" His telephone rings, and he picks it up.

"It's her. Claire," he says.

"Hi. Yes. What? You didn't answer though, no? Good. A voice message? Look, I'll come over." He begins to stand up.

"I'd better go. Giselle rang Claire, a bit angry by the sound of it."

"I'm sure she is," I say.

"Oh, being fired, that's not the half of it. She's just realised she can't get her dresses back."

This time his laugh is stronger, but he still doesn't look like a man who'd won a total victory.

"I'd best go."

I stand up with him, take his hand for a second.

"Thank you, Davey. I owe you, well, more than one."

He nods again, shakes my hand, then pats my arm.

"It's been fun, Charlie, anything you bring always is. I'll call later."

It has been fun, maybe not quite what David had expected, but at least the drain on The Great Night Out is solved. I'm buzzing a bit. I think it is from the moment when I thought Giselle was going to cough up the money.

I can't help it; things are going right, so I have to say it, keep the ball rolling.

"Oh, since you're seeing Claire, tell her that I'll have her money Thursday, when the exchange goes through."

David's smile widens.

"You're sure? I thought you could hear the sound of a shark approaching?"

"Yeah, yeah, I'm sure, just nerves, I guess. It's the first time Marianne and I have bought a house." I laugh, but it's not one of those that feels like it means anything.

David looks doubtful, glances at his phone, shrugs an 'if you say so' shrug, and says, "Okay, I'll let her know."

We shake hands again and David makes for the door, leaving half his beer behind.

I sit down, pick my glass up and take a further swig; yeah, it will work out, I'm sure it will, corner, check, turned, check.

How was I to know that a dark-hearted, knife-wielding mugger is waiting around that particular corner?

*

I don't like lawyers, never have. Most of them are professional pessimists, where me, when the world is falling down on me, I tend to think 'where can I sell this hardcore?'

So, it's normal that sitting in the offices of Turnip, Swede and Beetroot, or whatever Lance's firm is called, I feel nervous. It's normal, but I'm not sure quite why I'm here. I shouldn't need to be; today is completion of my purchase and sale, all done and dusted. Instead, I'm sitting in the reception area of Turnaround, Stop and Brake, waiting, and wondering.

It's a typical set-up. Large chairs that are supposed to be comfortable but where you slide off the leather, banging your knees on the glass coffee table and knocking the property and business magazines to the floor.

There's a receptionist sat on a high desk off to one side; he, very forward-looking, Transom, Stern and Big End, looks and acts like Giselle's brother. He'd brought me a drink in one of those china cups that are designed to slurp the coffee into the saucer as soon as you pick it up, and I dripped some onto my trousers, well, work-stained jeans, actually.

Perhaps that's what he hadn't liked. That and the plaster on my shirt and, I'm pretty sure, some on my hair. Tough, I'm busy and I'm a sexy multi-tasker, though right now, I also feel a bit worn down.

"Tallboy, Sideboard and Basin, how may I direct your call?"

I must have heard him say that thirty times so far, and always he makes it sound like he's just been interrupted doing something far more important, when it's his bloody job.

The sound level increases for a moment and Jennifer, Lance's assistant, appears at an open door down the corridor, and starts walking towards me. Very Trainee Lawyer is Jennifer, knee-length dark skirt, smart white blouse and business jacket, trim dark hair and maybe nearly twenty-two. She makes me feel old and I run my hand through my hair, picking a bit of plaster out of the back.

"Mr Mellon." She smiles, and for the first time I feel, if not welcome, at least as if I'm someone with a recognised part in this little three-act play. "Lance can see you now, do come on through."

Solicitors seem to come in two sorts. Either their offices are stacked floor to ceiling with piles of papers, or they aren't. Lance is one of the aren'ts.

He has a single blue folder on his desk. The cover has a thin strip of white tape that has been stuck with precision to the front of it by someone proud of their OCD. Typed on the tape are the words 'Tilsley-Mellon'.

"Ah, Charlie, good to see you, thanks for coming by." There is something about his voice, a slight whine to it, probably from perpetually saying, 'Ah, that might be an issue'.

"Oh, no problem," I say. "It's just a one-hundred-and-twenty-mile round trip, and it's not like I was up to my arms in half-made plaster moulds or anything important."

"Good, good," he says. Clearly he's not a partner in Sarcasm and Subtlety and this goes straight over his smart blond haircut.

"You see," he says, and for the first time I notice that he appears to be sweating slightly, a few expensive beads of legal perspiration on his brow, and it's not warm in here. "We have hit a small snag."

That's not my experience with solicitors. Firstly, it's never 'we'; it very soon becomes 'you'. In a bacon and egg breakfast, the client is always the pig, the solicitor always the hen.

"Yes?" I say, maybe sounding calm, only it feels like I've just stepped off a ledge, and I'm not sure how far the fall is.

"It's the—" He picks up the blue file and takes out a drawing. It's one of those architect plans of the development site, all the plots laid out in a sort of anal precision. Our plot, Marianne's plot, on the corner, has a nice red line around it.

"Look, let me show you." He turns the paper around and passes it to me.

"This," he says, "is the plot you are buying—"

"And selling," I say, to remind him.

"Yes, absolutely, and selling." Though he said 'and selling' a little as though it were a distant memory.

"And this," he went on, pulling out another piece of paper, "is the Land Registry record of the plot."

I look between them, shrug, then look again, harder.

"Erm," I say, "isn't the—" I look a third time. "The kitchen, isn't it not on the bit of land that… Marianne… is buying?"

He smiles, bright white, dentist-cared-for, teeth.

"That's right, Mr Mellon. You obviously know your way around."

Mr Mellon. A lawyer only calls you Mr when you're a millionaire or screwed, and I am not a millionaire.

"So," he continues, "she isn't."

"Who isn't what?" I ask, the ground in the canyon below the ledge now resolving itself, like five hundred feet below me.

"The other party, Mrs Tilsley, she isn't, won't, complete." He lets that sink in. "At the moment, until this" -- he tapped the Land Registry form - "gets sorted."

"But," I say, then nothing comes out, just a weak breath, and a pile of dust billowing up as I hit the canyon floor.

"But," I try again, "where does that leave me? Do I have to buy it?" Obviously, an iceberg has more of a chance surviving in the sun than me completing this purchase.

"Oh no, no, of course not. No, I wouldn't let you complete the purchase in those circumstances, not until we know where we are."

"Ah, Christ, that's all right, then. For just a moment—" I laugh, the relief running through me like a greyhound after a rabbit.

He laughs as well.

"Okay, well, that's okay then, and—" He stopped. "Mrs Tilsley, she's sent you a payment, for getting to the exchange; she understands you might need it. Half the ten thousand she promised, so..."

He examines a piece of paper as though this is difficult maths.

"So, five thousand pounds."

Even better, Marianne is paying me, I had given Claire a cheque, she had paid the VAT man, the world was perfect.

"She said it might help cover the interest. On the bridging loan."

Everything freezes. I watch as the second hand on the large silver clock on the wall doesn't move.

"Interest?" I say, in a voice so high-pitched that I swear I hear a dog barking in the road outside.

"Yes, interest. Your loan from Lloyds Bank for the deposit, the sixty thousand. Obviously, Marianne's deposit is in escrow, we hold it. So, your loan, it, well, the interest will need to be paid, until this gets sorted out. Don't worry though. That shouldn't take more than a couple of months, oh, Christmas, better assume six months. You'll be okay to cover that, won't you?"

As daft questions go, this was right up there with the buyer of the leaning tower asking, "So, it was meant to be like that?"

I leave Trashed, Stitched Up and Buggered in a bit of a daze. Numbers building and getting redder every time I think about them.

Actually, it isn't the interest that is the big problem. True, it is another drip into an overflowing bucket, but I know Rob expects the whole sixty thousand pounds to be repaid by the end of October, *at the latest*. Sixty thousand pounds. The more I say it, the redder it gets.

I know, too, that I'll have to tell Eileen, soon, very soon, but I can't, not immediately. Because why? Because sometimes I'm a coward, and sometimes, things just turn out okay.

Point in case, as I start out towards the A14 back home, the phone rang.

'Rob?' I think, then, 'Eileen?' Spinoza hit it on the head when he said there is no hope without fear. The dice of fate rolls me past the down snake of those two names, and lands me on an up ladder on the board. It is Van.

"Van, my man! Please, have some good news for me." Okay, I sound desperate, but not as desperate as I actually am.

"Ah, good afternoon to you, Mr Mellon."

Mr Mellon? Van's office voice, still at work. I glance at the car clock, just coming up to five, hence the hard drag to get anywhere in Cambridge.

"Oh, good afternoon," I say, mirroring his tone.

"Just a quick call to let you know, your shipment, I expect it to be dockside tomorrow afternoon. It will go straight to auction, I reckon, doesn't even have a consignee after Elsworthy sold the last lot off."

"Ah!" I nearly drive into a white car in front of me, which has ridiculously stopped at the traffic lights.

"So, you'll be there? Five pm, sharp?" Van continues.

This was all meant to be a bit vague for anyone else in Van's office, though I couldn't see that they'd care one way or the other; still, it kept him happy.

"You bet." The lights switch to green, but the traffic hardly moves. The 'call waiting' sign comes up on my phone: Claire. "Must go, Van, see you tomorrow, thanks. I owe you," I say.

"Hi, Claire, all okay?" Right now, bad news was flowing so quickly after good that I expected the roof to fall in.

"Hi, Charlie…" She hesitates, and the phone has that echoing sound it gets when you're listening on the car speakers. "Yes…" She pauses again.

"The cheque was paid all right, wasn't it?" I ask. Had Rob heard? Bounced the cheque? See, fear riding the horse of hope. "I've got more coming soon, the trainers are in." Now I was trying to offer solutions when I didn't even know I had a problem.

"Oh no, no, the cheque was fine, and the VAT is paid, only…"

"Only what?"

"Only, look, I've got Giselle here, at the shop, she's… Look, she wants to talk to you." There is a shuffling sound as the phone is passed to me, then Giselle starts.

*

That, though, that was all yesterday. I let her rant, she demanded David's number and threatened all sorts, claimed slander, libel, and theft, but I didn't worry too much. That was not my problem. I had plenty of other problems to deal with.

Today has been a good day. The moulds for my first launch of Give Me a Break are almost ready, looking great; and I'm on my way to Felixstowe.

Or I would be, but I can't get out of the track that runs past the house. Ahead I can hear shouting and see the flash of an orange light as it spins round. It's okay I have, I check my watch, I have, shit, only half an hour to get to the dock. The auction of 'unwanted, unclaimed and unpaid' items starts at five.

Already I've left it tight, but my lot won't be first anyway, probably it won't.

I'm out of my car and down to the orange light and noise. It's, oh shit, of course it is.

Terry Deck is standing talking to a guy in a hi-vis jacket, who is standing next to a tractor with a hedge-cutter and trailer for shredding wood.

"Ah, Mr Mellon." Terry turns to me, shouting a little over the noise. Why is it that 'Mr Mellon' nearly always sounds like it should come with a health warning?

"What's going on?" I ask. "I need to get out."

"Yes, I see," Terry says. "I did mention to Eileen, when we chatted, that we would be doing this today. Did she not tell you?"

"Well, I need to get out, now," I say, shouting a little over the noise of the shredder, which is whirring but not shredding.

"Okay, mate." The guy in the hi-vis jacket moves towards the tractor cabin. "I can shift it a bit, you should be able to squeeze—"

"Will that cause much delay? Mr Pulbright won't be paying overtime." Terry grabs the man's arm.

The driver looks at me, his eyebrows rise, and he shakes his head. He has a world-weary look that suggests he'd spent all day with Terry, but without the benefit of the Tao's advice on patience, or a half bottle of gin.

"No, I didn't suppose he would." He looks at me again. "Give me a sec, mate, I'll get this shifted." He pulls away from Terry.

Sure enough, he's as good as his word, carefully manoeuvring everything back and forth to give me space. Probably would have been faster without Terry Deck's help, though.

I now have twenty minutes to do a thirty-minute drive

and get to the auction. No problem.

After lawyers, I hate the A14 dual carriageway more than anything in the world.

I hate it most when the night is dark, the cars are slow, and the rain is starting to fall. More than that, I hate it when my phone keeps ringing and every time I answer, I'm told exactly how much closer I am to disaster.

The twenty miles between my cottages and the docks are engraved on my soul. The route runs like a scar of battle through my psyche. When I die and they cut me open, 'A14' will be engraved on my heart.

Over dramatic? Moi?

You try it, walk a mile in my shoes, or at least sit twenty miles in my car seat.

At the ten-mile marker, the phone will ring.

Van will say something that translates as '*You should be here*' but has a lot more swear words and is a tad more urgent.

Five miles out from the docks, you'll get another call.

This one will tell you that he's right, he's definitely right, he's absolutely right, and ask about your location.

Again, there will be far more words, much louder, and not so much sprinkled with adjectives as machine-gunned.

When you reach The Docks, the phone will ring again. You will be at the security gate, and will snarl at the phone, which the guard in the little gatehouse will misinterpret.

By the time you've smoothed his ruffled feathers and driven the last half mile to the auction room, you will have learnt that your journey has been an exercise in futility.

The whole purpose of your trip has changed; the universe has used it to give you a lesson in fortitude.

The shoes have been sold.

If you are anything like me, you will tell the universe to take that lesson and shove it where the sun no longer shines.

*

Chumbawamba's almost music is ringing through my head. That happens after you listen to a song forty or fifty times. It's a very Dao song, recognises that life is full of changes and fluctuations and all we can do is ride the wave.

Shit, though, right now, I'm not sure if I'm waving or drowning.

But what can you do?

Spilt milk is for wiping up and hoping that the smell doesn't last too long, even when you've been given a licking.

So, today is the day after the great *'who on earth would want to buy one thousand right-foot trainers?'* day. I am at home; I am, if not dancing, at least doing a vague facsimile of it.

Most of today has been about checking stock for Give Me a Break, labelling it and carefully storing it in the guest bedroom, very carefully, hopefully without leaving too much evidence for Eileen to see, at least until the accompli has been fated. Soon it will be shifted to Claire's, which is going to act as the hiring-out site.

It had been hard, but productive. Everything would

have gone faster if I hadn't had to call Van a few times.

David and I are now sitting in the back garden. The sky has that streaky grey, red, blue colour that tells you that evening is just around the corner, and I'm feeling tired.

I pass David a can of beer, and he gazes out into the lane and the woods beyond.

"No squirrels," he says in an absent sort of way, as if this is of significance.

As he says this, he clicks the ring-pull on the beer, and it explodes with a hiss and spray of beer. Note to self re dancing when holding a beer can.

David dodges most of the spray and, while he flicks the rest off his hand, I fetch a tea-towel and throw it to him.

"Thanks again, Davey, for everything."

"Hey, it's fine," he says, "after the last few months, it's good to be doing something so—" He pauses for a moment, thinking.

"Not simple, but unmediated." Trust David to come up with business jargon.

"I mean," he continues, "no directors to keep happy, no agencies to brief, just you, me, and the product. Back to basics. Oh, did you call Rob back?"

I wince a little, has he become my secretary? I ignore that, and ask, "So, what do you reckon? Will it take off? How big will it be?"

"Well," he continues, slurping a little beer from the top of the can, as it continues to bubble out. "It's easy. You take the whole market size, multiply by the percent who know about the product, then by the percent who are early adopters, and have a low resistance to the cost-benefit dynamic…"

"A squirrel," I say, pointing into the woods. He looks, and I pick up where he left off.

"The percentage who know about the product. So that's, roughly, you, me, Eileen, Van…"

"Claire," he adds.

"And pretty much nobody else," I say.

A chill wind blows up suddenly, and the woods look a little darker.

"The thing is, Davey, until, I mean, until I actually got these worked out." There is one of the failed plaster casts on the table, and I pick it up and wave it like I am shaking hands. "Until then, I didn't want to make too much of a song and dance about it."

He nods, and I am a little relieved.

"It's a tough one, and I get it. So, what's your plan now?"

I scratch the back of my head – it is a good question and I am still struggling a little for the answer.

Up to our left there is suddenly a flare of car-lights and the sound of a motor. I don't need to look up to know who it is; I recognise the slight knocking of the exhaust silencer not living up to its name.

We watch as Eileen pulls up and gets out. Her greeting and eyebrow raise has shades of 'Tuesday beers in the afternoon?' with echoes of recent discussions that had included phrases like 'proper job' and 'can't go on like this'. But, as always, she was polite and welcoming to David.

After a brief kiss, I offer her a beer. She pauses for a moment, then, to my surprise, nods.

"I'll just change, into something more comfortable," she says.

A few minutes later she is back, wearing jeans and an anorak, and we have a few crisps, peanuts and other nibbles on the table.

"Successful day?" she asks, looking around.

"Pretty good," I said. "We've got fifty—" I pause. "Made. We're just talking about marketing now."

Eileen glances around.

"Any ideas?" I ask quickly.

"Hmm?" She grabs a few peanuts and takes one like it is an aspirin. "Well, given your budget—"

"Which," David begins.

"Is zilch," I say.

"You've only got one option," she says.

David nods. At least he knew where this was going.

"Guerilla," says Eileen.

"Gorilla?" I ask.

"No, guerilla," Eileen corrects. "I learnt about it doing that management course work paid for. Part of my Professional Development." For a second those two words hang in the air, which, given how heavy they sounded, was a surprise.

David, though, is nodding.

"Yes, that's what we need. And I'm willing to bet, Charlie, that if there is anyone who knows a few guerillas, it will be you."

That got us talking.

In the end, I order pizzas, and we finish off the beers, and we talk some more and come up with a plan.

I'd have to say, overall, it was a good evening. Of course, even as we talked, I could hear a sound coming from the living room. Two sounds, really.

One is an elephant wearing a big sign that says 'who stole my trainers?' and the other is also an elephant. This one had 'Marianne's house' written on it.

Those are two elephants I had spent the day ignoring, but very soon, the pile of elephant dung on the worn carpet is going to be impossible to step around.

What I didn't know was that those existential threats were, actually, not the biggest of my problems. They were what actors might call 'noises-off'. No, the biggest fan-destined turd was sitting quietly in a brown envelope on the kitchen table, under the pizza box, unnoticed.

"Right," said David. "I really should be going. I have had an interesting email from someone who wants to share a significant fortune with me, and I've been working on a reply."

We both look at him. There's a new word, which I, being hip and up to date, already know. Mansplaining, and I get the sense that Eileen is going to launch into an example.

"Oh," he says, looking surprised at our surprise, "don't worry, I'm not *that* stupid. But I think I might have some fun. Anyway, Estelle has asked where I am, has instructed I get back home, ASAP."

It took a few moments to shift his car past Eileen's, but soon he was on his way, and we walked inside.

"That was… nice," Eileen says, and I can hear a softness in her voice that had been missing for the last few days, or maybe longer. Then she looks around the kitchen, and I feel her stiffen slightly in my arm.

"Yes, it was, and a good plan too. I'll get on to a few of them tomorrow."

I hold up the list of likely suspects we have identified. In my line of business, which is more a dot-to-dot drawing of a maze than a line, it's amazing just how many people you know.

"Yes, good," Eileen says, a little distracted. She has started to wash the plates and the bowls that had held the snacks. The water gushed and spluttered, a sudden spurt – you have to turn that tap a bit further to avoid that – and it sprayed water over the sink.

I saw her eyes close for a moment, and she breathed in. She was tired; a hard day at school, I guessed.

"Charlie?" she said, quietly, looking out at the woods, which were now just a vague dark blur in the light cast from the kitchen.

"Yeah?" I asked, moving towards her, my hands reaching for her shoulders.

She shrugged me off.

"Tea-towel's there." She nodded to the temporary hook I'd put up six months ago. As she did – it was that sort of look – the hook fell off, again.

"Charlie?" she tried again. "Do you ever, you know, get tired of…"

She hesitated, looking around, but I had the idea that she was seeing far more than just the kitchen.

"Tired?" In my head, I could still hear two of my favourite songs.

"Well, sometimes," I continued, "it would be nice for things to go... more smoothly." Absently, I looked at my phone. No message from Van.

"Charlie." Three Charlies in a minute; usually my radar is better. "I'm trying to have a serious conversation here. Put the phone down."

"I was just wondering if Van, you know, the trainers?" Surely, she'd understand.

"There's always something Charlie, the trees, the trainers, Claire. Even Claire gets more time than the house does, than I do."

I didn't need this. I was trying, stuff, life, the universe, was just having a go at me at the moment. We'd had a good day, got things ready, had a plan – why now?

"But you heard what David was saying. Give Me a Break could be big, really big."

"But when will I get a break, Charlie? When will *we* get a break? Always we're scrabbling from one big, not quite happening payday to the next."

"Oh that's..." I had been going to say 'not fair', but maybe it was true, a little.

"It's just, I'll find out about the trainers, and that will sort everything, I promise." I almost picked the phone up again – but managed not to. "And Marianne's house will—" Oh shit, shit, shit.

"What about Marianne's house? I thought that was done, completion a week away. You said."

'You said' – does it always sound like an accusation?

Or is that just me?

"Yes." Stop digging, Charlie. Jump in with both feet, tell the truth. The truth will set you free. As long as that doesn't mean a divorce. Christ, I'm even arguing with myself.

"Actually, that might, that is, there is, a problem there."

I know, I know, I should have told her before, but least said soonest mended, what you don't know can't hurt you, and fools rush in where angels fear to tread. See, not telling Eileen about the house, that was me being... angelic.

"I don't want to know," she said. There, I was right.

"I only want to hear that it's fixed and you've got the money for this, and everything else." She swung her arm round now, taking in the kitchen, the bills on the wall, and probably the car with the dodgy exhaust.

"It will be, I promise, you'll see, we're on the final straight now, honestly." I sort of believed it too; the odds had to improve, surely. Only, please God, Rob would let the bridging loan go on. Shit, another call to make tomorrow.

"I'm sorry," she says. That's Eileen, she understands me.

"I'm sorry," she continues. "But... really, I don't think I can keep going like this. Things have got to change, Charlie."

She didn't say 'or else', but I could hear it.

I moved a bit closer to her again.

She turned away, picking up the pizza box.

"Honestly," I said, "I get it. You'll see, it will get better. I'm going to be out there guerillaing away like there's no tomorrow and if—"

If it doesn't work, what? That was a bridge I'd cross, even if it meant getting a 'proper job'. I could feel the truth of it inside me, and it terrified and amazed me. Maybe, maybe America would be better; that had been the real gig economy.

"It's got to change, Charlie," Eileen says, more quietly now, but with much more weight. Tiredly, she picked up the pizza box and started towards the black bin bag in the corner.

I nodded.

"I get it, I really do. Tomorrow, I'll go see Van, and I'll sort something out with Rob. Then, up to the trees, Matt, up there, he said he might take them from me, then, the boys for the guerilla stuff. I'll live in the car till it all gets sorted."

Eileen smiled, a small smile, but at least it was there.

"And if? Just if?" We both knew what she was asking.

"Yeah. If. I'll, I'll find something more—" I swallowed. "More dependable."

"A job, Charlie, we're talking about a job, right?"

For Eileen, if that was the choice, my life – or my wife.

I nodded, slowly, though it felt like I was putting my head on the chopping block.

"Yeah. Hell, I'll join the commuters, Cambridge, Ipswich, even Norwich. I'll find something. I promise."

"Thank you," she said, opening the bag to put the box in.

She stopped. The pizza box had something stuck to the bottom of it, a large brown envelope.

She peels the envelope away from the bottom, leaving

a pale patch on the box matched by a deeper brown puddle on the letter.

We both look at it, with all the interest we could muster at ten-thirty in the evening and balancing on the edge of a much deeper conversation than I had really wanted.

Eileen glances at the address and nods in a way that is also a shake of resignation.

"It's for you, looks… official."

She passes it to me and waits. For a second I want to put it to one side, but it's surprising how much weight Eileen can put into an eyebrow raise.

I already have a good idea what it is, the 'Suffolk Constabulary' logo's a bit of a clue. It tears open easily enough, a thin serrated section coming away with a zipping sound that for a moment fills the room.

Everything about the contents look like they had been computer-produced, faint typing on clearly formal sheets of thin paper. Dire warnings and instructions about lawyers and fines, and even prison.

It is my speeding ticket, and in one disjointed motion, it sends a muck-spreading tractor careering through the linen shop of my plans.

For why? For because I already have six points, and this is telling me I'm due another six.

Which will be disqualification. And that will pretty much kill all my business plans, and my commute plans, and just about all my other plans.

SEVEN

Outside, the sun is shining through the trees at the edge of the woods, a low slanting sun, hazed by morning mist. The usual roe deer are peering through the garden fence, and the smell of morning coffee is tugging at me like some wispy finger from a 1950s cartoon.

Eileen has already left for school, breakfast things lie in the sink to be washed by my promise, and I have a million things to do.

Just for a moment, though, something is holding me down. I can hear the birds on the roof and in the garden, and I'm sure I caught the shriek of a buzzard earlier. This is my place, my life, it's what I've worked for.

And right now, it feels as solid as the mist wavering at the top of the trees.

The echoes of yesterday evening keep sneaking up on me, promises made in the night that can't be forgotten now. And I will keep to them. I'm not the Charlie Mellon who was married to Claire. That was a different Charlie, and his solution, well, that wouldn't work again. Would it?

Today, today I am going on a tour, a tour of pubs and clubs. That is going to require focus; I cannot afford to get side-tracked. While driving, I can make some calls. I'll chase Van up about the trainers, and try, again, to get hold of Marianne. Oh, and Rob, Rob, of course. Must, too, deal with the speeding ticket.

It keeps running through me, though, that tide going out feeling.

Okay. Enough of that. I know what I need. It's, yes, I know where it is.

Top shelf of the cupboard that will hold the plates and dishes, when the kitchen is done.

Yes. I take it out of the plastic case, pop it into the little CD player, turn up the volume, way up, way, way up.

The beat starts, keyboard, a single repeated note.

And I'm gone, shit, yeah, I'm gone.

I'm up on the stage; in front of me the crowds, heads bopping, arms waving, their voices rolling out, as we lay it on them. The music runs through me, the beat building.

I can see them; I can feel the energy growing and growing.

When we get to *that* point, the whole crowd stops singing, hanging waiting, then it comes, into the pure golden silence.

Fuck yeah, fuck, fuck yeah. That's what 'Chasing Cars' is about, chasing your dreams. It washes over me, and through me, and I look to see that it has gone past.

I'm crying, bloody tears; no one to see them, though, so maybe they aren't real.

Me, I'm Charlie Mellon. I go my own way, and I'm where I want to be.

Look out, world. I'm not knocked down – it's all dope a rope.

I turn to the dishes with a small snort of laughter; now, time to get shit done.

*

"Charlie Mellon? What are you doing here, at ten" – Jerry Manthers checks his watch – "ten-ten in the morning?"

He pauses for a second from wiping down the bright white bar top and looks at me through pebble-thick glasses under dark eyebrows and a forehead that would give a phrenologist itchy fingers.

"Come to think of it, what are you doing here at all? Not really your sort of hang out, is it?"

I look around; he probably has a point. He does have a point. The cafe-bar has that bright, just showered feeling that all gym bars seem to have. Dotted at the tables are a morning cocktail mix of youngish mothers, some with baby pushchairs. A television with the sound down has a rolling and slightly lagging auto-generated text running across it showing farmland that is vaguely familiar.

Jerry follows my gaze.

"Up Lakenheath," he says, "some poor Yank pilot's plane crashed."

Sure enough, the camera pulls out to a commentator who picks up the story, and I turn to Jerry and shake his hand.

"How's it going, Jerry – feeling your age yet?"

"Me? No." Jerry laughs his idiosyncratic cackle-laugh and one of the push-chair occupants lets out a small cry of fear.

"That was some do, wasn't it, Charlie?"

"Sure was, now that's what I'd like my fiftieth to be like," I agree, and for a few moments we both look around the cafe as though it were that evening again.

"Liz still talks about it sometimes," says Jerry, "especially the karaoke." He looks at me; maybe he expects me to colour a little at my drunken dyslexia, which means he doesn't know me as well as he thinks.

I'm almost ready to leap into 'Proud Mary', when I'm rescued by a thin, anxious-looking, guy who comes to the counter asking for a caffeine-free, semi-skinned, latte.

While Jerry busies himself there, I look around the club again, and wander to the noticeboard to the right of the long bar.

The board doesn't have a great deal on it: business cards from a couple of local builders, a small A3 leaflet advertising yoga sessions, and a bigger one, headed 'Back to The Future Day'.

Jerry finishes with the 'it might as well be water' buyer, who has, of course, declined sugar, and I turn to him.

"What's that about then, Jerry?"

He looks at the board.

"Oh right, 15th October 2015, that was the day Marty

McFly went to in *Back to the Future*, two. So, we're having a 'Back to The Future' fancy-dress disco tonight."

I smile; maybe the stars are aligning.

"Fancy dress, eh? In that case, let me show you this."

I reach into my rucksack and pull out the large cardboard tube.

Business with Jerry done, I make for the door, clicking my phone as I do. There are a few uncertain noises, a hissing, then, amazingly, a voice.

"Well, well, and to what do I owe the... pleasure... of hearing your voice so early in the morning? I'm just getting out of the shower. Don't you just love that spring clean feeling?"

"Hello, Marianne," I say, shaking my head slightly. I'm not sure if I'm trying to shake out the thoughts that come, or clear room for them.

"And hello to you too, Charlie. I can't imagine why you're calling." Her voice is slow, as if she is deliberately drawing this out.

"Well, I'm calling for the same reason as my last" – I look up into the air as if counting, not sure why, I'm on the bloody phone – "thirty or so calls."

"Oh, I know, so sorry, Charlie, I've been busy... entertaining, had my phone on silent and... vibrate." Again I shake my head. "Anyway, now I'm... available... what can I do for you?"

I thought I had balls, but Marianne has bigger ones than me.

"What can you do for me? What do you think? You could tell me just what the—" There are many words I want to use in that space, but I still haven't figured out the best approach with Marianne, and probably never will.

"Look, Charlie," she says, "perhaps we should meet, have a chat, what do you think?"

I think the last time I had a chat with Marianne Tilsley I had sixty thousand pounds less debt and wasn't on the hook for paying three hundred pounds a month in interest. But, then again, at least Claire has her money. I also think I don't have a great deal of choice.

"How about… you come to My Place?" she asks. "I've got a rented house, Capel St Mary."

Sure, great idea, the most positive part about it is the god-awful drive along the A12.

"Erm."

"I'm kidding, Charlie. I'm a little tease, aren't I? I've just finished Pilates, as I say, feeling very… flexible… Perhaps we could meet in the Crown at Claydon again?"

That can work, and somehow I prefer meeting Marianne in public.

It doesn't take too long to swing around that way, and when I get there, Marianne is already waiting.

She's wearing a different Lycra-tight set of clothes, perfectly respectable but also making her curve-side appeal very clear. John is putting a glass of sparkling water, with what looked like a piece of celery in it, on her table. John never leaves the safety of his side of the bar; enough said.

"Oh, coffee for me please, my good man," I say, walking towards them. John gives me a look that suggests he'll bring the coffee with a rubber tube and a sharply pointed nozzle, but I smile warmly. Really, I should know that John is better as a friend than an enema.

"Well?" Marianne asks, head cocked to one side and a smile that has me thinking of a viper.

"Well, what sort of mess have you dropped me into?" I ask. Might as well jump right in. I'm a firestarter, stitched-up firestarter. "Let's start with, why, why didn't you complete?"

"Oh, Charlie." She leans forwards, and for a moment I think she's going to tap my hand, but she must see the fear in my eyes, and she pulls back with a half-smile.

"That wasn't me, Charlie" – big emphasis on the 'me' – "that was Lance, after I… suggested… he check the boundaries."

John comes over with a cup half full of coffee and a saucer also half full of coffee and splashes it down on the table. I look at him and he shrugs a 'what did you expect?' look.

"You, you asked Lance to check?" I scrape the bottom of the cup on the lip of the saucer and lean forwards to take a sip of coffee without it dripping on me.

"Well," she says again, and this time she draws it out, like a train sliding into a station. As she gets to the stop, I know I'm going to hear the rest of the story.

"I might…" She hunches her shoulders, giving a sheepishly guilty look, but her attempt at innocence is about as convincing as someone claiming their tortoise can juggle chainsaws. Then she laughs. "Yes, I might have known all along, about the boundary."

Reflex causes me to drink more coffee, and I know

without looking that I've just transferred an errant drip from the saucer to the crotch of my trousers.

"You already knew?" I ask. There's no need to pretend confusion.

"I did. I mean, it's a nice enough house, as those piles of tat my ex builds are concerned. But did you really think I'd want to live there?" She hits the beat on 'really', 'I'd' and 'there' as though pointing out something so obvious that I should have guessed all along.

I say nothing. I've already convinced her I'm an idiot, no need to lay it on any thicker.

"You see…" She leans back in her chair and takes a sip of her water, deftly removing the celery first. The chair has a high back and, as she straightens against it, I can imagine her saying, 'No, Mr Mellon, I expect you to die'.

"You know I used to work for him, that two-timing lump of shit?" This time she's much harder, closer to Hannibal Lecter. "I used to buy up the plots, even did some of the layouts. Oh, don't look so surprised about me being an expert in laying out, Charlie. Or in plotting."

Just where this is going still confuses me, but it seems we are getting somewhere.

"So, when I saw that they'd squeezed one more house onto the site than I had ever been able to, it set an idea running. That was after I had caught him with his trousers down, of course.

"I never purchased that little corner plot for Tilsley's, and I didn't think he had either."

"But why?" Good with the penetrating questions, me.

"Because…" and she leans forwards again, her smile broad, white-toothed and disturbing.

"Because now, my shit of a husband is in a world of his own shit, half a million or more of house which he can't sell, but he has contracted to do just that. Revenge, Charlie, just about the only thing I like cold. He'll have to pay the lucky owner to buy that plot, if he can find them. I never could."

"But why?" I ask again, but this is a new question.

"Why you? Oh, really, as I said. No way would he have sold to me. He's a rat but he's not stupid."

"But… what?" Nailed it, I found a new question.

"What do you have to do? Nothing, Charlie. Lance will keep the pressure up, and at some point, everything will turn out okay, probably."

"But…" This time I keep going. "But I'm stuck with a bridging loan, and interest."

"I know. It's a pain, isn't it? You're resourceful, though. I'm sure you'll manage. And this way, well, I like a motivated seller. And, Charlie?" She puts down the glass and starts to rise.

"Remember, Charlie, you signed a contract to sell to me. Don't go running to my ex asking to get out of it. No, don't try that. Otherwise, well, then I'd have to sue you. Which wouldn't be as much fun as what I'm doing to him, but might make up a little for it."

She moved past me, picking up her Pilates gear bag, and twiddled her fingers at me as she left.

I stared into the abyss, and it stared right back. Bollocks to Spinoza, Nietzsche was the one giving lessons today.

*

It's lunchtime now, and I'm in the Spread-Eagle pub, in the centre of Ipswich. It's a real city centre bar that has that chameleon ability to meet the needs of the business types during the day and become a bouncer-doored pickup palace in the evenings. Its Tudor front is confirmed as no mock when you have to duck your head to get in, but the lack of height is made up for by a depth that is explained by it being on a corner.

I know what you're thinking: I'm drowning my sorrows. But no, you should understand now, I duck, I dive, I swerve, master of flexibility, me, so I'm here for several reasons.

One is to continue my delivery of posters; the other is that it is directly opposite the sandstone edifice that is the local Lloyds Bank branch.

I order a pint of Abbott and half a French baguette with two sausages in it, and a bowl of chips. The lunch of champions. John Britain, old school mate and day-manager, sends my request zipping through the electronic terminal, then asks, "So, what's that bit? At the bottom of the poster, in the red box?"

Good man, John; a few times I've had to point it out.

"Oh that?" It's hard to make casual sound casual when you've done it ten times, but I can fake sincerity if I really must.

"Well, you see." I bite my lip, like he's found me out.

"They, the casts, are strictly for fancy dress, right?" I

raise my eyebrows in a way that asks more questions than it answers.

"Right," he replies, but dragging it out uncertainly.

"So." I sigh, my well-practised 'people, eh' sigh.

"A few times." I pause, and shrug. "A few times we've had customers book them out for two weeks." Of course, right now, I'm not even sure what my booking system is, but faking it and making it are two sides of the same coin.

"A two-week fancy-dress party?" John asks with just the right amount of incredulity.

"Eggzactly!" I've done this a few times now, and maybe I'm getting a little too theatrical.

"So," I continue, "I asked a couple of them and found out—" I move to a stage whisper now.

"They've been using them to get preferential treatment, getting to the front of the boarding on the plane, even upgrades in hotels."

I shake my head.

"People – eh?"

John looks at me, small cogs clicking around in his head.

"Right. Do you think…" Now he pauses. "Do you think that, maybe, well…"

"What?" I ask, as innocent as a baby that saw the light just three hours ago. That innocence definitely tinged with the aftertaste of Marianne.

"Well," John looks concerned, "you know, putting in that big box that the cast is not to be used for that sort of thing, might—"

He clearly doesn't want to offend me. I follow his gaze

to the poster, as if seeing the bright red warning, saying not to use the cast for gaining advantage when boarding planes, for the first time.

"What?" I ask again.

"Well, you know, you might be… giving people ideas," John says, an idea perhaps dawning.

"Nah," I say. "I don't think that will happen. Oh, you have a customer." I take my beer and settle down to wait for the food. A warm feeling growing inside me. If this works, it doesn't matter what happens with Marianne snake-in-the-grass Tilsley.

The chips and baguette arrive in short order, and for a moment I relax, pulling on my beer and just letting the effort of the morning wash away a little. I still have twenty or so posters left, but half a dozen of them are destined to pub noticeboards around town, so maybe I'll deliver them all today.

As I eat and drink, I keep one eye on the main door to the pub. Mostly people are leaving, office workers with their two o'clock deadlines. A few new customers are drifting in. I always wonder just what they are doing here this time of day, salesmen perhaps, maybe people having a drink before going into The Bank, or after. Who knows what coincidences bring us all to the same place at the same time?

A young guy, tall, thin, in a dark suit, pushes the door open to allow a slightly shorter blonde woman in smart office wear to proceed him, laughing at something as he does. I know him, it's…

"Hey, Danny, how's tricks?" I call.

He looks across, hesitates, then nods and relaxes as recognition comes to him.

"Ah, Mr Mellon. Good, thank you." He's a second prize; maybe he's playing hookey while Rob is out of the office.

"Been a busy morning," he says, and I don't see any guilt in him. "Need a quick break before my head explodes!"

The blonde woman with him pauses on her way to the bar; she looks back and calls, "Usual, Danny?"

He glances around. "Yes, please, and the, erm, the BLT, no chips."

She nods and turns to the bar.

"Angie's Chris H's assistant," Danny says, and I guess that Chris is probably another manager.

"Ah, right. Rob around today?" I ask, trying to make it sound casual, but knowing that this is a 'poking a wasp's nest' sort of question.

Danny hesitates for a second, glancing around, as though about to share a secret.

"He's at a meeting in the Regional Office today, Cambridge."

Angie has stepped back from the bar, holding two soft drinks. She raises her eyebrows and looks across the pub to an empty table. Danny nods at her.

"Ah," I say, "I had hoped to talk to him, about," now I look around, "the bridging loan."

Danny nods, and his lips tighten as if he's just eaten something that didn't taste nice.

"Sure, sure. I think he was planning to write to you."

Danny is not a good liar. I sense the letter is already

written, maybe by Danny, just awaiting Rob's loopy blue scribble.

"Ah," I say again, but this is a different 'ah'. This one is like the sound you might make when a step you are expecting in the dark isn't there.

Danny looks pained again.

"It's. Well, he's laying out some timelines, options and—" He struggles for a moment, perhaps searching for an alternative, but it comes out anyway. "Consequences, interest rate increases, fees. If... you know." Now he flushes red, and looks across to where his sandwich is arriving at Angie's table.

I don't want to give him another ah, so I nod.

"Good, great," I say, as though he's promising me that a cheque rather than a time-bomb is in the post.

"Anyway, you'll— I, he's made some suggestions, about... cancelling the house purchase, within, I think, a month." Again he flushes. "I... need to... get my lunch," he says, moving away.

"Sure. Enjoy," I say, taking a swig of my beer to wash down the last piece of the baguette, which is suddenly cold and a bit lumpy.

Danny goes across to join Angie and sits down. They clink glasses. Never clink glasses with soft drinks; it's bad luck, or seven years of bad sex. Danny is at that age when that's a lot of bad sex he's going to be having.

Cancel the sale?

'*And don't think about getting out of this sale, Charlie, or else*' echoes through my head.

Looking around, the pub is nearly empty now, I sit for

a moment, a little worm of fear and hope stirring inside me. In the end, it's too much, and I hurry to the front door, waving a casual and confident goodbye to Danny and Angie. Time to do some checking.

Outside, I push the contact button on the phone, and listen to the chirping.

"Toiling, Soiling and Boiling," a voice on the other end seems to say.

"Hello, can I speak to Lance Tyler, please?"

"Hold please, who's calling please? I'll see if he's available, please." The receptionist rattles off his standard machine response.

It is one of those phone calls where you alternately want to throw the phone through the nearest window and reach down into it and strangle the person on the other end.

"Well yes, I could pull out of the sale." Hooray, Marianne was bluffing.

"Only, Marianne will take you to court." No, she wasn't bluffing.

"But—" Yes, a but, in my favour?

"I could sue Terry Tilsley – or Tilsley Building." Right, like I can afford that.

"Or you can just wait."

Just wait? I'm a ducking diving firestarter; Charlie does not wait – unless I don't have any options.

"Wait for what?"

A long, detailed explanation follows.

"The agreement to exchange and complete on the same day was only an agreement to do that within the terms of the contract."

A statement that seemed to be saying nothing really.

I hear a little legal sigh.

"The contract called for completion within ninety days of exchange, and, under a sub-clause— you understand what a sub-clause is, Mr Mellon? Under a sub-clause, if both parties agreed and were able, were able, Mr Mellon, a shorter period could be agreed. But that was only an option, an, if you like, a favour from one party to the other."

So, some favour, the opportunity to drop me into the mire. Every time I talk to a lawyer, I feel like I'm being thrown off a ten-storey building.

So, yes, I could pull out, and, if I did it before the ninety days, well, of course, I'd lose the deposit I paid.

"Or?" There must be an alternative. He's probably got me on some charging meter, as getting to the point does not seem to be on his agenda.

"Oh right, well, of course. You wait for the ninety days, then, if they can't complete then, then you get your deposit back and we might even be able to get some penalty from them. There is a contingency for that."

Right, ninety days, not a month.

I glance through the window of the pub. Danny and Angie are chatting and laughing, while I burn. Thanks, Lance. I can't repay the loan, and I can't not repay the loan without… consequences.

Danny seemed to sense me staring at him; he looks up, and waves his glass at me in a toast.

Great – enjoy your seven years of bad sex, Danny; you deserve it.

*

I spend the next hour dropping into my target pubs in the city centre. Those with noticeboards are okay with me putting the posters up, and I am soon back out on the road. Keeping busy, it's a way to ignore the things you can't avoid forever, while you can avoid them.

Actually, I'm getting an even better feeling about GMAB; I left quite a few thoughtful bar staff behind me. Next, a bigger fish to fry, but one worth it, I think.

Waldringfield Heath Golf Club is just to the west of Ipswich, looks out across to the River Deben. On a good day you can see the coast as well. Bit windy up there, and personally I never saw the fun in hitting and searching for a little white ball. Lots of people do though, rich people. So, maybe worth a poster.

I've been up there a few times, when Joe and Jess Wilden got married, and a couple of good New Year's Eve events, but it's not like I'm a regular.

I pull into the car park – nearly half four now but I can't help but stop and just look for a moment.

Sunset's a while off, but the sky is already getting that scattering of greys and reds that tell you it's going to be spectacular. Suffolk isn't ridiculously hilly, not a Yorkshire, but it's at least the well-developed big sister of the Fens; we got the curves. Today is one of those days when God, or whatever spirit it is that moves you, has opened up the curtains and laid out a scene that stretches down, then out across fields and little woods all the way to the dark smear of sea.

As always, the magic works, and the energy comes back to me.

Shit. I'm ready. This will work out, the loan, the interest, the kitchen, even the bloody speeding summons, which just this second leapt back into my mind, all of it. I'll get it sorted.

There are about twenty or so cars in the car park, Beamers, Audis and even a Rolls with a personalised number plate. I park my van over in a far corner. Most of the members probably won't even notice it, and if they do, it's just one of the staff.

So, I march my way to the clubhouse, little tote bag over my shoulder. The trick now is to make it look like you belong; if you can do that, most times, no one even asks the question.

The clubhouse is nice. It's a low red-bricked building with a big conservatory looking out over a practice green. It has a sloping brown tiled roof with a few small windows. Perhaps The Committee meet in some room in those eaves, black-balling potential members like me.

Inside, most of the area is taken up by a long bar, beechwood panelled front and real marble top. Tall beer pump sentinels stand guard in front of optic-bottomed bottles and the biggest coffee machine I've ever seen. The bar area seems split. About a third is pastel softness, a few potted palm trees; a sign, 'The Bistro', tells you what's on offer.

The rest of the place is more traditional. Sets of tables and chairs, also sofas and a few big leather settees. I can imagine evenings of red-faced golfers downing whiskies while bemoaning that they can no longer be wreathed in cigar smoke.

Actually, I don't need much imagination for that. There is a group of six men who appear to have slipped past 'one more for the road' and might be edging towards 'good morning, Judge'.

One in particular catches my attention. He's sitting, taking up a good half of one of the settees, holding a whisky glass and laughing. If he were standing, I'd guess he'd be six foot three or four. He's slung his grey suit jacket beside him, and even from here I can guess it must be worth at least three months of bridging loan payments.

He has blond hair, which lies in a fringe across his face, and before he takes another mouthful of drink, he flicks his head back to shift the hair from his eyes.

All the attention is on him, and I take my chance. There is a noticeboard to one side: details of club competitions, rules, committee notes and a few posters. I walk across, all businesslike, trying to be so obvious that no one will even notice me. Sneaking, that's what gets you seen.

"No, no, it's not easy nowadays, got to keep on top of everything," the big man is saying.

"I got the impression that that was where your problems came from," says one of the others, and there is a burst of laughter, which the blond guy joins in with.

I get to the board, and look for a good place. I need it to look official. Maybe this wasn't so bright, but, hey, what's the worst? They just take it down.

"Sure, sure, have your fun—" The big man is fighting back now.

"You certainly did, Terry – and it's costing you." Again more laughter.

Terry. I try to think where I heard that name recently, but it's a pretty common one.

I have to move some of the other notices stuck to the board to find space for mine. The pins have been driven in with a mallet it seems, but after a tug they start coming out.

"Fucking Charlie Mellon." The voice makes me jump, and I spin around, nearly dropping the Tee Off times for the Ladies Invitational, whatever that is. It's 'Terry' who said my name, but he's not looking at me. He's still talking to his entourage, whisky glass in hand and face red.

"Did a great deal up at Martlesham," he continues, "just moving into profit, and then this guy Mellon's lawyers get all shirty."

Terry. Terry Tilsley, Marianne's soon-to-be ex. That's who it is. Well, of all the golf clubs in all the world, I had to wander into his. His voice changes slightly, and I can almost hear the weasel-up-his-nose whine of Lance Tyler.

"Do you actually own that land, Mr Tilsley?" There's something in Terry's delivery that says he's got that same deep-down loathing for lawyers that I have.

"Well of course I fucking own it – pardon my French." Though none of the crowd around him do seem to mind.

"Only" – now he shakes his head, and the sofa shifts slightly under his weight – "that bitch Marianne, she didn't do her job properly, it's a pig's ear and I'm left looking to find out how it happened. Now I'm stuck, and this Mellon character, he's digging his heels in. A deal's a deal, he's telling me."

I'm lost for a moment. I'm just standing there, listening in like I've every right to be messing with their noticeboard, and I'm hearing all about me as if I'm some character in a play. It's weird.

"Actually," Terry continues, "he's hiding behind Lance 'do not try to talk to my client' Tyler. But I'll find the little prat. I'll explain to him, offer him one of the other plots. I'm a reasonable man, aren't I?"

One of the larger of the group leans back; he looks more like a builder, probably a bodybuilder, than a businessman.

"Oh, you're a very reasonable man, Mr T, and, if this Mellon guy, if he still says no…" He cracks his large left fist into an even larger right hand. "I'll make him an offer he can't refuse!"

The whole group burst out laughing, and that wakes me from my trance.

I think for a moment. The Give Me a Break poster has an email address, of Charlie@CMEnterprises, but nothing that mentions my surname.

Sod it – I'm not hanging around here. I turn quickly and make for the door. Terry is still complaining,

"Bloody Marianne, how the f—" – his French is improving – "she messed that up, I don't know, but…"

The heavy wooden door swings quietly shut behind me, blocking out whatever Terry had been about to say, and I make a quick dash across the car park. Home time.

I've done weird, I've had weird done *to* me, but that was certainly up in the list of strange. The promised amazing sunset is building out across the Deben, but the red and orange hues look more ominous now, and I'm glad to reach the vague safety of the van.

Time to go, get home, a beer to celebrate, and wait for the orders for the plaster casts. And if they don't come? They will, they will.

Tomorrow, Wednesday, is Bury St Edmunds Market Day. Time to lug the records out again, crank up the CD player and draw the crowds in. It's fun, and I've got my regulars, and I need the money. The records and CD sales keep the wolves from the door, everything else, and Eileen, keeps the roof on the house.

I get the van going, down the darkening track that leads from the golf course and back onto the main road.

Van.

I haven't heard from him properly since the auction. He'll have left work now, after six. So, I give him a call, skipping through the fast-dial numbers to his, while watching the bumpy road.

It rings out, quite long for Van. I swear, he usually answers real quick because he's got few other people to talk to.

"Hello, Ch— Charlie?" I've got my little Bluetooth head thingy in, look like a real twat, but I embrace technology when Eileen threatens me if I don't.

"Hey, Van, how you doing?" I shout. It's weird how you always need to shout when you're driving. Of course, I don't really mean 'how you doing?' – I really mean 'any news about the buyer?'

"Hey, Charlie, good thanks." He stops, and stifles

a laugh. "Actually, yeah, really good." It's like he's got a private joke going.

"I was wondering," I say, "you know, about the trainers."

There's a moment's hesitation, then he's back.

"Oh right, yeah." He pauses and for a second everything goes quiet, and I wonder if I lost the connection.

"Yeah right." His voice comes back. "I'm trying to track them down, but the buyer—" Again the phone falls into silence, crap reception as I drop down to the main road.

"I missed that, Van," I say.

"The buyer, they paid cash, and I've got to… find an excuse… to see the accounting stuff, not really my job, you know, and…" He pauses again and I'm sure I hear another voice, a woman's voice. Is he with someone? A female someone?

Don't get me wrong, I'm sure there is someone for everyone; it's just that I sort of thought that Van's someone might be hiding somewhere, like Thailand.

"Ah, sorry, Van, have I interrupted you?" I have a grin on my face, which I'm glad he can't see.

"No, well, yeah maybe, a little, w— I'm out having a drink with… a friend," he says.

Ah, that would explain a lot. I realise I actually feel happy for him; Eileen will be as well. I stifle the urge to pull his leg. Life is strange.

"Right," I say, "look, I'm on the market tomorrow. You can call me anytime. I really need to know about those trainers."

"Sure, yeah, I'll do that, Charlie. Sure yeah."

"Hey, Van, I'm up at Waldringfield, how about I join you? A quick beer would be good." My smile is growing.

"Oh, what now?" He's nervous or maybe embarrassed; I should be ashamed of myself.

"Yeah, I could do with a wind down after my day."

"Sure, yeah, no. I mean, thanks, Charlie, but I'm, I'm with someone."

Yes, I knew it.

"Anyway, I've got to go," he stammers slightly.

The line goes dead, and I smile. If there is hope for Van, there is hope for us all.

*

Eileen is pleased for Van. She's never been his biggest supporter, but subscribes to the view that says a man is always better off with a woman, even though the reverse is not necessarily true.

We're sitting now, at the end of a long day, when, I think, things moved forwards.

Okay, the kitchen didn't, but tomorrow, tomorrow, or Thursday, it will. Eileen can see that I'm on a sort of high, and knows that it's a bit precarious.

"You should have seen them, darling," I say, "the way their brains started clocking over at the message on the poster, it was…"

I can't quite find the words, but instead do a fist pump and smile, like I scored a goal, and she laughs with me.

"And, so, Claire, she's all set to go too?" Eileen belongs to the 'trust but verify' school of marriage.

"Yeah, they're part of her stock now, if people want to rent. I'm not sure; they might just buy."

I glance again at my phone, checking the emails, but no orders yet, too soon, too soon.

I take another mouthful of the wine, the day running through my head.

"What is it, Charlie?" Eileen asks, and I wonder which of the what-is-its her radar has picked up.

I can hear 'Fucking Charlie Mellon' from Terry, and also see Marianne, laughing at me in the Crown. Rob had warned me about the Tilsleys, Claire too. And still I got burned.

"It's…" Before I can confess, she interrupts.

"Is it the speeding ticket – have you answered?"

Oh shit. It's been a long day, and for a moment I'd managed to put that into a box marked 'stuff I can't handle right now'.

"Yeah." I sigh, as if I was just about to get up and do something about it.

"Yeah, I'll have to, you know, appeal, I guess."

"Well, you can be very appealing, when you try, Charlie." Eileen gives me that look that tells me she's on my side, though I never doubted it.

I push down on the chair arms and lever myself up, moving towards my computer in the corner.

"Where's that bloody letter?" I ask, looking around.

"Stuck to the noticeboard," Eileen tells me. The noticeboard, which is on the floor in the kitchen because the nail came out. I nod, make the quick trip back and forth, then return, looking at the letter.

"You can... Elect to..." I read the instructions aloud. Eileen pulls a chair in from the kitchen and sits beside me.

We get through to the website, tick and click buttons, check numbers, read fast, and then more slowly, through the options.

She looks at me. "Were you speeding, Charlie?"

"Well, technically, but it was either that or have a live deer jumping around in the van with me." I sound a little whiney, even to me.

"Well, it does say that you can present extenuating circumstances. You never know, if you get a magistrate who's reasonable."

We both stop at that point. In my world, there is only one person who will be on the bench that day, I can be sure of it. None of the letters in Reasonable are even in his initials, let alone his middle name.

My finger hovers on the mouse, getting ready to click the 'Yes I am sure' button that says I'm being honest and truthful and understand that a court decision may impose a higher penalty than detailed in the charge notice.

I look at Eileen. "Am I sure?"

"Charlie," she says, "you have never been sure about anything, but that doesn't stop you."

I smile, lean across and kiss her, and click the mouse.

I'm going to have my day in court, for good or bad.

EIGHT

There is something in a thing being not quite finished that I find exciting. I mean, when it's done, it's done, right? And then, well, there's a lack of potential.

On that basis, it's quite obvious that the kitchen has a great deal of potential. Yes, opportunity oozes from every corner of it. Today, though, today I have promised I will start down that road to completeness which in my Daoist heart I know is just an illusion.

First, a walk in the woods to clear my head, a bacon butty, which I had to make for myself, and coffee, while checking my orders for GMAB.

That latter doesn't take long. There are three email messages, all headed 'test' or slight variations of that, all from me. But that's it. I had expected, I don't know, more; well, I certainly couldn't have expected less.

Right, enough. Do nothing, as far as GMAB is concerned; effortless action there, which means action here, in the kitchen.

Bomb site, Eileen calls it the bomb site. Okay, so, deal with that. Bomb sites have mess strewn around. Deal with the mess, find places for some of it.

If I put up a couple of the units, that will clear the floor of their boxes, and create space for things to be stored. Plan, action, move it.

Have you ever noticed how difficult it is to get a boxed kitchen cupboard out of the box it's been boxed into?

First the box itself has been wrapped in tape and then glued down, heat-sealed, and slathered with sweet and sour sauce. Well, the latter was perhaps me, but the rest is the manufacturers making sure you have a workout.

They also draw cryptic runes over the outside, portents of the instructions to follow. Those runes I decipher, as my Stanley knife cuts into the cardboard, as meaning 'don't cut into this cardboard with a thin-bladed knife'. I am, though, spared the wood-being-scratched sound of doom and manage to slice open the box without scoring anything other than a brilliant result of a box I can now get into.

Still, I nearly break a thumb trying to peel the end of the box over the corners, not helped by the extra lashing of brown tape. But, at last, I can see the unit in the box.

Quick check of my phone. No messages, no emails, and, still, nothing from Van. I must call him later, find out how his date went and if he knows where my bloody trainers are. I need those trainers for, for instance, a proper floor for the kitchen.

I turn the box over and let the unit start to slide out.

This is a gentle operation, much like a midwife delivering a baby, I imagine. Which goes to show both that I have little imagination and that I have not been present at a birth.

The unit stops. There is extraneous packing in there, a very thin piece of polystyrene, which is stopping the unit from falling out. At least, half of it is doing that; the other half of that sheet has come out and is creating a small blizzard of white particles as it fragments. These are swirling around the kitchen and settling in places that will cause no problems later, like the hob, and the open drawer of the air fryer, which I know I'm supposed to have washed up.

I slide the unit back into the box, and plan a further cut, caesarean style, down its full face.

As I do, I hear a sound outside, a car slowing down as it turns off the road to attempt the rutted track that leads to my back door.

It's not Eileen, or even Terry Deck. They both know to keep to the right to avoid the big stone on the left which… Clunk. There is an expensive-sounding noise as the front of some vehicle finds the dodgy surface under that stone and drops forwards.

From where I'm standing, I can see my van. As it happens, and it is just luck, it is angled so that the window on the driver's side acts like a mirror, reflecting what is up the track.

If you wanted a list of the things I didn't expect to see, a Rolls-Royce would be pretty high up, probably jostling with a herd of wildebeest and the postman arriving with my lottery winnings.

But there it is. Big grill, silver lady leaning a little further forwards than she should be, posh exhaust gases billowing at the back, and a personalised number plate, TT 007.

Everything falls into place like someone dropping a bull onto a china shop.

TT, Rolls-Royce, the car park of the golf club. This has to be Terry Tilsley looking for… what had he called me? Oh yeah, Fucking Charlie Mellon.

I panic. All right, I admit it, I go full *Mission Impossible* and James Bond, or maybe 'Five Go Hiding from Smugglers'.

As the Rolls backs up the track, coming to a halt with its caravan-sized boot just short of the main road, I dive for the hallway door. I do mean dive, good commando style, almost wriggling forwards on my elbows. I can hear the music. I reach the 'dinnnah' bit where normally someone pulls off a silicone mask, when I hear the rapping on the back door.

Heavy rapping, on the edge of banging, but that might just be because the rapper is the big body-building guy I'd seen at the clubhouse. With fists like he has, the range of door banging available probably starts at 'pounding'.

Now, we are at a slight impasse. From my position, on the floor in the unlit hallway, I don't reckon he can see me. But, from his position, and with the Rolls blocking the track, I'm not going anywhere.

He knocks again, then puts both hands to the glass of the door, peering in. With how big he is, it's like an eclipse, and I pull myself closer to the wall. Why? Part of me is saying 'why?' or rather 'why not just go talk to him?' The other part, another part of me, is saying 'doing nothing is also making a decision'.

The eclipse passes and I hear the door handle rattle. The door is never locked. Who is going to break in? A deer? An odd squirrel? The door opens and, I know it sounds dramatic, but I pull out my phone, screen not broken, thankfully, and start to dial, nine, nine—

A voice shouts, a distant, leaning out of a Rolls-Royce, type of voice.

My door closes, footsteps fade away. Then the Rolls reverses into the main road. I listen for a squeal of breaks and a crash, but nothing comes. I sit there for a while. Maybe this is a trick of some sort?

Then, reality comes back. Terry Tilsley had come, then he'd gone. He wasn't some gangster, probably. But right then, I didn't want to find out.

Okay, panic over, back to the flat-pack.

At last, it all slides out, the final flurry of polystyrene making a marshmallow-style puddle in my coffee.

I need another coffee anyway, so I tip the old cold cup away in the sink, rescuing the polystyrene, which as I pull it free, leaves a trail of brown across the two-ring hob. I'll clear that up in a minute.

The kettle boils, coffee is poured, and I look at the pieces of the kitchen unit. It all looks pretty simple, nothing I can't get to grips with.

I lay the pieces out, identifying each one and opening the bag of little screws with my teeth. After I collect the screws from the floor, I hear a car again, but this doesn't have the pure purr of a Rolls-Royce; it has the throaty diesel chug of the post van.

Recently that noise too has had me diving to hide behind the door, but I fight the urge. In the back of my mind, I have the sense of people reaching for their computers to order from GMAB, and those messages are all about to flood to me, and wash my problems away.

Kevin waves at me through the back door window and I shake my coffee cup at him in invitation. He declines with a shrug, hands me the post and is off in a dark cloud, and leaving one behind.

Amongst the junk mail and renewal notification for the tax on the van is a suspiciously white and professional-looking envelope. I recognise the typeface through the little clear window and the anonymous PO box return address on the back. It's from Rob, the promised 'update' re my bridging loan.

I weigh the letter in my hand, trying to decide. Is this a sit down in defeat sort of missive, or should I keep standing? Ready to run, fight or flight. Or, maybe, just do nothing. Pop it on the mantelpiece for later, least read soonest fended off, or something like that.

I take another mouthful of coffee, hold the letter up, trying to read through the envelope. Sod it, go for it.

Dear Charlie, blah blah blah. Unexpected situation, concern re failure to complete the contemporaneous exchange... contemporaneous? Danny wrote this for Rob to sign. Lending outside policy because of long good relationship, however, but, none-the-less, dire consequences.

It's basically what Danny had warned me, but before, in the pub, that had been hearsay and rumour; now it's black and white, or blood and thunder.

I need to find those trainers, buy them, sell them, and get my life straight again.

Or, failing that, a little trip, not far, maybe America.

Where the very fuck did that idea come from?

No. Not again, not this time. I couldn't do that to Eileen.

Like I couldn't do it to Claire?

That was a different me, that was Charlie Mark I, not the me I am now.

I reread Rob's letter. I have until the middle of next month to get this sorted, to find the sixty thousand, sixty fucking fuschiaring thousand that Marianne duped me into the hole for, to get out of this mess. I can't cancel the sale, and I can't complete it. My money, the bank's money, is lying in Trouble, Strive and Bollocksed's bank account and I'm cuffed and stuffed.

I slap my forehead with my phone, and as I do, the phone rings.

For a moment I think I've broken it, but no, the screen shines, unknown number.

Maybe a GMAB enquiry? Hope springs eternal.

"Hello, CM Enterprises," I manage to say.

"CM Ent? Oh right, should have guessed you'd have some stupid name."

The voice is female, hard with a hint of merciless. It's not Marianne, who's all black widow and teasing; it's—

"Giselle?" I ask, confused.

"Oh, you're smarter than you look, Charlie, which I guess isn't difficult," she replies.

I shake my head for a second. I've still got one eye on the window of my van, wondering if this is some weird tag-team that Tilsley and Giselle have cooked up.

More likely it's just the universe, which has an aversion to completed kitchens.

Her call is no higher on my list of things that I expected to have happen today than the clouds opening and a choir of angels beckoning me homewards. All I can do is ask, "What can I do for you, Giselle?" I sound as if I've suddenly become a doctor or therapist.

"Well, let me think," Giselle replies, though there seems very little actual thinking going on. It's all coming direct from the heart, by-passing the higher functions. "You and your poncy little friend David fucked up my life. What you can do now is sort out the mess you made."

I laugh; what else can I do? A vague part of me is impressed, but the rest is thinking that if it hadn't been for Giselle, then Claire wouldn't have needed her money back, I wouldn't have met Marianne, and most probably the kitchen would be finished by now.

"Listen," she says, and there is a weird, slightly frightening intensity in the way she's speaking. "Claire's stolen all my dresses, and I want them back. She's blocked my phone and won't talk to me. You dropped me into this mess, now you can get my dresses back."

Again, I shake my head, but the little silver ball that should roll into the hole marked 'sense' still seems to be circling the one labelled 'WTF'.

"I?" I manage, but it again comes out with a laugh at the end of it.

"It's simple, Charlie. Even for a man of your limited capacity. It's your fault I lost my dresses; you can get them back for me."

I'm waiting for an 'or else', but it doesn't come. I have, though, the sense that it's lying there in the shadows somewhere. I can hear the glow of two red rat's eyes in her voice. I know, that sort of synaesthesia takes a bit of triggering, but I was right.

I try to get my head around what she's saying. The kitchen unit is still lying like an accusing set of jig-saw piece puzzles on the floor and the least I say the sooner I can get mending.

"What do you mean, Claire's stolen your dresses?"

"My stock, she won't let me have them back."

"The dresses you were using to steal from her and nearly ruin her business?"

"I bet, Charlie, that you almost admired what I did. Me and you, we both look out for ourselves and the main chance. It was business, not personal."

She's right of course, not that I would have been quite the cuckoo that she had been, I don't think.

"Don't kid yourself. No, I won't help you…"

"Oh come on, Charlie. You know, it will just go bad if you don't." Her voice has that tinge again, and I can definitely feel something snake-like and slimy running over my foot.

"Or?" I ask. Might as well find out what she's plotting. There's a flash of shadow movement in the garden, but it's just a couple of walkers going down the lane. It's, Christ, it's half-ten now, and the kitchen is still looking like it's yesterday.

"Well, you know, I think the police might be interested in how Claire stole all my dresses, don't you?" Giselle is saying.

"Stole them? Oh, come on, you don't really think that will work? You'll have to try harder." She really is crazy.

"I don't know, maybe it would, maybe it wouldn't. Or, perhaps, I'll call the Inland Revenue. If they came and did a spot-check, they'd have a few questions about just how Claire got all those extra dresses. I'm sure she'd enjoy a VAT audit as well. All I need to do is make a few phone calls. I have the hot-line number right here."

There is a sort of joyful malice in her voice, but I'm still not sure I believe her, and in any event, is this really my problem?

"Well, tell her that. Why drag me in?" Though I know, even as I say it.

"Because she won't talk to me, will she? And you know, I'd like to handle this with discretion."

That's not what she means, not really. I squint a little, thinking.

"So that, so, you can start hiring out again, somehow?" How many dresses are there? I wonder.

"Maybe, you know, competition is always healthy."

"How do you expect me to convince Claire?" I want, really, to again ask 'why me?' Actually, all I want is to be alone with my flat-packs.

"Oh, she listens to you, Charlie. Still got a soft spot, I reckon."

The sun shines through the window all of a sudden, a beam hitting the last few particles of polystyrene as they rise in the draught from the wind that must have cleared the trees. It casts directly onto the kitchen unit.

"Okay, okay. I'll ask her." Anything to get Giselle off the phone. "I'm not promising, mind."

"Oh, I'm sure you'll get it sorted, Charlie, one way or the other, or…" There is something about her 'or' that sounds like the hissing of a dynamite fuse.

"Or?"

"Oh." That was three 'ohs' in a row; I can feel her drawing a line through them. "You'll see, Charlie, you'll see. There's always a plan B."

She puts the phone down with a slight click.

I turn back to the flat-pack and my cold coffee.

I hang on to the phone for a moment, and tap it against my teeth, thinking.

Freewill is an illusion; I've always known it. Of course, that's never worked as an excuse as to why the dishes haven't been done or how it was that I had an expired visa, but at least I understand those things are never really my fault.

Which explains what happened next.

I take a final look at the cupboard pieces, check my watch, throw the remains of the coffee in the sink, and go out to my van. I need to go talk to Claire. I don't want to call her because… because why?

Because she'll be busy in the shop, can't answer the phone. Because in my mind Terry T and his big builder buddy might be dropping back soon, and because I hate fucking flat-packs.

Whatever, at least on the way I can hurl something at a second bird. Even as I pull out onto the main road, ignoring the lurch in my suspension from the big dip at the top, I push the button to call Van.

It's office hours, so I won't be interrupting any pre-coitus discussions, though I still have problems imagining Van has got *that* far. The phone rings a few times, then: "Admin, Tracking, Turner."

Wow, Van is giving it the whole nine yards this morning. I almost forgot his real name is Michael Turner. Anyway, I can take the hint; he's probably recognised my number, but he's not free to talk openly.

"Ah, good morning, Mr Turner. I'm seeking an update on certain urgent deliveries."

"Oh, right, let me see, you would be Mister—?"

"Mellon, L, E, M, O, N – as in feeling a right one."

I hear the vaguest uncertain chuckle, but Van doesn't rise to my bait. Then there is some clicking on a computer keyboard. I use the half silence to ask, "So, you had a good night out yesterday, how did it go?"

His breathing halts for a second and it sounds like he had to tab back on the computer.

"No, nothing I can tell you at the moment. Still, it's early days." I'm trying to parse the possible double meanings, when a Rolls-Royce flashes past me on the other side of the road.

For a moment I think the driver is going to slam the brakes on and do a U turn, but no. Either they didn't recognise me or I'm just becoming paranoid.

I bring my attention back to the phone. Van is talking and I'm not hearing.

"Sorry?" I say.

"I said, still haven't tracked down the buyer, leastwise not contact details, sorry."

In my head a small bell is ringing. Maybe it should have been clanging away earlier, but I'm the trusting sort. Now, well, it all seems a little strange.

"That so? Seems a bit weird."

Again, the phone goes quiet, then Van says, more hushed this time, "Look, sorry, Charlie, I can't talk right now. Perhaps catch up later?"

I need to look into his eyes, I reckon.

"Yeah, I've got to come over that way, a house up at…" I hesitate, then say, "Kirton. The Slubber's?"

A further pause. I can imagine him thinking; this level of hesitation is typical of Van when he's trying to keep two different ideas straight in his head, or when he's tying his shoelaces, for that matter.

"Yeah, that should be okay… um, let me check. I'll get back to you with a time."

Get back to me with a time? Van's diary is usually blanker than the *Blankety Blank* contestants. You might think I mean the boards they use, but I don't.

"Sorry, have to go, Charlie. I'll, I'll call you." The phone goes dead.

I check my mirror. I'm almost expecting to see the grill of the Rolls-Royce looming behind me, but no. The road is eleven-thirty in the morning clear, and I'm soon pulling up at The Big Night Out.

Claire's behind the counter when I go in, chatting to a couple of women, and taking a dress in over the counter.

"Great, thanks, glad you enjoyed it," Claire is saying, eyes running over a very classy black dress, then checking some white gloves that look long enough to be used for delivering a calf.

"These all look fine, thank you."

The women don't move. Then the taller of the two, whose legs must have looked great in that dress, asks, "The deposit?"

Claire flushes. "Oh yes, of course, do you have the receipt?"

They go through a complicated little shuffle of bits of paper and credit card payments, the women leave and Claire says, "Bloody Giselle! Another bloody, dam, buggering fifteen pounds. I'll have bought all her bloody stock by the time this ends." My best guess is that she's a bit annoyed.

"What's happened?" I ask, though really I think I already see. I just don't have the sense to keep my mouth shut.

"Giselle took deposits for all her dresses; well, we do that. But now, now every one of hers that comes back, I have to repay the deposit, from my own account." She flushes and slams the dress down on the counter, not that that has much effect. "I'll have paid for every one of her bloody buggering dresses at this rate. Now, what do you want?"

It's not often you hear that question sound like a declaration of war, and if you do, tread carefully. Do not follow through on your real reason for visiting.

"Ah, I was just passing," I say. "Thought I'd drop in, see how you were doing."

I've 'just passed' Claire's shop probably every other day of the last five years. Aside from the loan stuff, you can count the amount of 'dropping in to see how she's doing' on the middle finger Giselle would probably hold up to me.

"Charlie, just ask," she says, and her scowl switches to an almost smile.

I run that through my head for a moment, then: "Any... any interest in GMAB?" I ask. Claire is the pickup and drop-off spot. Good plan, even if I say so myself.

"Actually, yes, we had two hires today already. Saw your poster in town, apparently. Didn't you see the messages?"

"Two? What already? Yes, yes, yes – I knew it." I do a little jig and reach out for a moment to pull Claire in. Then we both stop, as we remember our history. This sudden entente cordiale is as unlikely as me turning French.

"Did they... they hired, for, for how long?" I ask, fingers and everything else crossed.

"Both for the minimum," replies Claire.

A week. The pricing had been tricky for a hire; I mean, just how much is getting to the front of the queue worth? So, I'd set it up to make it easy.

"And?"

"Yes, I used your terminal, don't worry. The money should be with you now. I'll send my invoice at the end of the month. Though if I have to keep paying for bloody Giselle's dresses, I might need it earlier."

Now to get back on that track – the reason I came. Not sure why though, as I could already see the swirling water of my plans to get Claire to return the dresses spinning down the plug hole of you've got to be fucking joking.

In any event, I mean, really, it wasn't my problem. Giselle though, she could become a problem, so maybe a little try.

"You, have you heard from her? Giselle? I would have thought she'd want the dresses back," I ask. It's like I'm stepping out onto a minefield.

"Oh yes, the little— I mean, the cheek of it. Made all sorts of threats, going on about police and theft—" Claire's face goes red again, but I wonder if I see a tiny hint of fear in her eyes.

"Could she, could she cause problems?" I ask, carefully stamping on the minefield while holding my hands to my ears.

"Oh, I don't think so. The police wouldn't know where to start."

I reckon Claire is right, but it's the tax man I worry about. Again, I'm not sure why I care, but once you're in the minefield, it's hard to turn around and get out.

"Might it be, you know, easier, to let her have them back, maybe you could charge her for those deposits?" My last attempt before I give up – not my fight. And anyway, I want to tell Eileen about GMAB, and, shit, I've still got to do some more of the kitchen.

"What? And let her set up in competition? Why would I want that? I'd rather burn her bloody dresses."

That's the Claire I knew, and, well, yes, and loved. There's the same tiger in her eyes that nearly ripped me apart when I got back from America. I hold my hands up in surrender.

"Okay, okay, I'm not the enemy!"

She laughs.

"Sorry, Charlie," and her voice softens. She looks at me like she used to, a long time ago.

"It's good, you know, us almost being back to, well, not like before before, but proper friends."

I nod; it is. No, we'd never go back and relight that bonfire – I only have wood for Eileen now – but, friends, that's what it's about, isn't it?

I don't say anything about Giselle's other threats; if they come true, I'll hear, and we can see how we deal with it then. No point trying to cross bridges when you're not even sure that's the route you're taking.

"Right," I say. "Great news about GMAB. I must get back; I have a kitchen to do something with."

Claire's eyes roll and she shakes her head.

"Charlie, really?"

For just a moment we both seem to wonder if we're going to peck-kiss goodbye, but we've not quite reached that stage. I wave vaguely and make for the door.

"See you again soon, oh, and send your invoice when you like. I'm in the money!" I call as I leave.

*

I start my drive back home. Singing, "I'm a firestarter, sexy business-starter." Maybe the words don't sound quite right, but where's the shit I give? GMAB is on its way, and next, next I'll find out who bought the right trainers, then.

The dark clouds start to roll in a bit. On one side I have the feeling that Van is holding out on me, and on the other side is the Terry Tilsley shaped avalanche that Marianne pushed me in front of.

I'm like a yo-yo at the moment, but hopefully spinning along, not at the end of my tether.

I'm soon home. Confusingly, the flat-pack is still lying there just as it was. I had hoped that maybe some elves, or at worst the woodland creatures, would have come in and finished it for me.

Lunch, something good to match my mood, an omelette, and maybe a few strips of bacon, and, well, some fried potatoes, mushrooms, and I'm sure there are some tomatoes. It won't take long, and you need to keep up your strength if you're going to be an entrepreneur come kitchen builder come wheeler-dealer.

Then I see it, and stop.

It's a small card, jammed in a gap between one of the windowpanes and the frame.

I pull it out. There are three things that catch my attention.

One is the name printed on the card: Terry Tilsley – Managing Director, Tilsley Building.

The second is the black pen scribble. 'Call me' it says, but the pen looks like it has carved the surface, scoring deep, uneven grooves.

The third thing I see as I turn the card over – it's a reddish-brown thumbprint. It looks like blood.

Or maybe it's just a dirty thumbprint. I try to convince myself that that is what it is, but, for a change, I'm not very convincing.

I look around. The woods are quiet, too quiet. It's that

sort of silence when you know the bit-part actor is just about to get an arrow in his chest. I shake my head. It's the pressure of being stuck indoors all day, not good indoors, me. That's why I love the market: outside, chatter, banter, witnesses.

I could call Tilsley. Just call him. What's the worst that he and a six-foot-six bodyguard can do? I mean, I know they have access to foundations, and concrete, and burying implements, but really? Why not just call?

Because not doing something is doing something. Because I'm already riding several stormy seas at the moment, and right now I'm managing to wave, not drown, that's why. It's not a good why, I'll maybe admit. Procrastination is not just... well, I'll think about that definition some other time. Right now, doing nothing, it's my choice.

And anyway, again it's not really my problem. Marianne, Marianne is the one who set this going. She, the two-timing, scheming, threatening to sue me piece of femme fatale, that's who should be sorting Tilsley out.

By this stage in my careful calculations for the remains of the day, I've managed to beat the egg for the omelette, and have assembled the ingredients. A small part of me, the bit that keeps tripping over the flat-pack on the floor, mutters something about *that* being the only thing I've assembled today. I'd ignore it, but it has Eileen's voice, so I carefully move the cupboard pieces before I drop any – any more – tomato on them.

Omelette made, consumed, and plates dropped into the sink with the others, which I will definitely do before Eileen gets back, I'm ready to start building again.

My phone rings. I jump. Suddenly I can see one of those spinning wheel things they have on game shows. I mean the sort where everything blurs when it's turned, then slowly the prize, or something bad, is revealed.

In my mind I can see Terry T, Rob, Giselle, Marianne, and even the tax man, whizzing around on the phone screen, but, miracle of miracles, it's Van.

"Van, my man!" I call. Relief floods through me. He's calling me; that's a good sign, I hope. "How's it going, any news?" If he is about to screw me, this is not a very good start. This is me waving a flag marked 'desperate'.

"Charlie, hi." His voice is the croaky one he uses when he's in the pub. I always expect him to say something like 'hardest game in the world the old import clerk game', but he continues:

"Sorry I couldn't talk before, you know, walls have ears." This makes no sense, or at least as much as Van usually achieves, so I nod in the hope he'll guess he should continue.

"Yeah, right, well, I might…" He hesitates. In my mind's eye I can see him looking left and right to check he's alone. Van is pretty much always alone; there's something about him that encourages aloneness, almost like he carries a four-foot circle of space around with him.

"Anyways. I, that is, yeah, I might…" He's taking hesitation to a grand art today. If this is his idea of building tension, he's nailed it.

"You've found the buyer, Van? Have you?"

"Yeah, that's right. How did you guess?" I want to slap the front of my head, but don't. Focus.

"Great, well done, so, what's the plan?" What's the plan? I'm asking Van what the plan is. I can hear his brain working through that, then, all my slurs and calumnies are sent packing.

"Yeah. I've, I've talked to… the buyer. They want to meet up, see if we can do a deal."

Holy shit shit, first GMAB gets going, now the trainers come marching to my rescue. Get those out of the way, and I can face up to Terry T, and if I can show Rob some money to meet the loan costs, he'll be interested.

"When and where?" I ask, before it slips from his mind.

"Oh right, yes. They said, how about, now, well, five, when I get off work, in the… Sl—"

"In the Slubber's, five o'clock." I cut him off in my excitement, checking the wall – presently on the countertop, leaning against the air fryer – clock. Shit, it's two-thirty now; where did the day go? But I can do this. I have to do this. There are no options.

"Super, great, yeah, I'll be there, no problem." I think he should have got the message.

"Okay, I'll let… them know. Have to go, just popped out, they'll be looking for me, I reckon. We'll see you at five." The phone goes quiet.

I stare at it for a second. That was the weirdest call I've ever had from Van, and what was the 'we' bit? Like he and the buyer were together in this. No, I'm just getting paranoid.

The thought goes through me and I check my van outside, angled nicely so that its window mirrors the lane. All clear.

Right, I have – I calculate – two hours, well, an hour and three quarters. Don't want to be late. In that time, I can— Shit. Must get the new records catalogued, market day tomorrow. Or, maybe, I could do them this evening? No. Do it, think, act.

I pull the box of LPs from their position on the sink. Eileen will be pleased to see they've gone, and I set to work.

*

Four-thirty, the Slubber's, relaxing but also a little on edge. Waiting for Van and the buyer of the trainers. If I can pull this deal off, everything will be plain sailing, the only rocks being the bridging loan, and the driving licence thing.

The driving licence, The Summons.

Ten minutes, for ten minutes I had the wonderful feeling that stuff was under control, then that leaps from the wardrobe of my mind waving a knife. I had an email telling me my court date, next month, ages away. But I'd better start getting my argument sorted out.

I'll check that, think about it more, when I get back.

Right now, though, I stare at the bubbles in my beer, glancing up each time the door opens, and chill. Talking of chill, a cold wave runs through me – not sure I did the dishes before I left. I glance at my watch and do some mental calculations.

Van gets here with the buyer at five; half an hour to become best friends and strike a deal, that's half-five. Rush hour traffic out of Felixstowe to Cambridge, allow forty-five minutes, that makes it quarter to six. Eileen home at six. Sweet, cool, I can get stuff tidied up in that time.

I spend the next ten minutes in the blissful state that only vast over-optimism and very poor mathematics can provide.

At ten to five, I call Eileen.

"Darling. How's it going? Hey, GMAB made some sales today," I say by way of grabbing the conversation.

"Hello, Charlie, all okay?" Eileen's bullshit and suspicion radar are working in tandem, then she processes what I said. "Oh, that's great about GMAB, well done." The congratulations are genuine as always.

"Thanks, ah, have you, are you leaving school at the normal time today?" It's hard to make that sound casual, but I try. As I do, Van walks in the pub door.

"No," Eileen says. I make a little fist pump. She's going to be late. "No, I'm just about to leave actually. To be honest, I've had enough for today."

Dam, that just adds to the challenge, but, in any event, I'm having trouble keeping focus.

The reason is Van.

It's Van, Jim, but not as I know it. For a start, his hair looks like, at the very minimum, it has been washed. It might even have been cut, certainly combed. His suit jacket and trousers – *suit?* – match, and his tie, well, not only is it a sensible colour, but it also seems to be working in sync with his neck and shirt.

"Sorry – sorry to hear that," I mutter into the phone to Eileen. And I am sorry, for lots of reasons.

"Hey!" I say, as though the thought has just struck, and

it has. "How about a meal out? I could meet you at the Crown."

Van has gone to the bar, and is ordering himself a drink. Van buying his own beer when I'm sitting here? That's the same as a declaration of independence.

"Why?" Eileen asks, using her 'have you left the kitchen in a state, failed to move things forwards?' and 'are you serious about getting a proper job?' voice.

"Well, to—" I choke for a second as the door to the pub opens again. "Celebrate. GMAB," I say in a high-pitched voice.

High-pitched? For why? For because someone has just walked into the pub, marched over to Van, and kissed him on the cheek.

That someone is Giselle Turner.

NINE

Two days later, more precisely a little short of thirty-nine hours later, I am knocking on the door to The Big Night Out. I am alternately holding my hands to the window, searching for movement inside, and, yes, I admit it, shouting. I like to think I am shouting politely, but I'm probably not.

I would have been here sooner, but being a man of infinite patience and calm, and having to make a living, I was at my Cambridge Market stall yesterday.

It was not the best of days, but I had covered my costs and petrol and, in the last hour, sold a very nice *Aladdin Sane* album for six hundred pounds, so had made a profit. That, though, did nothing to clear the mental hangover and pain from my meeting with that low-life, two-timing, backstabbing, naive moron, Van.

Over those two days I have been cooking up my righteous anger. The ingredients include Van's duplicity and Claire's betrayal, all with more than a dash of flavour from Eileen's questions about a full-time job.

"All right, all right, I'm coming, for God's sake."

A voice then a shadow and finally a Claire appear from the back of the shop.

"Now, what on earth's the— Charlie?"

I can remember only three occasions when I have left Claire speechless. One of those was when I stood at her door, suntanned and with a small suitcase, and said, "Hi, honey. I'm home."

This time I think it was my violent kicking at her – now open – door that distracted her. That, and my looking not so much like an ex-husband as a future axe-murderer.

Not that I ever would, of course; I just look like I might.

"Charlie," she tries again. "What's wrong? What's happened? You'd better come in." Her concern is obvious.

Now this isn't fair. Instant calm and concern as weapons against two days of brewing anger is underhand.

Claire starts towards the back of the shop, perhaps noticing that I've put the 'closed' sign on the door, perhaps not.

"Claire," I say, before I'm even halfway through the shop, "did you, by any chance, ever talk about Van with Giselle?" This question is as loaded as Bill Clinton asking if Monica has the dry-cleaning bill.

"Did I?" She stops on her walk, and glances back. She's putting two and two together, and perhaps working out that I'm intending to give her what for.

"Well, not as such, I mean…" She goes silent; it's the sort of silence that you get when pennies drop down a very high well. "We... Look, what's this about, Charlie?" She's made it to the back room and is absently reaching for the kettle and sorting out teabags.

There is not going to be enough tea; it will take a whole Boston Harbour full to sort this out. I fight the urge to go all courtroom barrister. It's hard to maintain righteous anger in the face of concerned tea-making.

"Look, I know you did. She pretty much told me."

"Told you? You talked to her? How could you be talking to her, after what she did?" Now Claire's voice rises, and I take a step back. Her anger with Giselle is as raw as a sushi chef's cookbook.

"No. I did not talk to her; not like you mean. But also yes, because she's now Van's... paramour." I scrabble for a word and fail to get a double-letter score.

"Paramour?" Claire asks, and she almost breaks into a laugh. "Where did paramour come from? Are you going all *Rumpole of the Bailey* on me?" The kettle boils, and she turns to it.

"I don't know the right word," I say, drawn into unnecessary detail. "She's not quite his girlfriend, not for want of his trying, but he's hooked, that's for sure."

"But that makes no sense. How could she even know about...? Oh." Claire hands me a cup, and, despite having been in the direct line of the steam from the kettle, goes pale.

"Oh?" I ask. It's a good 'oh?' I learnt it from Eileen; it means just what the listener knows it means. Claire starts to talk, quickly, hoping she can somehow change the facts.

"Well, I guess, maybe, I mean sure, I mentioned... I

mean, Charlie, it wasn't a state secret, was it? It was funny, about the trainers, and Van and…" She fades away for a second and I can see her piecing together the broken crockery of my shattered dreams.

"What?" Claire asks. "What has that low-life, two-timing, backstabbing, scheming bitch done?" I'm impressed that we both managed to come up with the same adjectives for different people.

I take a sip of the tea. That's the thing about Claire and me: we've got so much tea that's gone under the bridge that we always end up just calmly discussing the latest disaster.

"Well," I reply, "Van bought the trainers, the right-hand ones."

Claire looks up in surprise and real delight. "Oh, that's amazing! Great, so now you can—" She stops. I'm the book she can read whenever she's drinking tea.

"What happened?"

"What happened is that he won't sell them to me, or do a deal with me, unless…" I pause, wondering if she'll guess.

She thinks for a second, then asks, "What has this to do with Giselle then— ah." The ah has the sort of sound you might make as your head is finally covered by quicksand.

"Ah, yes. He wants me to do a favour for Giselle, his very good friend Giselle, who he met only a month ago. A few days, as far as I can tell, after you asked me for the money back, and I mentioned the trainers." The fog is clearing for Claire now, and I draw the picture in more detail.

"Giselle just happened to be in the Slubber's one

evening, and they got chatting, as you do, and as Van has never done in his life."

"Ah," she said again, a small bubble rising to the top of the quicksand. "And this favour is?"

"I have to convince you to give Giselle her dresses back." In for a penny, in for a pounding.

"Never, no, no way, that thieving little— do you know how much more I've had to pay out? It's not going to happen, Charlie. I mean, I'm sorry for you and all that, but no." She stops for breath and to wipe some spit off the wall the other side of the office.

I don't know what I had expected; well, I do, and this was pretty much it. But I have to try.

"Look, Claire, I get it, but... Is there any way? Look, if I sell the trainers, I can refund the deposits you paid back." It would be worth it, I was sure. I could see it in her eyes, she wavered slightly.

"Charlie, it's not just that money. She'll find some way to set up again, to undercut me. I bet she's got all my client names."

"Maybe I could convince her not to." I had no idea how; when you're drowning, you grasp at the least floating straw.

"But why would she?" Claire asks. "I mean, why get the dresses back if she's not going to hire them out?"

It is a pretty good question.

I sigh, thinking. I need those trainers. If I can close that deal... not just for the money, but to show everyone. Everyone pretty much being Eileen.

Now, I do what I do best, do what led me to America,

and back. I sit and think. I can see little lines of this way and that. I know where I have to go, and where I've been.

Where I've been has all the things I can use to get where I have to go. It has to. The way of the Dao, the bridge to your future is built on the timbers of your past.

It comes, welling up from inside me. It's a beautiful idea, which fills me with warmth and brings a smile to my face.

Claire knows this smile. She leans back because, in our past, this smile would have led to a kiss, and with the door locked, quite a lot more.

"Oh, do I have an idea," I say. "Look, let me make some calls. I think you might be able to give Giselle her clothes, but not worry about her competing with you."

Claire looks at me, head tilted, appraising.

"Look," I say again, "let me do some digging. I mean, it is partly your fault I'm in this shit."

She flushes again, then nods.

"Perhaps partly," she agrees.

I don't barge the open door down, just leave my foot in it.

"Thank you. I need to do a bit of checking. If I'm sure, I'll come back, and we can talk again, okay?"

She shrugs. "I guess so, okay, I owe you at least that."

"Great, good, thank you." I bounce up again, full of certainty that it will all come good. Then, I'm out the door and looking up a phone number faster than you can say 'premature ejaculation'.

TEN

After that meeting with Claire, I spend most of my day getting plastered. Isn't that what Saturdays are for?

When I say plastered, I mean the white powder version, which, with dexterous adroitness, I turn into lightweight, holiday-starting add-ons. GMAB is going great guns. I'm spurred on by Claire ringing me saying she was going to need some more and telling me that two hundred pounds is on its way to me from the sales. Okay, it's not Bill Gates type money, but it will help keep the wolf from the door.

I'm working in the shed. It's the end of October chilly, but the low sun has got around to see me late in the day, so it's been all right. Most of the time I've been zen-like and focused on the now.

Which is all very well. But pretending the future isn't barrelling down towards you only works as long as it doesn't arrive. And it always does. I step back from the last mould, look up, and can see patterns in the trees, patterns that morph into darker thoughts.

Rob has arranged a meeting next week about the loan, and I can't tell him much. Marianne is away on some girls' trip to Prague, Lance won't answer my calls, and everywhere I go, I think I see Terry Tilsley's Rolls-Royce. The trainers won't be rushing to my rescue unless I can pull off a miracle, and I'm soon going to run out of material for GMAB.

I shake my head; there's something else. Eileen.

Eileen has never been 'something else'. She's the rock foundation of my world; I can't imagine life without her. There is, though, in that lack of imagination, something terrifying. Or, maybe, the terror comes from knowing just how close I am to having to choose: my life or my Eileen.

She's coming out now, bringing a mug of tea. There is a splash of dark on her leg.

I stop what I'm doing, pull up the mask, and move towards her. We lock eyes and I glance down at the wedding ring on the hand holding the tea. She misunderstands, thinks I am looking at her leg.

"I caught the mug, coming out. Sorry, you lost a bit."

I can't help but look at the kitchen units stacked by the back door, where I moved them after the washing machine started leaking again.

"How's it going?" she asks. There are six arms standing up to dry, and she adds, "What's that?"

"Ah, my latest triumph," I say. "It's an ankle cast, special request. Apparently the guy already has the crutches." I laugh, and a second later Eileen joins in, but it is the pause I hear, not the laughter.

It's been like this since, well, I'm not sure. It's crept up on us, or maybe worn through to us, eroding what we had, to expose what we have.

"Will, will it be enough, Charlie?" she asks.

"Oh yes, sure, this will keep Claire going with the orders she has," I say.

"No." Eileen reaches out and touches my arm. "I mean, what with the loan, and Rob, and, well, you know what winter is like, everything slows down. The markets die, and…" She stumbles. Eileen never stumbles. "And, what if, the court case… If you lose your licence. What then?"

She's not accusing. She's asking the questions I had managed to ignore as I timed plaster and wrapped bandages. She's seeing her world, while I'm ignoring mine.

I put the cup down on the small table next to me, and pull her in.

She sinks into my arms, and I feel the warmth of her against me; we let ourselves go, blend into one another.

After a time I can't measure and am not even sure existed, we pull apart, and she leans up and kisses me.

"We'll be all right, won't we, Charlie?"

I want to say yes, I know I should, but for once, I'm honest.

"I don't know," I say.

We stand like that for a moment, then the sound of a car slowing at the turn-off catches my attention. I jump and pull away.

"What" – Eileen looks up the track – "is it?" I've told her about Tilsley, though, since the first attempts, he's not been in contact.

The sun is low and the car has its headlights on, but I know straight away it's not a Rolls-Royce. It's a Range Rover, a big ugly brute of a car, which is not really designed for this track.

Even as we watch, it bounces in a pothole and a large chunk of hardcore I had pushed down into the dirt last year pokes up. The car lurches forwards a few more feet, oblivious. Then there is a grinding screeching noise.

Range Rovers should not make grinding screeching noises, not in a good way. The car stops in a sudden cloud of exhaust, and the driver gets out, slamming the door.

If the tide had already been going out on my hopes, here's the earthquake that drags it further, before the tsunami. The driver is Arthur Pulbright, my land-owning, lord of the manor, neighbour.

He doesn't look happy, but then I can't remember him ever having been happy. As he bends to peer under the car, I edge forwards. My guess is that the lump of hardcore has punctured the silencer.

"Shit – fuck," he says, in a very upper-class but ungentlemanly way. Well, I guess I'd be annoyed as well, though the dent in his pocket will hardly register, I'm sure.

I don't want to help him, but something British in me still feels I should make the offer.

"That didn't sound good," I say, which I admit is stating the obvious, but we're on bad enough terms, so that actually anything less than telling him to piss off my land is like saying hello.

"I can have a look under if you like…" I hold out my arms. I'm wearing a plaster-smeared boiler suit; he's got fancy plus fours and a shooting jacket. He's probably going to check the blinds for a shoot. He shouldn't really drive down here, but parking on the main road is a pain, so I usually just ignore him.

"What?" He turns, red-faced, and pompous little pig eyes staring at me. The swirl of fear and worry that I've managed to keep bottled up for the day slops over, and I feel it rise.

"You, Mellon, I think you've done enough already." He makes a vague motion for his phone, then squats down to have a closer look at the under-carriage of the car.

"Bloody great brick or something, rammed right in…" He stands slowly. I can see it was an effort for him to squat like that.

"You," he says, turning to me again. "You're supposed to maintain this track, you know, it's one of the bloody covenants. Like not running a business from the premises. What are those?"

His gaze has gone from the car and track to three ghostly arms that are drying on a line I've strung out.

"Those, that's just a hobby of mine," I say, wondering for a moment if he's seen the posters at the golf club.

He snorts in a way that, while it clearly takes practice, he probably perfected at Eton or Harrow when he was Pulbright Minor.

"As I said," he starts again, "you're supposed to

maintain this track for access, my access, to my land. I'll be sending you the bill for this, nigh on two thousand pound, I would guess."

I shouldn't rise to him, I know I shouldn't, for lots of reasons. But he's an odious, entitled little twat, and I've had enough.

"Really? The covenant you say? I have to pay for the damage?" I know Eileen is somewhere behind me. I can almost feel her saying, "Don't do it, Chas, he ain't worth it," but I'm pretty deaf at the moment.

"Yes," he confirms. "Not that you would understand that type of thing, I'm sure. Goes back a long way. You'll find it in the deeds, should you ever get to own this place outright, I mean."

I nod, look like I'm thinking, which I am.

"So, tell me," I say, "was it a dog cart or a single horse shay that was damaged?"

"What?" he asks. He doesn't do confused very well, though I would have expected it must be something he encounters every day.

"A shay, was it? Or could you not get two horses abreast down the lane?" I ask again. I am enjoying this. I shouldn't. I know that I am not building a bridge to the future here, but setting fire to it. He shakes his head, as though that tells me something, and I continue.

"Yes," I say, "a hundred years ago or so, a covenant was put on these cottages because the blood-sucking landowner of the woods, that's you now by the way, saw a way to screw a little more money out of the farmhands who lived here."

He waves his hands, in a sort of 'there you go' gesture.

"That covenant required them to maintain the path suitable for..." I make a pretence of thinking. I looked this up ages ago. I can take note of this sort of thing.

"...suitable for the passage of a single horse shay or a dog cart, or, as I said, two horses abreast. It does not require me to provide a path for a two-ton motorised monstrosity. Go look it up, or get someone to do it for you."

He's gone quiet now, but it's not one of those good quiets; it's more like the one when the red counter on the bomb reaches zero.

"Is that so?" he asks, and I laugh. I can't help it. Is that the best he can manage?

"Yes, and," I add, "I think there is some by-law that prohibits parking on this track, so I'd be grateful if you'd clear the way, so I can pass without – what's the term? – let or hindrance, I think it is."

Then I turn to go back into my home, my castle. I feel, yeah, I feel great.

There is a sort of comical spluttering behind me, then a car door opens and slams shut. I have to turn, though I was enjoying the whole walking off into the sunset bit.

Pulbright is at the wheel of the car, revving. From the way it rocks, I'm guessing he's in reverse. This is not good; this is about the worst thing he can do. I screw up my eyes as there is another terrible grinding of metal on rock, then the Range Rover leaps backwards.

The roar of the engine is momentarily drowned by more scraping, then a loud clang as the exhaust falls off. Who would have thought a car could make so many different noises?

He reverses into the road and away, and I walk back to the exhaust. It's still hot and steaming slightly, like its owner, I would guess.

"Well, that showed him," I say to Eileen, as I walk into the house, feeling, yes, feeling good.

Eileen looks at me. It is not a good look.

*

Next morning, Sunday, lie-in Sunday, often 'get reacquainted with Eileen Sunday', if you know what I mean. That was especially on my cards given we have an extra hour in bed, but no, not today.

The weather outside is warm for an October, but inside everything is very frosty. It doesn't help that the thermostat for the hot water died when I was adjusting it for the clock change, but that's just one small cockroach amongst many on the New York tenement floor of my challenges.

The largest brown scuttling Arthropoda is either the one waving its antennae in the air and holding a sign labelled 'bridging loan' or possibly the one scuttling across the ceiling looking like a lawyer going to court to discuss my impending driving ban.

Okay, enough of the metaphors. They do, though, give a sense of where I am, mentally.

I made Eileen breakfast, the closest I could get to a peace offering, but I know it is going to take more than a full English to recover from the previous evening's discussions.

Those could be summed up as an in-depth analysis

of just why it is stupid to antagonise the local magistrate a few weeks before going to court. Given that that does not take a great deal of working out, it was surprising how long the discussions went on, and where else they reached. As we talked, I had a sense of flood water spilling out from a fenland drain and running across miles of seedlings.

Enough of that. But no, today, getting up again is proving a challenge.

Eileen is upstairs, so I pull myself together and reach for the wall calendar, which is still on the floor, now beside the fridge.

The court date is already on there, in Eileen's handwriting. Of course it is. I know, I'm getting knocked down, and setting up again is proving a challenge.

Okay, Google time, let's try asking the question, and seeing what clever answers there are.

Before I reach the computer, my phone rings and I jump to find it. I left it by the dishwasher when checking the pipes; the leak has stopped, at least. I catch the phone on the last ring before it goes to voicemail.

"Hi, is that Charlie Mellon?" an uncertain voice asks, but I recognise it straight away. It's a call I've been waiting for since I left Claire's shop.

"Hi yeah, how you doing? Thanks for getting back to me."

We chat for a while, not long, just enough to confirm that the small bond I thought we'd formed was there. He's decided to keep the records I held out for him, but is making sure they are better stored.

Then I get onto the point of my call.

It takes a while for him to see what I want, but I can hear him shrugging on the phone, like it's something and nothing. Eventually, he agrees.

"Yes, okay, Charlie. You were good to me, so, sure, I owe you that much. Three weeks, you reckon?" he says.

I make a little fist pump sign, just as Eileen walks in. She smiles and comes over to give me a slight kiss; we're thawing.

"Yes, Dave, that should be plenty." A lot can happen in three weeks, I hope.

"Good news?" Eileen asks, and for a second I feel that that is a loaded question, like a request rather than an enquiry.

"Maybe," I say. "Maybe you could say a small step along the way."

She gives me that 'oh for fuck sake's, Charlie' look which suggests there's still a lot of ice in the water. I breathe in, getting ready to explain.

My phone rings again. I've programmed this tune: it's the stripper music. Probably not a good choice in the circumstances.

"Hi, Marianne?" I say, inwardly cringing, but in a way happy that Eileen is watching me. This is a call better to have in public.

Eileen's eyes go up and she gets that questioning look on her face, though I know as much as she does.

"You back now, then?" I ask.

She is, and it was wonderful, but very tiring days – and nights. Prague is such a… cosmopolitan city, don't I think? I want to sigh and tell her to get on with it, but something, maybe yesterday's discussions, is telling me to make sure my brain is engaged before speaking.

Eileen is hovering, and I switch the phone to speaker mode and wave her closer.

"So, Charlie, darling," Marianne is saying in that long drawn-out and affected way she has. That brings another look from Eileen, but I give her my best innocent shake of the head, which I think she accepts.

"I know," Marianne continues, "I know that the house, and the loan, and everything, they must be a real trial for you, and I'm sorry." She sounds about as genuine as the Prada bags I once sold on the market, but I say nothing.

"I was wondering," she's saying, "if we could… meet up, lunch maybe, and I can explain. It will be worth your while – I promise." For a moment I wonder if inviting Eileen to hear this has been a good idea, but, on balance, it probably is.

"Er, when?" I ask, my eyes glued to Eileen's.

"Well, always grab the… opportunity when you can, that's what I say. How about today? Lunch, I'll treat you."

Eileen's jaw drops a little, and I pick up the challenge.

"Yes, okay, that would be" – I'm going to say 'nice', but switch at the last moment – "good, to discuss… business."

"We can discuss whatever you want, Charlie." I shift backwards a step as Eileen reaches for the phone.

"Good, yes, I need to talk about a few things." My agenda has Terry Tilsley at the top.

"Wonderful, shall we say, oh, one o'clock today? It will take me a while to get ready. How about the Hole in the

Wall, Wilbraham? I know it's a little out of the way, but I've always liked how… cosy… and discreet it is."

I don't know it, but am sure I can find it. I nod, then say, "Er, yes, right, one o'clock then."

"Wonderful, Charlie, wonderful." Her world is full of wonder. "I'll look forward to it." The phone clicks off and I feel a sudden sharp pain in my shin.

*

The Hole in the Wall at Wilbraham is an old coaching inn. You drive in under an arch between the main property and what is now a garage, and was probably a stable back in the days of Dickens and Dick Turpin.

In the car park I see there are a number of very expensive cars, including a sporty silver Mercedes with personalised plates, MT 53XY, and I guess that Marianne is already there.

Sure enough, she's sitting at a small table in the main restaurant to the right of the bar. The set-up inside seems not to have aimed for anything in particular, 1950s middle-class dining room chic, perhaps. It is not quite dark enough to be off-putting but not light enough to be welcoming.

Marianne's eyes widen as we walk in and her smile falters, then switches to a sort of knowing grin.

"Hello, Charlie," she air-kisses me, "and this, this must be your lovely wife, Linda?" Marianne extends a hand to Eileen, who picks it up and returns it unopened.

"What a lovely surprise. I'll get them to lay out another

place." Marianne can roll with the situation; I'll give her that.

"Eileen," Eileen says. "Linda is Charlie's mistress." This throws Marianne for a second, then she laughs.

"Oh, right, sorry, Eileen. I won't make that mistake again. Now, what can I get you to drink? I'm having the Chardonnay."

We sit. The waiter bustles over at Marianne's waving, sorts out the extra place and then returns with drinks. I opt for a bottle of a local beer; Eileen follows Marianne with the wine, a large glass.

"Well, isn't this cosy?" says Marianne. "And," to Eileen, "I'm so glad you could make it. I know the invite was a little hurried." Eileen and I share a quick look, and I actually feel her relax next to me.

"Look, Charlie, I wanted first to apologise, to you both – about my, near enough, ex."

We've picked up the menus and are browsing as Marianne talks. The food looks good. If it tastes as well as it reads, this is going to be a great meal. That, though, may be a little ambitious; I'll settle for getting out alive.

"Actually," I say, "he's not been around since the first time. So, no harm done."

"Well, that's good. Lance is… effective, when it comes to warning people off."

Now Eileen stiffens again. "Lance, your solicitor?"

"Yes, Terry rang him, shouting and threatening. Saying you were being deliberately difficult and should listen to reason, and that he would…" She turns to me, extends a hand, then withdraws it at Eileen's glare. "I think he used the phrase 'sort you out'. Anyway, Lance soon squashed all that nonsense. I'm glad he's backed off now."

And actually, I believe her. Eileen perhaps does as well; I'm not sure.

We select food. Eileen chooses the most expensive starter, a steak tartare. I suspect that tells me something about her mood, and to follow she chooses lamb chops, rare. Yes, I'm getting the message. I settle for a terrine and fish and chips. Marianne simply says, "My usual."

"Look." Marianne picks up the conversation after a moment studying the retreating waiter. "I know I got you into a lot of trouble, but really, well, it was Lance."

"Lance, how's that? I thought he was the wonder-boy?" Eileen's first real contribution sets a tone. Marianne smiles. I think she is enjoying this.

"Oh, he is, and he's overprotective of me. You know, I would have gone through with the purchase, sent my deposit, but he absolutely wouldn't let me, when he knew of the land problem."

"Why did he let Charlie exchange, then?" asks Eileen, with the ringing sound of a hammer hitting a nail on the head.

"Ah, he explained that to me," Marianne says. Her smoothness is either rehearsed or simply well practised.

"His assistant was overseeing Charlie's purchase, to keep… a little bit of distance between the contracts, you know?"

We mull this for a moment. It sort of makes sense, and I'm about to ask the obvious question, when Marianne rises.

"Must go powder my nose," she says.

As she leaves, Eileen looks at me.

"Did you see that? About pretending she'd invited me? I don't trust that woman, Charlie." This is no more news than the sun rising, but I'm more and more pleased I brought Eileen along. I need her.

Food arrives while Marianne is still busy powdering. She seems to have some avocado and crab concoction, which I didn't see on the menu, and Eileen's looks beautiful. My food is still awaiting delivery and the single waiter is distracted by the phone ringing. Eileen tucks in anyway, and after a short while, the phone call over, my food is delivered as Marianne returns.

For a while we focus on the food, it is worth the attention, then Eileen says, "Look, Marianne, I don't understand really – why can't Charlie just drop out of the purchase, and the sale to you?"

"Oh really." Marianne gives a look that suggests Eileen has just left infants school, and I wonder if I should go powder my nose or maybe ring the bell for the start of the fight.

"That would be, well, he's got a contract with me, and, much more importantly, there's a nice little bonus coming." Now Marianne stares at me. If I were alone with her, I think the entendre would have been doubled, but this time, I'm sure it's money she means.

"Really?" I ask. That's not good negotiating, but I can see Eileen's white-knuckle grip on her knife, and want to hurry things along.

"Well." Marianne leans forwards, pressing pleasingly

against the dark silk blouse she's wearing. I focus on my food.

"Lance tells me that he's suggested to Terry that he drops the price by forty thousand. If he does, we can split that, a twenty thousand bonus for you, Charlie."

"But how? The kitchen isn't on the right land." I had been counting the months of not having to get a 'proper job'; Eileen asks the better question.

"Oh." Marianne waves her hand in the air vaguely. "I think he's sorted that out now, found the owner, and is doing a deal there as well. Hasn't it worked out well?"

Should I ever need the perfect example of a smirk, I'll hold hers in my mind.

"Now, tell me, Charlie," suddenly Marianne's attention shifts, "what is all that stuff about Snow Patrol? Claire said I should ask you."

*

It could have been a great meal. The food is wonderful, and my raconteuring excellent. Marianne is suitably amused by my deep dark past, and even Eileen laughs at the five-word fragment of 'Rolling on a River'. But, as we leave, there is the inevitable autopsy.

"I just don't trust her, Charlie, never in a million years, and certainly not as far as the double bed she'd like to throw you on." Eileen, never backwards in coming forwards.

"At least," I say, "I've got something to tell Rob, some hope that this will all be cleared soon, and I can make a profit."

"Maybe, let's hope so, otherwise, who knows what The Bank could do."

As it happens, I know what The Bank could do.

They've got the deeds to the cottages as security for any lending. That was the only reason Rob agreed the bridging loan in the first place.

If I don't get the loan cleared soon, Rob can throw us out.

"Oh, it will be fine, I promise."

She looks at me, and smiles, that smile that makes it all worthwhile.

It comes back to me, how I came to meet Gary Lightbody, in my Tina Turner tribute band days.

I sing 'River Deep Mountain High', not quite on key, but with feeling, and Eileen laughs.

*

Next day, Monday the 26th of October, bursts onto the scene with dark clouds and rain. I ignore these portents of doom. I'm a pretty good ignorer of doom portents when the day before I've had a good afternoon of rest in Eileen's arms.

She, of course, is already off to work, and I am about to get going as well. A busy day beckons; some more arms to drop off to Claire – GMAB is going great. Also, I have my little idea to run past her. Fingers crossed I might be on the way to getting my hands on those trainers.

The rain slows me down, but I'm walking through the ringing door of The Big Night Out just on ten, and Claire is already hard at work.

"Very nice," she says, admiringly. "You off to get married, Charlie?"

I do a little turn and pull my tie tighter. "You approve?"

"Oh, you could always scrub up well, Charlie, but if you think that that is going to convince me to let you have those dresses, then you've got another thing coming."

I put my hand to my heart as if she's shot me.

"That's so unfair, Claire, you know me too well. Now, how's GMAB going?"

"Really well! It's ridiculous, but you've obviously tapped into something. I had three more orders on the website overnight. There'll be some more money coming your way tomorrow." Her smile grows again; this is helping her as well.

Today is going to be a good day, I can feel it. Ever since the trip back from Wilbraham, Eileen and I singing in the car, it's been good.

"Great, and you can see, I've got my arms full – of arms, as it happens!"

I hand Claire the big blue carrier bag with five more plaster casts in. That's pretty much used up my supply now. I'm going to have to order more plaster and silicone.

"Wonderful," she says. "Do you have time for coffee, or is the registrar's office booked early, or—" Her face clouds. "Oh, you're not off to court today, the speeding thing?"

"No, no, couple of weeks yet." I make yet another note to do some research on that. Every day I try, but every day something more urgent turns up. "But coffee would be good, and a little chat?"

"How little a chat, Charlie? I'm busy." Claire's goodwill has its limits.

"Twenty minutes, tops. I have an… an idea. I think you'll like it."

Claire sighs, turns the shop sign to 'closed' and we go into her office.

Fifteen minutes, that's all it takes. I am the man; I still have it. If my performance with Danny and Rob later is anything like that one, they'll be paying *me* interest.

Claire sees me out of the shop, and she's smiling.

"And you're absolutely sure this will work, Charlie?"

"I reckon so. I mean, two weeks should be plenty, don't you think?"

She nods and smiles again.

"Yes, that will take us up to, well, early November, and no way she can get set up for Christmas orders, or beyond. I'm—" Claire catches her bottom lip under her top-tooth in a way that used to have me wanting to kiss her.

"I'm only agreeing to this because, well, the Marianne thing, and Giselle finding out…"

I put my hand up.

"I know, but, shit happens, and all we can do is make lemonade."

We both laugh and I give her the lightest peck on the cheek, purely platonic. Claire flushes a tiny amount, then, as she closes the door: "Two weeks minimum, though, Charlie, okay?"

I nod. "Two weeks it is. I'll pick them up soon, tomorrow, day after. Okay?"

"Sure, let me know. It will take me a few days to get them all separated."

We have a plan. What could go wrong?

*

The Claire visit has got me buzzing, almost there on that, then the trainers, and 'I'm in the money, I'm in the money'. Actually, not my most favourite or usual song, but, what with everything the money means, yeah, I'm going to sing.

A slow drag up the A14, eventually crawling past an enormous earthmoving vehicle chained to an even larger transporter lorry. The lorry has a sign, 'Abnormal load on board', which explains why the traffic is so constipated.

Having scored a strike with Claire, I'm buoyed up for my meeting with Rob. As I get closer, though, the daydreams of success start to evaporate under my fear of the beating sun of bank policy and caprice.

Caprice – sounds like it should be an island in the Mediterranean, but the way things chop and change for me, it could just as easily be one of the more spiteful fairies from *A Midsummer Night's Dream*. See, my mind is as slippery as an eel in a bowl of jelly right now. I need to focus.

I nearly collide with a taxi, which was blatantly indicating the direction it was going, and then going there. That sort of unlikely behaviour is what gives taxi drivers a bad name. We shake our fists and swear at each other amiably and I take a quick left into the multi-storey car park.

Again, I'm not thinking. Charlie Mellon does not pay

multi-storey car park prices, nor does he refer to himself in the third person. But, today, it seems I do both. So, I park up and make my way down to the city centre, and Rob's branch.

Rob is running a bit late. Danny comes out, apologises, then vanishes. I study the way he walks and use my X-ray vision on the brown file in his hand, but both tell me nothing about what awaits behind Rob's green office door. A weird melange of a song comes to me. Some 1970s government warning ad, to the tune of 'Green Door', which featured a 'mad bad axeman who is deep in sin', behind the green door.

I nearly get up to leave, but then I really would be in for the chop. In any event, the door opens and Rob waves me in with a smile.

We shake hands. He vanishes for the walk to behind his big desk and I squat in the little child's stool he has for customers. We scoot around the 'do I want coffee?' question, the vague comments about Ipswich Town, and he tells me his arm is okay now, but it will be a few weeks before he can play golf again.

I toy with saying 'face-boverred?' to him, but keep up the appearance of deep interest and concern.

Then, at last, he says, "Anyway, it's good to see you again, Charlie."

He opens the brown folder, which I last saw in Danny's hands, and studies it for a few moments.

"What's happening, Charlie? With Give Me a Break. You've had—" He looks again. "Nearly seven hundred pounds in over the last week or so."

As a starter for ten, it's a great question, and I wonder if it's the key to unlocking the chink of light at the end of the tunnel. Pulling myself from that morass of metaphors, I lean back into the office chair.

"Yes, going really well. Claire thinks we'll have them all hired out soon, might need to make a few more."

"That's great, Charlie. I must admit, I had my doubts but" – he puts his hands up as if in mock surrender – "but you read the room on that. And," now his voice shifts slightly, "do you need to invest more, to grow it?"

I hate this sort of question. If I say 'yes', will he shake his head and say he had worried that that was the problem, start using words like over-extended and under-capitalised. Observations my English teacher at school also used to make. Yet, if I say 'no', will he say that I need to boost my income? I leap into prevarication and obfuscation, which, if they aren't a firm of solicitors, really should be.

"That was, the options I mean, exactly what I wanted to get your thoughts on," I lie, but so convincingly that within half a second, even I believe it.

"Really? Well…" He scratches the back of his ear and glances up into the corner of the room.

"Actually, we need to get the bridging loan clear first."

Clear, as in seeing our way forwards? Or 'cleared', as in 'no longer outstanding'? I want to know. I jump in.

"Right, I was discussing that with Marianne, only yesterday."

"Oh, really? And how was she? Full disclosure, Charlie, I had a brief chat with her on Friday, at the Rotary dinner."

Shit. Well, not really shit. I don't know what Marianne

said to Rob, but, on the other hand, perhaps she told him what she said to me, then it might be okay. I don't commit myself. Rob goes on.

"Yes, she was having a fine old time. Of course, she was in grander company than me, the lawyers and magistrates of our fair county."

"What, Lance from 'Tinkerbell, South Paw and Blue Fly'?" I ask.

"Yes, and Magistrate Pulbright, and his man, and a few others."

Suddenly, it's like I'm back on the naughty chair. I can feel my face going red, then pale. The memory of my lunch with Marianne at the Ivy runs in like that man from the Tango ad and slaps me around the face. The way Terry Deck had happened to be there. It even goes through my mind for a moment to wonder if Terry was meant to come to the Hole in the Wall. Marianne had disappeared for a while, maybe to warn him Eileen was with me?

This is like three seconds of thought, bits of mosaic falling from the sky and arranging themselves in a pattern that forms into a much bigger mess than I had realised.

"And what did she say, Marianne?" I ask, and I know my voice has got that squeak noise in it, but I can't control that.

"Well," Rob shrugs, "she said that she thought Terry was going to give in, sort out the land, and she'd complete the deal, and you'd get a bonus."

I nod, though inside I shake my head. Of all the mean despicable tricks, she's told us both the same thing.

"And, how, what do you think about that?" My voice

has dropped an octave in the right direction, and the legs of the kitchen chair I'm sitting on now seem less rickety.

"Well. To be honest, Charlie, we, The Bank, we're more, jam today sort of people."

The chair wobbles. Rob continues.

"But, what with GMAB bringing in the money to cover the interest, we can give it another month, or so. You keep those sales going, and we can let it run for, say, let's say until after Christmas. Should be done by then, surely."

I want to leap out of the big office chair Rob keeps for important customers like me, but instead nod sagely, indeed nod the whole bloody herb garden. Yes, yes, he leaps, he scores. I'm a lucky punter, bloody lucky punter.

So, that's it. For now. Eileen and her fears about Marianne are unfounded. I've got twenty grand to look forward to, and more when I do the trainers deal. Life is great. I might even leave my van in the multi-storey car park all night, just because I can.

Rob and I chat about this and that, but really, I want to get out of there, before he changes his mind. Least said, soonest lended, that's my motto.

So, I'm soon back out in the main square, Rob's promising me a letter of confirmation, and I decide a quick beer is in order.

Maybe, at the back of my mind, I can still hear a nagging voice saying, 'So, what was that about, Marianne, Pulbright, Deck and Lance all together? Coincidence?' I ignore it. Always a good thing to do with nagging worries, ignore them.

*

I choose the Cricketers for my celebratory drink. Two down, one to go. If I can get hold of Van, tell him that Claire will give up the dresses, then today will have been the best day since Eileen said she'd marry me.

The Cricketers is, at quarter past three in the afternoon, quiet. A few lonely old men and unsavoury characters, like me, are keeping their beers, and either newspapers or phones, company. A large television has a news channel, cycling through this and that, with scrolling sub-titles. Their brightness is added to by a bank of slot machines. Slot machines that accommodate five- and ten-pound notes, I notice.

I order a beer from the single server looking after the bar. She isn't quite run off her feet, but she's not left standing for more than a few seconds between the serving, cleaning, stock-checking and whatever other jobs Mr Wetherspoon keeps her busy with.

The beer slips down wonderfully. Within moments I'm in one of those little golden fugue states that sneak up on you every now and then and surprise you with just how good the world can be.

I'm feeling the love, for the drinkers here, for the brewers of my beer and even for the chemists who made the E-numbers in my crisps.

"It's too quiet." Somebody should say that; somebody with a grizzled face and scars that show experience and wariness. Or maybe the camera should pan around the pub and focus on a mean-looking stranger with an empty glass, whose gaze lingers a little too long on my back.

Something, anything to warn me would have been nice, but no. It just leapt out of the shadows wearing a white skull mask and waving an impossibly large knife.

Up on the TV screen, the picture has switched to an airport, Stansted, I think. It doesn't look quite dominating enough to be Heathrow.

The sub-titles are scrolling jerkily, spilling the story in a slow leaking-pipe trickle.

'Fight at Stansted airport. Check-in desk problems delay Ryanair flight to Prague.'

It catches my interest in no more of a way than if the door had opened and a cold wind had blown in. It has, but just not reached me yet.

The story is one of those human interest, no one has invaded anyone, no bombs have gone off and no politicians have been caught doing something they shouldn't, stories. But the news team are going to town on it.

'Fifteen stag-party members of an Ipswich rugby club denied access to the flight…'

Ah, a local story. I see now that this is BBC Suffolk reporting; that explains the focus.

An Ipswich rugby club. I wonder if I should get one of my posters up over there.

If I haven't already.

Slowly, climbing from the depths, is a sinking feeling which would rival the last seconds of the *Titanic*.

There is a live camera on the scene now. It's slightly out of focus, then zooms in on a group of men, ages ranging between twenty and forty. They are all wearing rugby shirts, a few have half-full plastic beer mugs, which they wave at the camera when they see it.

That isn't what really captures my attention, though. There is one other thing that stands out. Something that marks them as brothers bound together in adversity.

Every one of them seems to have a broken arm.

That cannot be good.

Okay.

It could be a coincidence.

Rugby players break bones all the time. I'm sure there is a legend of the great match of 1927 or some such, where thirty players between them broke one hundred and two bones, and the windows of the clubhouse in the drinking afterwards.

Then again.

The players have vanished from the screen now. The afternoon-soft and blandly dressed commentator makes a final comment and we leap to the weather report. Apparently, Storm Eileen is brewing to the west of the region. I marvel at the prescience of meteorological science.

I saw the plaster casts the team were wearing; they burned into my mind in the few seconds they were on the screen. I am not a Picasso, I do not sign my art, but... I do have enough pride in my work to recognise it when I see it. Those casts were mine; I just know it.

So, don't panic. Do... not... panic... That is the key.

I consider my options for a few minutes, which seems like a year.

My passport is... where? In the top drawer of the bedside cabinet, on the left. No, the brief flash of what my life would be like without Eileen is enough to send that thought off.

Is there a law against what has happened? I'm not usually one to leap to the small print in my defence. The smallest print I have on my stall is the sign in six-inch-high letters that says, 'Check for scratches before you go go; I don't refund later, no no.' Then again, I've never seen my product playing a leading role in a thirty-second, afternoon, local-TV news item.

I order another beer; this will have to be the last. The warm feeling of ten minutes ago has shown itself to be emanating not from the heated car seat of life, but something much less welcome. Right, think, I mean, who actually *watches* afternoon TV? Especially the news items. Local news is for getting up and making tea or going to the loo, rushing back for that moment when Columbo says, 'Er, just one thing.'

'Who are you trying to kid, Charlie Mellon?' The voice in my head is loud and insistent. This is serious; when I start asking myself questions, I know I'm in at least two minds about a situation.

I put down the half-empty, definitely not half-full, glass, and make for the door.

As I walk out back onto Crown Street, I am amazed that cars are still going past, and people are shopping and chatting as if nothing has happened. Maybe it had been an illusion? The sum of my fears adding up to a momentary break with reality.

You can tell how bad things are when you start banking on a psychotic event as a way out.

I glance across the road as I walk back towards my van lounging in its ruinously expensive parking place in the car park. On the other side of the road there is a newsagent with one of those whiteboards that summarise the headlines in six or fewer words. Today their evening declaration is 'Airport flight chaos for Rugby Team'.

I speed up and make for the van. Suddenly I feel hunted, though all around me, nothing, nada, no reaction. It's like there's been an earthquake and I'm the only person who's invited.

Home, home, and hide. No, not hide, prepare, plan, talk to Eileen; she'll not only have something to say anyway, but will know what to do. Sure, major corporate PR disasters are right up her street.

Once in the van, I feel better, a bit more normal. The cocoon of my little metal office has a comforting familiarity. The act of driving, of being in control, is good.

My phone rings and I glance at the screen, thinking, in order, who I do not want it to be.

Worst, worst would be Eileen, then Rob, probably Rob, after that, well, Claire or BBC Suffolk hiding under the disguise of an unknown number. And it's... Claire.

That's fine. Claire is probably ringing to ask when I'm going to pick up the dresses. Of course she is. Naturally she would stop her busy work in the shop to check something we'd already agreed: Wednesday, two days' time.

"Hello, Claire, how are you, everything going wonderfully still?" I answer cheerfully, noting that the 'still' has been delivered in a near castrato high pitch.

"Charlie, that you?" Claire asks.

"Yes, of course." I drop my voice several keys and for a moment it still sounds like I'm running my fingers down a blackboard at school.

"Charlie, I've – the plaster casts – I've had a reporter ringing me."

Claire's got it under control more than I have. There's not accusation in her voice, not quite, yet it's more than just a statement. There is a question, a request and a plea in those few words. Pretty good going for, what? Eleven words.

"Oh, yes?" I say. "Really? What did they want?"

'Oh, come on, Charlie,' I hear myself saying. It is clear that denial is not just a big river in Egypt.

"Haven't you seen it? On the news? Where have you been, Charlie?"

"Oh that!" I say, immediately annoyed that an exclamation mark has barged its way in where a question mark had been invited.

"Yes, that!" Claire could always out-match me when it came to verbal dexterity; that was one of the reasons I had to get two thousand miles away.

"Right, I was just about to call you, to discuss – what did you tell them, did they ask about me?" Crass, I know. There is no I in team and some of those other pointless business posters come to mind.

"I'm sorry," I recover. Time to tap the baton of life on the lectern of 'another fine mess' and face the music.

"Are you okay?" I ask. "What do you want me to do? What should we do?"

"Oh, I'm fine, Charlie." Claire sounds a little calmer

now. "But, well, I thought I should tell you, in case you didn't know."

"What did you say to the reporter?" I ask, genuinely interested.

"I asked how many he wanted and gave him the price list, of course." She laughs.

I sigh, and feel a tiny fraction better.

"But, Charlie," she continues. "I think you're going to be getting some calls too, you know?"

Even as she says this, my phone tells me an unknown number is calling me.

"Thanks, Claire," I say. "Look, I'll have a think and get back to you."

"Okay, Charlie. Oh and, Charlie?"

"Yes?"

"You'll get back to me soon, yes? Not like eighteen months from now?"

It's a low blow, but fair enough.

"Sure, tomorrow, I promise."

I click her call off, and let the 'unknown caller' go to voicemail.

By the time I get home, I have fifteen voice messages.

*

Home, safe and sound, yet also under siege.

I did listen to the voice messages. Initially, they were from someone describing himself as a researcher for BBC Suffolk. I have his name somewhere, in what is becoming a pantheon of media gods – BBC, ITV, Sky, Channel 4 and others whose initials I've consigned to the darker realms.

Eileen and I are sitting on the bed in our bedroom with the curtains closed and the lights off, talking and watching the news channels.

It's not that my plaster casts are the main news item. Typically, they are tagged on at the end, as an 'and in other news' human interest story. Of course, it's not the mainstream media – see, I'm getting this jargon from Eileen, the mainstream media – that are the major issue.

Someone videoed the whole check-in desk disaster and now it has over one hundred thousand likes on YouTube.

Just what did the team think they were doing?

The video catches the first player dragging his carry-on bag up to the check-in and looking no more unusual than the normal range that you see at a Ryanair desk. Then one by one, they all troop up, and you can see the check-in team getting more and more suspicious. Then the captain of the team hobbles in, to a big cheer, with a crutch and the ankle plaster I made, and the shit hits the fan.

"Okay then," Eileen says. "What are you going to do?"

"Well," I reply, "Davey B reckons I should shut the website down and be grateful for what I have made. But—"

"But you're probably thinking now is the time to put up even more posters, ads with 'as seen on TV'?"

I turn to her, smiling, but she cuts me off, shaking her head.

"No, Charlie, this is *not* where you get me to admit later that it was my idea."

I look at her sheepishly, regretting my blatant wool over eyes pulling attempt.

"What do *you* think I should do then?"

She sighs and for a moment glances at the closed curtains.

"Number 1 – I think you need to talk to a reporter, and keeping your face as straight as you can, say this is all a big shock to you—"

"Which it is," we both say in unison.

"And," she continues, "for once I'm in favour of the old wu-wei."

"What?"

She nods, smiling.

"Do nothing, it will blow over, probably sales will drop off, but *you* have done nothing obviously wrong."

I mull that. It makes sense. Of course, there is one little outcome, issue, problemette I have to deal with.

My mind flashes back to, what, eight or so hours ago? Rob saying, 'As long as the money keeps coming in from GMAB, then we'll be fine.'

That can wait. Tomorrow is a mystery, yesterday a dream. I turn to Eileen.

"You know, since we're up here, on the bed, with nothing else to do…"

"I've noticed," Eileen says, leaning towards me, "that this is one aspect of our lives where you seem to forget Daoism entirely."

"You're right," I say, reaching for her. "This is much more a carpe diem type situation."

*

Despite any impression you might have formed, I am pretty much a man of my word.

So, next morning, even though I should be going to Bury St Edmunds Market, I'm first driving out to see Claire. This is a bright and early trip organised by phone.

Bright and early for a lot of reasons.

First, I still need to get to the market if I can. Second, well, right now the track outside is clear, and I'm hoping it will stay that way. If it does get busy, well, with luck, neither Eileen nor I will be there.

So, quick load up of the van with my records, then a scoot over to Claire's, and dawn has only been peeking over the horizon for half an hour or so.

Stowmarket is sleepy town quiet when I get there. A few punters buying cigarettes, newspapers and packed lunch supplies from the newsagents, and the early morning cafe doing a slow trade in greasy breakfasts and hot coffee.

Claire's shop looks dark, but she said she'd be there. So, I drive up around the back and see that the little yard has her red Ford Focus in it. I pull my van in, hop out, and knock on the door. For a moment, I feel like I'm in some spy movie.

"Claire, it is I," I say, pulling my hoodie top off.

Claire gives me her very best 'stop pissing around' look, and I get a feel for just how chilly the waters are.

"No, Charlie, you're not going to laugh your way out of this. I had reporters here, Charlie, *reporters*. Lots of them. It very quickly went from funny to something a lot more serious." She manages to get the full-strength italics into that, as if they were the Spanish Inquisition. I know enough not to say that.

"I'm sorry, Claire. I mean, we—" The tiniest twitch of her face tells me not to make this any part of Claire's responsibility, though she did know. "I mean, I, I never thought this could happen."

"You never thought, Charlie, you never do. This could ruin me, everything I've worked for." There are tears in her eyes and suddenly I understand, and I reach for her.

It's spontaneous; we have a lot of history, a lot. She looks at me and then comes forwards into a slightly awkward hug.

"You've got to sort this out, Charlie, you've got to, somehow."

We pull apart and I nod.

"Well, I'm here, aren't I? I said it wouldn't be eighteen months. Eighteen hours, that's pretty good."

Claire gives a little sniff and smiles. I know how she feels. She's spent a lot of time getting the business right; I know how the fear of losing it eats into you.

There is a knock on the front door; it rattles through the shop to the back office. We both jump.

Claire turns to go. We both know that no customers will be banging at the door at – I check the clock – seven-thirty in the morning. I take her arm.

"Shall I go?"

She looks at me. She would have gone, but she nods.

"It's you they'll want anyway, Charlie, thanks."

I shrug. "Well, it's my mess."

Annoyingly, she nods. I go to the door.

I pause for a second. Zone out, and I am standing backstage in Boston. The bass guitar placed around my shoulders feels like a cross between a noose and an Olympic medal.

The crowd are whistling and calling, getting restless. The Roadies are where I should be, doing the last second adjustments. Gary and the others are standing next to me, each showing that weird mix of tension and excitement I've come to learn during my time with them.

All except Pablo, who is somewhere between crying and hysteria as the paramedics work on his ankle. Which is why I'm here, last minute, last second replacement.

"Charlie, you can play bass, yeah?" Gary asked as we stood around, hearing the end of the support group's set and seeing Pablo writhe in pain.

Never say yes to a question like that.

It helps now, though; that's the thing about experience: you need to experience it. If I can walk out onto the stage and mime my heart out for ninety minutes to a crowd of twenty thousand, then I can answer the door to BBC Suffolk.

I open the door.

An attractive young lady is standing there, smart nicely styled blonde hair, dark-rimmed glasses and a sensible red anorak with a BBC logo on the left side.

"Ah, hello, is Ms Faye there?" she asks, in a soft Suffolk accent.

"Hello to you too," I say, engaging open and approachable mode. "Ms Faye is otherwise engaged." I stop. That's bullshit PR style talk; WTF has got into me?

"No cameras?" I ask, the disappointment sneaking out.

"Sorry." She jerks her shoulders up in a slightly embarrassed shrug. "I'm just BBC Radio." She holds up a tape recorder the size of a small bar of chocolate, then puts it down and puts out her hand.

"I'm Abigail, Abigail Fisher, BBC Radio Suffolk, and you are?"

It's a smooth move, nicely done. I shake her hand and open the door a little wider.

"Charlie, Charlie Mellon," I say. "Would you like to come in, cup of coffee maybe?"

She smiles. It's a shame she's on the radio; she has a good smile.

"Thank you," she replies, walking in quickly. "So, what's your connection to the shop, then, Charlie?"

And before I even know it, my first interview has started.

By the end of the interview we are all best friends, near enough. Claire must have been listening in for a few minutes, heard how it was going, and joined us.

"No, we particularly said they were not to be used for aeroplane queue-jumping."

I stick to the party line, and although I reckon Abigail is far from convinced, she is just as interested in the 'small business suddenly in the glare of publicity' angle.

Then, somehow, we get on to our, Claire and I, having been married, and that takes us down the whole Snow Patrol blind alley. Soon, though, her phone rings and she says she has to get going, but to be ready for a few more calls until the whole thing dies down.

Claire lets Abigail out the front door, and turns to me. "Well, could have been worse." She shakes her head. "Now I have to get back into the 'normal' world."

"Yes, that was up there with the weird," I say.

Part of me still wants to talk about Snow Patrol, how I first met Gary, when I was doing my Tina Turner act down in Ipswich, but this is not the time.

"Right. I must get to Bury. I'm already late. Look, I'll pick the dresses up tomorrow, okay?"

Claire nods.

"Yes, I've got them all stacked in the back. Still the same plan?"

"Oh yes," I say, smiling.

"And, I mean, should we?"

"Yes, definitely we should. Giselle deserves it," I say.

"I mean, what about Van?" Claire asks.

"Oh, come on, Claire. Giselle is just leading him on, but he can't see it. He'll thank me eventually, you'll see." This is no time for Claire to get the wobbles.

"I suppose so. Okay, what time tomorrow?"

"Early I think, very early, will that be okay?"

"Early?"

"Well, I've got to be ready for interviews, autographs, you know."

Claire shakes her head.

"Seriously, what time?"

"Well, still early, before you open. How about eight-ish?"

"Fair enough, Charlie. And, Charlie?" She looks at me, suddenly more serious.

"I'm sorry it didn't work out, between us, and glad, glad you found Eileen. Thanks for not running away this time."

"I'm sorry too, Claire, and, yeah, with Eileen behind me, and knowing how I hurt you, no more running away."

We stand in the sudden silence for a second, then I give her a hug, or she hugs me, I'm not sure which, and I make for the door, feeling good.

*

"Daniel ain't travelling tonight on a plane." Big Mike, who runs the fruit and veg stall, has been singing that for the last hour. At first it was funny; now it's sort of losing its gloss.

Of course, it is better than Jenny, with the nice watercolours, on the other side of me. Her rendition of "oh this year we're not off to sunny Spain" is painfully out of tune.

I'm treating them both to my very best dignified silence, which only causes more laughter.

"Hey, you got any early Aerosmith?" a suspiciously un- Aerosmith-fan-looking sixth-former asks me. "You know, *Get Your Wings*."

As it happens, I do, worth about ninety quid. I start to sort out the stock behind the counter.

"Yes, I think so, a first pressing," I say, but when I look up, he's gone.

It's been like this for a week now, though it is dying down. It wasn't quite fifteen minutes of fame, but, thankfully, not even fifteen days. Now I can get back to the real world.

I sort of miss it, I suppose. It was… well, it was fun in the headlines. The big problem I had was keeping a straight face while claiming that I had never expected anyone to even dream of trying to take advantage. In the end I started resorting to jokes about it all being a bit of armless fun, and that it gave someone a little extra elbow room, and things like that. That soon had them all leaving in droves.

What I do miss, though, what I do miss, is the money.

Really, the person who is making that loss more obvious is Rob. I made the first interest payment, and think I'm okay for the next one, but arm cast sales *have* slowed down, well, stopped virtually at the moment. He's getting all antsy again. There is still no word from Marianne about the house, and the Terrible Sons of Buggerall are no help either.

Soon though, I reckon I'll be able to come marching in with the trainers, and things will be okay. I hope. Another week or so should be enough.

A little wave of something not so nice runs through me; it has the shape and vaguely unpleasant smell of Van. He's going to be pissed by what happens, I know he is, but, well, he has himself to blame. I can't understand why he doesn't see it, why he can't understand that Giselle is just stringing him along, for the dresses, and probably for his share of the trainers money.

Love isn't just blind here; it's bound, gagged, and left in a black sack in the cellar.

Problem for another day – I have plenty of my own for now. And older guy comes to the stall and starts rifling through the Barbra Streisand section, a small select group of aficionados check out that box. He selects a pretty good quality copy of *The Way We Were* and I take his fiver, relieved that Barbra never sang 'High Flying Adored'.

"I'm not leaving, not leaving on a jet plane." Mike begins singing a new tune, but to a very old song. Today is going to be a long day and all I can do is suck it up.

*

It is a long day at the market, but *'this too will pass'* turns out to be true even for the fifteenth time you hear 'Fly Me to the Moon'.

Eventually, the day peters out, then rain begins to fall, and I close up. It's been a good day overall, and there's enough money to refill the little rubber cat I keep my spare cash in. Yes, slowly my kitty is growing again.

My day isn't quite over. I've arranged to meet up with Van, to talk about the trainers and the dresses. We've chosen the Royal Oak in Stowmarket because there's no way I'm traipsing all the way out to Felixstowe, which is now sort of alien territory with Giselle around.

Getting out of Bury is like trying to siphon rice pudding through a straw, and it's half six by the time I get to the pub, but by then I don't really care too much about the timing.

Inside, the Royal Oak instantly soothes me. It's one of those pubs which just oozes 'sit down, have a beer, have a chat, stand up four hours later'. There are a few faces I recognise, and though I get a couple of smiles, and bloody John Taylor the resident joker pretends to fall off his stool and break his arm, it's not too bad.

Van is waiting for me; that's a first. He's alone, which is a relief. I'd psyched myself up for Giselle. When he sees me, Van jumps up, and I think for a moment he's going to make a run for it. But no, he beats me to the bar and with raised eyebrows asks what I want. Another first.

We're soon settled again, settled in the way that two people balancing on a chair with a single leg on a high wire above the Niagara Falls settle. He's looking at me as though I'm about to pull a gun, Han Solo like, and shoot him under the table. It's crossed my mind, obviously, but instead, I draw the lethal weapon of small talk.

"Giselle not with you?"

He blinks like I've swatted a fly in front of him, bites his lower lip for a second, then says, "No, she… She's gone to Colchester. She's got a sister out that way, not feeling well."

It's strange hearing Van talk about something like that, something vaguely domestic and touching on human relationships, and it throws me.

"Oh?" I can't bring myself to say I'm sorry, not that I wish anyone ill, but Giselle's absence is like six of your best friends turning up to a surprise party.

"Yeah, she's been there a few days. She's good like that, better than you know, Charlie." His voice still has that croaky, fifteen too many cigars last night throatiness, but maybe there is a touch of softness somewhere in there.

"Right," I say, not going to be drawn there, so I get to business. "Look, I've sorted the dresses, with Claire."

Van smiles, I mean really smiles, a smile crossed with shock. He looks like a man who just won the lottery.

"You have? That's fucking amazing, great, how, I thought, you know, Claire." In his excitement he gulps down the last of his beer and says, "This calls for a drink. Giselle, she'll—" I don't hear quite what Giselle will do, but whatever it is has got Van excited. He's got it bad. I hope that it's the real thing for him. I mean, I can't forgive him, but maybe I understand.

He brings me a second beer, a great stout, and we cheers. I gaze at him for a moment through the dark glass, and perhaps I see.

"So, when, when can we get them, the dresses? Then you and I, Charlie, we can, we'll sell the trainers and, and Giselle and I can set up—"

He's all over the place. I've never known him like this, and I put my hand up. I've already been bitten once by Van; I'm not going to let it happen again.

"Hold on, hold on. Look, Van. How do we do this, I mean? If I just hand the dresses over, how do I know you'll come good, on the trainers?"

His face sags and his jaw drops. Either he's a great actor or his imagination is no better than a snail asleep on its holiday.

"Charlie, no, I wouldn't rip you off."

"You already have," I say.

"Well no, not really. Giselle, she said it right, I mean, you weren't there, those trainers could have gone anywheres."

Which, of course, is true in its own small way, but I can't be bothered to argue about promises, agreements and past favours from me to Van. Raking over those coals will just get the fire going again.

"Whatever. But how do I know it will be okay this time?"

He looks at me, right into my eyes.

"Look, Charlie. This thing with Giselle, I mean, you know my luck with women. If you can help me get the dresses, then, what with those and my share from the trainers, we'll be set, you know, like in a flat, together."

I can see how much it means to him, and for a moment a pang of regret at my questioning him runs through me. But it's done, and I can't change it now.

"Okay, okay. Well, good luck to you." I can't bring myself to say 'both'; Giselle makes her own luck.

I sigh, take another pull on the beer.

"Look, Claire is sorting out the dresses," I lie. "She reckons they'll be ready in about a week." Given I've already got them, I can be pretty sure about the timing.

"Tell Giselle, let's say…" I look in the air, as if thinking. "The, what, it's the 3rd now, say the 11th?"

Van looks deflated; he has the face of a kid who just realised Christmas is still a month away, and he wants his new bike *now*.

"That long?" he says.

"Yeah, I think so. It's been hard enough to get Claire to agree at all."

He nods his head back and forth, weighing the truth on some very dodgy scales.

"Okay." He sighs. "I'll call Giselle and let her know."

After that we sort of lapse into a quiet silence. I'm pleased this bit is done, but pissed that it has even got this far. After a moment or two I pick up my glass, still two thirds full, and wander across to John.

"Well, thanks, Van, I've got to go see a friend now."

He nods and looks like he wants to say something, then nods again slowly, raises his glass in a vague farewell and turns to his phone.

*

Two days after meeting Van, I'm at the Bury St Edmunds Market. The only good things about it are that the rain isn't snow, and nobody is slinging.

Here, last week, most of the stallholders had been wearing slings when I arrived. Today, today that's old news and we can do little more than jump around with our hands in our pockets and consider what evil this penance should allow.

It's ten o'clock and I've got to make a phone call. I've got to make a phone call because I've received a phone call. Mine was from Rob.

Rob is not happy. His loan inspectors are in, and they are asking questions. His answers along the lines of 'Charlie's a good guy and this will come right' apparently don't meet Bank policy. They want more concrete suggestions, detailed proposals – timelines.

I'm more of an arm-waving sketch man, the details do appear eventually, the picture, and the kitchen, do get finished in the end, even if I'm never quite sure how.

So, I'm calling Marianne, in the vague hope first that she'll answer and second that she'll have more news than Lance at Totalled, Shitfaced and Bollocksed.

As I gaze out at the five good folk of Bury who have decided to come watch the rain run off the plastic sheets that make the roofs of our stalls, the phone rings out. Just as I get ready to click it off, a sleepy voice asks, "Ola, Buenos Dios." The words are strange, stranger more for being in a Suffolk accent.

"Hello. Is that, is that you, Marianne?"

"Oh, Charlie, hold on a second, I'm just…" She makes a sound a bit like a cat purring, and mutters, "Oh yes, just there, I think."

Then says more clearly: "Sorry about that, Charlie. I was just having some sun-tan lotion rubbed into those important little places I can't quite reach myself, and… well, some I could, but it's much more fun if someone else does it. How are you, Charlie? It's ages since we chatted."

There is a sudden squall of wind, the plastic roof of the stall flaps, and a wake-the-fuck-up of water splatters across my face.

"How am I?" Despite the cold, I can feel myself getting hot.

"Well, I'm freezing cold, up to my ears in debt, and stuck in some land-buying legal limbo which is costing me a fortune I wouldn't want to pay, even if I could afford it." The last bit is shouted.

"Oh, I'm sorry, Charlie. I know, it's so tiresome, isn't it? I had no idea it would drag on this long, or get so… complicated." I'm not sure, but it sounds to me like the last pause had a different flavour than her normal style, like she was distracted rather than distracting.

"Look. I can't get hold of Lance. He's never in the office

when I call. Just what the fuck is going on?"

There is a silence for a moment, and I know my anger is getting the better of me, but she needs to understand. Rob was talking of me having to sell the cottages if I can't get this clear.

"Lance?" Marianne ignores my outburst. "Let me see if I can… reach out to him." I could swear there is something of a double meaning in this. "What do you want him for?"

I shake my head, trying to rattle the meaning into place.

"I want out. I want to understand why, since Tilsley's didn't complete, we can't just call everything off, and I get my money back."

"But, Charlie, you know that. You signed to sell to me, and I still want to buy. If you cancel, then, well, Lance says I have to sue you, and we wouldn't want that. It was all in the contract."

I know. I should have used my own solicitor, but, but it was never supposed to get this complicated, unless… I take a guess.

"Can I just speak to Lance? Put him on."

There's a much longer and deeper silence. Then, "He's, he's just gone for a swim, with Terry, I think."

I don't know if she said that deliberately, but suspect she did, just to let me know how deep the rabbit hole goes.

"Now, don't worry, Charlie. It will sort itself out one way or the other, eventually. As long as Rob at The Bank doesn't get tiresome, you'll be fine. Now, I must work on my tan, and I'm sure you're busy. We'll catch up when I get back."

"When, when is that?" I ask, grasping at a straw as though it could give me some support.

"Oh, we're off for a couple of weeks. We'll be back around the 20th. Oh, and, Charlie?"

"Yes?"

"We're flying first class. No need for any subterfuge for us. Now, I must go. Bye."

The phone clicks off. Water runs down from a small hole in the roof into my collar. I let it run. It's the best thing that's going to happen to me today.

*

It's dark, my breath is frosting the air like cigar smoke in a cheap saloon, and my nerves are stretched as tight as a two-dollar dress on a three-dollar whore.

I just need to add the sound of a zither playing and I'd have the perfect movie set-up.

Part of me knows this is ridiculous, but another part, that part that maybe likes the theatrical, is enjoying it. Face it, I've had little else to be cheerful about in the last week.

The weather has run the full range from cold rain through to warm snow and back again. Rob has asked me for definite loan clearance plans and Eileen, even Eileen, is making louder noises about me looking for a… a proper job.

And right now, where am I?

Well, it's crossed my mind to book a plane ticket to anywhere, vanish for another eighteen months. But I won't; I know I won't. That was a different Charlie.

No. This Charlie is sitting in the dark outside a house

in Claydon, waiting for *the switch*. That's how it sounds in my head, with the italics.

This whole thing, meeting up with Van, agreeing the time and place for *the switch* like we're in some spy film, it's got the air of the ridiculous. Now I'm just waiting for Giselle.

I've a CD on in the van, Snow Patrol.

It takes me back to my first meeting with Gary. That had been an evening.

It was back when I did my Tina Turner act; those were the days when I had the legs for it. The little club by the Ipswich docks is long gone now, ripped up and turned into flats.

What a night, nine years ago, summer. Latitude was about to start, and Gary and Paul were down slumming it for a quick break. Of all the gin joints in all the towns, they had to walk into mine.

Yeah, I was right into 'Nutbush', where I would get the crowd going and joining in, and suddenly up jumps Gary on the stage with me. Takes a few seconds for me to clock it, but even if I didn't know the face then, I could tell the class. This wasn't some drunk wanting to take over the stage; this was a true professional.

So, we hit it together, and the crowd loves it, and—

There's a knock on my van window. I'm dragged back from better days and see the cold and pale face of Giselle looking at me. For a moment I just want to leave her there and join Gary and Paul back at the bar, but that was then, and this is now.

I get out and for a moment we stare at each other.

"No Van?" I ask. She looks at me, seeming a little confused in the dark, and points to an old Bedford van pulled up behind me.

"I meant as in" – I search for and find Van's real name – "Michael."

She shakes her head. "No, he's working late tonight. Just me – and you."

I nod. That's about par for the course; now I suppose I'll have to help shift the dresses.

"Whose place is this?" Giselle asks as we walk up the driveway. I pull out my phone to turn on the torch and find the key safe on the wall.

"Oh, a friend of mine. He owed me a favour, and we needed somewhere to store the dresses," I answer, looking first at Giselle then back at the key safe as I dial in the numbers.

She looks at me as though surprised I have a friend. I ignore her, slip my phone into my top pocket, should be safe there, and make for the door.

"How's your sister?" I ask, small talk being so much more acceptable than GBH.

"My sister?" She looks confused.

"Colchester, sister?" I repeat.

"Oh yeah, yeah, she's fine now." She gives a small smile, which flashes so quickly I'm not even sure I see it.

I get the door open, and we go in. The house has got that slightly damp and tired smell all houses get when they are empty. I reach for the light switch and thankfully it comes on. Dave had said the electricity was still connected, but I hadn't been sure.

"It's a bit of a dump, isn't it?" Giselle comments. "Where are the dresses, they all right?"

I sigh.

"They're fine, the bedroom, up the stairs. We laid them out there, keep them off the floor."

If either of us think it's a bit weird going up to a bedroom in a stranger's house, we don't say anything. Giselle is focused on the dresses, and me, I just want to get it over with.

"First on the right," I say. She's pushed past me and is already at the top. The single light bulb on the landing giving just enough brightness.

I catch up with her as she clicks on the bedroom light.

The dresses are there, as promised, laid out on the double bed, some on top of each other. They've been there two weeks now, with regular swapping around, to give them all, I hope, enough exposure.

Giselle looks at them, smiles again, then turns to me. It's now or never.

"Okay, I know how many there are, fifty—"

"Fifty-eight," I say.

"Eight." She nods. "Looks like we have a deal, then," she continues, "only—"

"Only?" I ask, alarm bells tinkling slightly.

"Only, well, look."

I wait.

"You're a clever guy, Charlie, I can see that."

I say nothing.

"And, well, you can see I, I, I'm always full of ideas."

I give a nod-shrug, not committing to anything.

"So. I think, you and I, we could do a better deal than we have."

Is she going to back out? I feel a small itch on my neck, but don't scratch.

"What do you mean?" I ask.

"Give me a hand with these, will you?" Giselle picks up a stack of the dresses, holding them close to her to carry as many as she can. I don't move.

"What do you mean?" I repeat, my voice sort of echoes a bit in the room.

"Well," she says, "I mean, Van, he's, well, you know what he's like, he's a bit… clingy." She's holding the dresses and clearly expecting me to take a bundle, but I want to hear this out.

"Clingy?"

"Needy, overall, just a bit too much, but—"

"But?" Everything seems to be going quickly now, but also very, very slowly.

"Look, let's get these down to my van, then maybe we could talk about your trainers."

I pick a bundle of the dresses up, holding them low; they are bulky rather than heavy.

We go down the stairs and out to the van; it will only take us a second trip and we'll be done. We're soon back up. Giselle scoops up most of them, and I pick up the few remaining ones.

"So," I say. "What next? Some code you send to Van to let him know the deal is done?" I hope she can see I'm joking but I sense she doesn't know irony from ironing.

"Well, I could tell him, yes, or—"

"Or?" Part of me wants to hear this, part of me does not.

"Or, well, I know where the trainers are. You and I..." She looks at me.

"You and I, what?" I want to make sure I understand.

"We could go into business ourselves, no real need to include... Michael, is there?" She smiles at me, and again I think of a snake.

"You and me? Cut out Van, is that what you mean?" Okay, I'm laying it on a bit thick, but I want to be certain.

"Of course, for Christ's sake, do you really think I want to be with that loser?"

There's more fire in her eyes now, and she starts down the stairs. "Bring that lot, will you? Let's get out of here." Then she softens. "Sorry, Charlie, I'm just a bit on edge. What do you think?"

I say nothing. We go downstairs and put the last of the clothes in her van without saying a word.

"Well, you and me, Charlie? We could make a good team, I think." Giselle makes one final attempt. I shake my head.

"I don't think Eileen, my wife, would be in favour, thanks all the same."

"She wouldn't have to know."

"Oh, I don't think that would work." The idea leaves me cold.

"Well, it was worth a try. No doubt Michael will want to stick to his deal, though I can always try to talk him out of it. I can be very persuasive." She's in the van now, looking down at me.

I nod. I'm sure she can be.

"Last chance," she says. Her hand flicks at the line below her neck distractedly.

"Oh, I think we're past that," I say.

"Your loss," she says, switching the engine on, and pulling away.

I sigh. Part of me hadn't wanted it to end like that.

I turn back to the house, need to lock up. I feel an itch in my head. First, though, a shower and I'll dump my clothes here; don't know what I might have picked up moving those dresses. That bed certainly had been infested. Poor Dave told me it took a week for *his* bites to go down.

I go indoors.

Van's waiting for me. He's come out of the other bedroom and down the stairs. He looks like someone ripped his world apart.

I grimace and look at him. I want to do more, but think it probably best I don't get too close until I change my clothes.

"I'm sorry, mate," I say, and I mean it. He gives me a sad sort of nod.

"I guess, I guess I knew really," he says.

"Still," I say. "We live and learn, onwards and upwards, one door shuts another opens."

"Charlie."

"Yes?"

"Shut the fuck up. You got time for a beer?"

"Sure, in a minute," I say. "I need a quick shower and change."

He looks at me, confused.

"Why?"

"I'll explain in the pub. You go wait in the van." I toss him the keys.

He makes his way downstairs, and I search out the bathroom and my clean clothes.

*

Two hours later, and we're in the Royal Oak. I can see that Van is going to be spending the night at our house, and that we're both going to have to get a taxi back to collect my van and his car in the morning. I don't want to get a ticket, which reminds me of next Monday, and the speeding case, and I still don't know exactly what I'm going to say. Today's Wednesday, I've got time.

"Cheers, mate." Van interrupts my slight drift off. His head wobbles a bit as he says it and I guess he can see at least two of me.

He's not as down as I might have expected. When I explained 'Operation Itchy and Scratchy' to him, he brightened up a lot.

"Genius, Charlie, pure genius. It makes me itch just thinking about it, the look on her face when she finds out."

"Oh, she'll spot the problem pretty soon, I reckon." I laugh and then have to wait for a second or two for that to reach down into his brain.

"You know, Charlie?" He leans forwards and for a horror-struck moment I think he is going to tell me he loves me, in a blokey sort of way, of course, but, thankfully, no.

"I. I would never have actually screwed you over, I was just doing it to, to help, you know, to get, Giselle."

I nod. I sort of get it, but it still pisses me off.

"Anyway," I say, "next we need to find a buyer. You're sure these are the right match?"

"Right match!" He laughs. "Good one, Charlie."

"No, I—"

Van's still chuckling, and while talking sense with him is never easy, trying right now has all the likelihood of succeeding as Giselle does of getting home not covered in bed-bug bites.

"You, you always come good in the end, Charlie. I should have knowed it." Van pats my arm, trying to catch my attention. It is a few seconds before he realises that I'm looking at him; when he does, it's obvious he's forgotten what he was going to say.

I'm quiet for a moment. Sure, the trainers are going to help, for a while. But I'm getting a little old for the whole 'and with one bound he is free' stuff, something Eileen has mentioned.

I don't blame her. I get it; leaping from one stepping stone to the next, and never knowing which one is actually a mine, it gets tiring.

"Van," I say, and my tone catches his attention.

"Would, do they have, like, any jobs going down at the docks?"

I don't want to say those words, but no matter how they feel, Eileen and I can't keep going like this.

This sobers even him; he pales and looks shocked.

"What? What, for you?"

"No, Eileen. What do you think? Of course for me."

"But, Charlie, you're, you're a free spirit. You're the man who got dumped in the middle of nowhere in America, and still got back. You don't want to be in an office, do you?"

I swear there are almost tears in his eyes; he's more upset than I am.

"That was a long time ago, Van, and now, I'm older, and wiser, and" – I wave vaguely – "have responsibilities."

"No, no, Charlie." He's drunk serious now. He shakes his hand at me and doing so wobbles the table, which slops some beer from a glass on the table next to us. The old guy sitting there looks at us and takes it in with one glance.

I raise my eyes in apology, and he shrugs back, no big deal. Van, though, he's gone.

"Do you know?" he says, looking at the man. "Who this is?"

The man shakes his head. I can see he's hovering between wanting to avoid a scene and interest. The Royal Oak can be pretty boring.

"This," says Van, "is Charlie Mellon and he once played guitar for Snow Patrol!" He says it like it's an amazing discovery.

I mean he's right, but it was only the once. As soon as Paul recovered, I was back to being a roadie.

"Annnd," Van hasn't finished yet, "he was so good that they had to dump him before they got in some big fight about who was to be bass player." The man looks both confused, impressed and disbelieving – pretty good going for a single look.

"Tell him, go on, tell him," Van urges.

And okay, I've had a few as well, and I love an audience, still.

"He's almost got it right." I pat Van on the shoulder.

"Thing was, well, it was either me or Pablo, Paul, who was going to keep playing. Him with years of experience and knowing all the songs, and me with my natural charisma and style." Which is sort of how it went, but they never actually were going to take me on.

"So. One night, they upped and left me, couldn't face the argument."

Which again has half a grain of what actually happened, and half a grain of clouded memory. It's what it had seemed like, a bunch of cash, expired visa, and dumped in, well, Baltimore, which can feel like the middle of nowhere.

The memories came back. It had been good. I drifted south, then over the border at Mexico. Going out down there, they hardly check anything, and eventually back to Claire, and, well, a different sort of music.

The old guy looks impressed, not very, but a little.

Then we all get to chatting, and some of the regulars join us, and, yes, it all gets a bit blurry until I wake up next day at home.

*

"Six thousand. That's brilliant, Charlie. You've got to be pleased with that – we should celebrate."

Eileen is being cheerful and enthusiastic, but even

though she isn't saying, we both know the truth: it's not enough, not nearly enough.

Sure, we, Van and me, it didn't take us long to find a buyer for the trainers, only… Well, first off, by the time the second half arrived, it was nearly nine months since I bought the first lot.

Nine months is long enough for a night of passion to turn into an 'isn't he cute?' and way too long in trainer fashion terms.

Add to that, I now had a partner in Van. He bought the trainers while I was still not even on-site. So, of course, I had to share the sales money with him; that took a big chunk out as well.

"What did Rob say?"

Eileen tries another tack, handing me a glass of red wine she's just poured.

"Well." She's picked up a good point. "He said that it buys me a little time on the bridging loan, but…"

Banks, that old thing about them lending you an umbrella when the sun shines and asking for it back when it rains. Rob, or his bosses, was proving the point. 'It's all a bit too erratic for them, Charlie. With you, it's always feast or famine, and well, they'd like a bit more consistency.'

"He… He reduced the overdraft, by four thousand," I explain. "Said The Bank wanted to see an overall reduction in my indebtedness, or some such bullshit."

So really, out of all that work, all that time, I've got two thousand pounds. I shake my head.

We are standing looking at each other, and the kitchen, the still incomplete kitchen. Looking out through the windows into the dark of the forest, I see our reflections. We both look pale and drained; it's how I feel.

"So, what does that mean, for, for us?" Eileen faces it with her strength as always; she rolls with the blows and looks forwards.

"Well." I shake my head. "I mean, I've got two thousand pound, net. That's enough to cover the bridging loan for a while, and the next VAT bill, so yeah, we survive another three months, but…"

"It's not the big payday you were hoping for?" She's good enough to make it a question rather than an accusation.

I know Eileen is as disappointed as me, but she won't kick me while I'm down.

"I'm sorry," I say, and I am, and more than that.

I feel drained. All that time trying to get the trainers, and the thing with Giselle, and all for nearly nothing really. I don't say 'What's the fucking point?' but maybe she sees it in my eyes.

"And?" This time the question is there.

To be fair, I told her, I started it.

"Yeah, I'm going to see Van's boss next week, end of the week. She, well, she seemed, excited, after we chatted."

Eileen smiles. I see a flush of something good running through her, though, maybe, perhaps her eyes glisten a little too.

"That's marvellous, Charlie. Of course they'd be excited to have you on board, what with your contacts and skills and…"

She's watching me, and lets her enthusiasm vanish into

a gulp on her blackcurrant juice and a turn to check that the veg are cooking okay on the gas ring.

I don't say anything. Those trainers, they were meant to give me the big payday – if not an outrageous fortune, at the very least enough to bat back the slings and arrows of life.

In the end, they've given me a breather, a reprieve, but that's all, and, well, it's just not fair on Eileen, on us.

I know. I've known for a while, at least since the last week, since the news. It's time for me to step up, grow up, and get ready to become a father.

And I can't do that if I can't provide properly. So, no more ducking and diving, no more deals, time for nine-to-five oblivion. For Eileen and the little grape that will become a Mellon.

Eileen can read me, not just like a book, but all the way down to the smallest letters on the bottom of the eyechart.

"Charlie, I think, we could still manage, even with—" She touches her stomach and smiles at me.

I shake my head.

"No, that's not right. It's not, not what you should have, not just to, to manage."

"But I don't want you to hate me, Charlie, to hate us."

Then, shit, it boils up from so far and so deep inside me that I can't believe it. What she is for me, what they will be for me.

The smile that comes to me pulls my face tighter and fills my body so completely that there's no space left for anything other than love. It tells her everything she needs to know.

But I tell her anyway.

"Eight hours a day at work gives me sixteen with you and... The Grape. Sixteen hours a day with you – that'll make me the best paid man in the world. Nine to five, hah, I won't even notice. You'll see."

And of course we hug. We stand there in the half-light of the one bulb in the kitchen ceiling, and I know it will be okay, not what I want, but okay.

And sometimes we just have to settle for... okay.

ELEVEN

You see, that's why I follow the Dao – inaction, simplicity and living with nature.

Now, I know that sometimes it doesn't seem like that's what I'm doing, but inside, inside I am. So today, the day after quite a night before, both in the kitchen and later... elsewhere, I am at peace with the world.

That doesn't mean I'm not working to make my personal world all it can be, just that I am also ready to accept whatever that is.

I'm a Daoist monk yeah, simple Daoist monk, hey, *you* try fitting that idea to the tune of 'Firestarter'.

So, this morning, and even now, two o'clock in the afternoon on a Saturday, I'm studying.

Eileen doesn't know I'm studying. We've not talked about the speeding ticket for a long while, and I've not told her about my research – we're trying to do *calm* this weekend.

The laws around speeding fines are complicated and confusing, and no matter how much I flit around the internet, none of the sites really seem to give me the answer I want. The answer I want, of course, is 'not guilty, leave my court and please accept this chunk of cash as an apology for ever having asked you here'.

I know, this is just the magistrates' court. Almost certainly my good friend and neighbour Mr Pulbright will be there to greet me. The Dao says something about that as well, about how the wheel of fate turns, only this bit of the turn is where it moves towards him.

Eileen is outside, getting the garden ready for winter, doing a little bit of weeding around my garlic beds, catching the best of the low afternoon sun.

I click the other page I've been looking at.

The little semi is in Barham, three bedrooms, a garage, which you might just fit a pram in, and a garden, which will be great for a cress crop, if we don't want more than one round of sandwiches.

The point is, the price, one hundred and ninety-nine thousand pounds. Our place here, it's got to be three hundred thousand plus, even with the kitchen as it is.

If I sell up, I can clear the mortgage, then I can buy that little box of Barham bland and have a bit of cash in the bank. The bridging loan will sort itself out over the next few months and we, the three of us, can begin our new lives.

Eileen comes bustling in, a little red-faced, but smiling.

"That doe came poking around whilst I weeded. I threw some shoots to it, and it ate them. It's getting really tame now."

"Sorry," I say. I push the lid of the laptop down and go over to her. This weekend is one where we are just us, where the outside world doesn't exist.

"Oh, that's alright, Charlie. You and 'switching off' are not exactly best bedfellows."

"No, I'm usually turned on with my best bedfellow," I say, reaching for her.

She skips back a step, laughing.

"Maybe, later, I need a shower after the gardening. Why don't you have a walk as well? Shouldn't you just be drawing in the spirit?"

There's a tiny joke in her voice, but she knows that that is exactly what I should be doing.

"You're right," I agree. "Why don't you have a bath? I'll take a walk before the sun vanishes entirely, and we can see what happens from there."

She gives this no more than a few seconds' thought, smiles and says, "Okay. No tea, then?"

"No, I'll go clear my head, feel the woods."

We kiss briefly and I go outside. The doe is still there; it looks at me, a sort of 'and just what are you doing in my garden?' look, then half scampers, half wanders off.

All things pass, nothing is permanent, holding on is what causes things to shoot from your hands. I know, I know. But that doesn't make it easy.

Enjoy the now, and the next couple of hours. Tomorrow, who knows what tomorrow and Pulbright will bring.

I push the thoughts aside and wander down through the garden to the bridlepath. A walk in the woods, that's what I need.

In a few moments I'm taking the track into the woods.

It's calm today, and already getting colder. The air and the light have the feel that things are closing down for the winter. The woods are full of their usual muted sounds, blue tits and goldfinches, a robin flits past me, and in the distance, I can hear a crow arguing with a squirrel.

I'll miss it, I know I will, but it won't miss me, and that's more important.

I reach the proper footpath, which will take me along and up to the road, and I take that. Up ahead, another figure is on the path, walking towards me. Shadowy in the dying light, it takes me a few seconds to pick him out. Flat cap, wellingtons, shooting jacket and, yes, a twelve bore, broken open, under his arm.

I know, even before he gets a few feet closer, it's Terry Deck. Just what I need.

He continues towards me, watching vaguely. I can tell that he's thinking because he's slowed down and almost tripped over himself – not really a multi-tasker, Terry.

"Well, Mr Mellon, and how are you today, out for a walk?"

"No pulling the wool over your eyes, Terry, is there?"

He ignores the sarcasm, and I can't say I blame him. I take another look; he's looking very fit and, well, tanned, I would guess.

"Not suffering with a broken arm then, Charlie?" He has his 'there, that got him' look on his face.

My turn to do the ignoring, then he continues.

"Of course, I'm sure there *is* a covenant about not running a business from the cottages; no doubt Mr Pulbright could look it up."

I was trying to walk away, but this pulls me back.

"Well, even if there is, it's a bit late. I'm not making those anymore." I don't really know why I've told him; I guess it's time to be facing up to some home truths, and this is just another one.

"Oh really?" he asks, but he doesn't look surprised. "That's a shame, always good to have a few side-lines, isn't it?" It's almost like he's reading my mind. He continues, "I mean, I don't imagine old records and Christmas trees have the cash rolling in."

"I do all right," I lie, and it must show, because although he was just beginning to walk away, now he turns.

"You know—"

Despite myself, I can't help but see what it is I know.

"What?"

"Should you ever want to sell up, you know, downsize from three cottages to something smaller, I mean, if, for instance, you ever find yourself with debts you're having trouble with."

He lets that hang in the air. Now he's really got my attention.

He nods vaguely. I notice again his tan and think back to my phone call with Marianne and *her* holiday. There is the sound of a penny dropping into a very large pile of cow-shit and splattering all over my life.

"What do you mean?" I ask, in a voice that hovers between threat and disbelief.

He puts his hands up with about as much conviction as a man in a striped shirt and carrying a bag marked 'swag' claiming his name is Chris Kringle.

"Oh nothing, but, if you did, well, I'm sure Mr Pulbright would make you a good offer for them."

He nods back down the track to where the light from the cottages has blurred the rising mist into something dismal and unpleasant, which makes me think of Pulbright again.

Deck continues, "I mean, even with the kitchen not finished, it's got to be worth something."

I really don't know what to say. Me, Charlie Mellon, lost for words. The last time that happened was when Eileen said she'd marry me.

"I—" But what can I say?

"Terry?" I recover slightly.

"Charlie?"

"Why don't you wander off and see if there are any birds for you to kill, or whatever other reason brought you out today."

He shrugs; this is just water off the back of the duck he probably plans to shoot.

"Okay, Charlie, that's fine. We, at least, are not going anywhere."

He walks off into the mist, and I turn and go in the opposite direction.

The light has almost faded now, and the mist has appeared in the way it does when you're not looking. I should have put my wax jacket on, but even if I had, I don't think I would have felt any warmer.

*

Despite my encounter with Terry, the rest of the evening flowed nicely, and I managed to get to sleep okay. Eileen can do that for me, push everything into perspective. Yes, I'll miss this place, but a place is just a place, and Eileen's the world.

Talking of whom, she's shouting at me now, as I enjoy the last of a lie-in. Magistrates' court this afternoon, and I'm not really as prepared as I should be. What I can do, though, is turn up and plead not guilty, then try to find someone who can help me get off. I mean prove I'm not guilty. See, even when I'm not prepared, I have a plan B.

Eileen calls again, slight sharpness in her voice.

You might remember what I said about today, how it was going to be 'unusual' – well, this is how it all started.

"Charlie." Volume and tone shifting to defcon three. "You're going to be late."

I'm out of the bed now, scratching vaguely and shaking my head.

"I've got plenty of time, my case isn't until 2pm."

Eileen walks in, dressed for work, but looking confused.

"That's not what the paper said." She's holding a brown envelope in her hand, black letters and a crown. I recognise it, in the way you might recognise the Four Horsemen of the Apocalypse galloping up the high street. It's the one from the JCSB.

"Holy shit-fuck." I say, which tells Eileen nothing in detail but communicates the general idea.

"What?"

"The calendar…" I mutter vaguely. Seeing just exactly

what happened, while praying it didn't.

"Yes," she replies. "Where I wrote 'court'?"

"Court as in magistrates' court," I say, with the sort of certainty Galileo had when telling the Catholic Church the position of the earth in the solar system.

"Court as in Crown Court, for your jury service." She says, shaking her head, but with fear dawning in her eyes. "Charlie, you didn't—"

I didn't. She's right I didn't.

The number of things I didn't can't be counted, but we can begin with not realising my jury service and speeding case court appearance are on the same day.

The world spins, and for a moment I feel I've fallen off a cliff into the crack of doom, and not in a good way. I jump up and start looking around for clothes suitable for jury service and magistrates' court.

Eileen recognises the panic in my face. Last time I looked like this, the bathroom ceiling was sitting on the living room floor, with the bath. Thankfully it had been empty at the time of the rapid descent.

"Charlie, how could you?" she asks, but it's too late for explanations, and anyway, she's the one who's just Jackson Pollocked my beautiful Mondrian of a day.

I'm busy stumbling into my trousers and hopping across to the wardrobe, hoping that there is a clean shirt and thinking, *Just where the fuck are my ties?*

Fifteen minutes and twenty-eight seconds is now officially the world record for getting dressed and down to my car in order to race to the Crown Court in Ipswich.

TWELVE

Racing to Ipswich Crown Court is not dissimilar to hurrying to Felixstowe docks for an auction, and about as easy to do. As I drive, in between shouting at the traffic, the world and Pan, the god of mischief, I try to read the letter from the JCSB.

There are some key points which are clear. First and foremost, in clear high letters, which really should be written in blood, are the warnings about trying to cancel my attendance for anything other than serious illness or a death in the family.

The traffic opens for a second and I scoot past a slow-moving tractor, pushing close to the speed limit before recognising the irony of getting a speeding ticket while rushing to court. An on-coming driver flashes his lights and presumably says something descriptive, but I don't catch the detail.

As I get more into Ipswich, any hope of moving

quickly vanishes in the stop-start grind of cars against humanity. All I can do is thump the steering wheel and recognise that in a thousand years' time, none of this will matter.

At last, I reach the centre of town, and the opportunity to use another large proportion of my bank account balance on a temporary home for the van. Of course, lots of other owners don't have a problem forking out a fortune to keep their vehicle comfortably stabled. So even finding a place in the car park is only possible by going up to levels usually frequented by yaks and yeti.

The lifts are either dead or being used as toilets by early morning drunks, so I give up pushing the call button and opt instead for rushing down the endless right-hand-cornered stairwell. Eventually, in a timespan measured if not in lifetimes, then at least the period Theseus spent looking for the Minotaur, I reach the bottom.

Against all reason and as a tribute to setting yourself goals even if you don't think you can succeed, I crash out onto the street at eight-fifty. Ten minutes to make the fifteen-minute dash to the county court.

I channel my inner rugby and basketball players and slip-slide, skid and twist my way past the crowds of commuters who, if they do nothing else, demonstrate how soul-sapping most nine-to-five jobs are.

All the time, as I run, there is a mantra coursing through me: *don't let me get selected.*

That, of course, would be the perfect result. I arrive, fresh, probably very fresh, at the court, and don't get selected to serve. Then, then, hanging around the court

I absorb all the legal knowledge I need, to get over the speeding ticket.

Worst case? What exactly is the worst case?

Well, that would be not turning up for jury service; right now, this late, that's contempt of court, fines and up to three months' imprisonment, so says the polite invite from the JCSB.

And if I don't go stand in front of Magistrate Pulbright? I don't get to plead my case and am found guilty in absence.

Which would mean, well, six points, a ban, and, and what follows doesn't bear thinking about. Of course, *he* wouldn't want me to suffer financial hardship, would he?

As I said, trapped between the dock and a barred place.

I run. Up the stone stairs, through the wooden doors, spin around looking for the sign to point me in the right direction. Then down the tiled corridor, ignoring the surprised looks and shouts of people with less to lose than I have.

I hit the double glass doors and stumble into a pinewood panelled room laid out with round tables and blue-cloth-covered chairs. Four tables, four chairs at each table, all but one of the chairs has a person sitting at it. It's not hard to guess who's missing.

As I crash through the doors with a gasp and sudden stumble to a halt, as though that's how I always arrive, a young lady with a clipboard looks up.

Glasses, dark hair, blue knee-length skirt, white blouse, and a look that comments about tardiness and just how close I am to contempt of court in a single glance. This must be Emily from my call, two months or so ago.

Sixteen faces turn to me, and I wave and smile, like I needed to attract attention.

"I'm Charlie Mellon," I say, and feel like adding, "and I'll be here all week," just to break the tension. I can already see it will take a bit more than that – a fan dance with me in a luminous green mankini, maybe.

"Good morning, Mr Mellon," says Emily. It's not often that 'good morning' sounds like a declaration of war, but she manages. Then she softens it. "Delighted you could make it; we were just about to get started. Please take a seat. You'll find some guidance notes to read at your leisure, or at least before you get called."

The room was quiet when I arrived but is even more silent now. I sense a certain relief that I'm the centre of attention. I walk through to my table, and, of course, have to work my way past the other three to get there.

My table has the sort of odd mix that the jury lottery should result in. A woman, probably aged around fifty, short grey hair, red blouse and white cardigan and slacks. She has the air of someone who manages people and commands situations, and is pleased with the opportunity to play a part in a different drama. Opposite where I sit and on this lady's left, a mousey man with eyes that flit back and forth has watched my entrance with amusement. He gives a tiny nod, and I immediately sense someone who would enjoy a lunchtime drink. But that's an error I've made before, which I think is called confirmation bias. The final occupant of our table is a younger woman, blonde, business suit somehow making me think of an American lawyer as they appear in TV shows.

We settle down, and Emily continues.

"So, as I was saying, it is important that you read your guidance notes, and that you do not discuss anything about any of the cases outside of the court." She pauses, looks around the room, then, as her gaze falls on me, she continues.

"Now, as you probably know, the jury consists of twelve people, and you will have noticed that we are, now, sixteen."

So, my heart leaps, and I hope she's going to call for volunteers to give up their place. See me win the Ipswich court reverse musical chairs finals. But no luck.

"So, we will draw lots for who is required for the first case today. I have been assured that this case will last no more than two days, so the expectation is that no one will need to request to be excused service because of the length of the case." Again, I feel the weight of her stare on me. I need a case lasting, let me think, no more than four hours, if I'm to get to the magistrates' court next door, so it's all pretty academic.

What I can do, though, is pray to the gods.

Four in sixteen are not going to be called; those are reasonable odds. I'm not a betting man. Actually, if I were a betting man, I would recognise that these are three to four odds on. Those are only marginally better than I can get on Ipswich Town not being promoted in the next five years.

Emily is still talking.

"On each of your tables are four plastic numbered discs." I look at my table.

The young American Lawyer holds up a disc, followed by Switched-on Business Lady and Mousey Man. I look on down, there is a disc in front of me, with the black numbers one and three on it, thirteen. Great, they've left me disc number thirteen. With that sort of omen, the best I can hope for is Ipswich being relegated.

Now there is a sense of tension in the room; maybe something about the competition has focused everyone. I wait, wondering what Emily will do. Is she going to get one of those ball things and draw them out with lights flashing?

But no. Instead, she peels a printout off her clipboard.

"In accordance with Court processes, this list was generated under the scrutiny of myself and the Chief Clerk. Only with the arrival of our last potential juror is it permissible for me to announce the result of the ballot."

It's already been drawn. Wu-wei, free will go take a running jump. I came in last; the other jurors have already selected their numbers. Predestined or what?

This little lesson in the futility of thinking I have any control over my life is comforting. It's more than that; it's reassuring, really – life happens, what will happen will happen. Go with the flow.

"The following jurors have been selected for today's trial. If your number is not called, you will be free to leave."

An idea strikes me.

"And, before I announce the ballot, I do need to make it clear, it is an offence to solicit another juror to change number with you."

Well, never mind about that, then.

"The numbers are sixteen." American Lawyer-lady smiles.

"Five, eleven, twelve, one, two, four, ten." Eight down. The odds of me not being called have got better, or are they still the same? I vaguely recall that is only the case if I can change my number now.

"Nine, fifteen." Mousey Man shrugs; yes, a man after my own heart.

"Thirteen." Thirteen. My die is cast.

Such is life. I'm not getting to plead not guilty; I am going to get a ban, no avoiding it. Well, any vague dreams of 'and with one bound he was free' see me leaping straight into the frying pan.

I shake my head. Then, I can't help it; I laugh slightly. What else can I do?

We, the lucky winners in the lottery, are directed out of the back of the waiting room. The four losers being told to wait around until they are released, then to return tomorrow for a second chance. Which is more than I'm getting.

Our trip is just a short one. Down a pale green carpeted corridor to another pine door, which has 'Jury Room' printed on the outside, and one of those sliding notice things.

Emily pushes the sign to 'OCCUPIED' as we go in, which, as I'm in the shit, seems appropriate. A police officer at the door holds it open to let us pass, then shuts it closed behind the last of us.

American Lawyer-lady walks to the end of a large table that fills most of the room, and drops into a chair, which makes her the centre of attention. I follow Mousey Man and Day Off Businesswoman and we take the next few chairs. The others fill up the remainder. Once we are all sat down, Emily takes control again.

We then use up twenty to thirty minutes of time being read something which is described as the rules but seems more like the riot act. Having checked our identification, in case someone sneaked in, we are reminded what we can and can't do. Most of the can't do stuff can land us in prison and fined. About the worst thing we can do, after 'disclosing the substance of our discussions', is fail to return to court after a break in the trial.

Next, a few questions about a Mr Adam Wyatt of Nacton Road, whom none of us know, which apparently improves our ability to judge him.

Then, at last, we are ready to start.

It's ten o'clock. I estimate in my head the likelihood of this trial being over in time for me to get to the magistrates' court next door, this afternoon. The number is so small that it might as well be the average credit balance I have kept on my bank account in the last three years.

What it adds up to is that my chances are nil, zip, nada, it ain't going to happen. I am destined to sit in limbo while the sand in the hour-class of reality buries the gravestone of my dreams.

This is okay. This is not about me *doing anything*; I'm not trying to change the universe, just understand its intentions.

The court room is… well, it's pretty much empty. This is clearly not the trial of the century; indeed, not even the trial of the week, I would estimate. 'Pretty empty' means two people at the front. They have the relaxed work-a-day attitude of those who clearly not just feel they belong here, but do.

A man of about fifty-five, dark hair, smart blue suit and an incongruous smile on his face, is sitting in what even I know is the dock. He looks about as concerned as a just-fed kitten in a basket full of roses. That level of smug already has me thinking he must be guilty, and even if he isn't, I sort of want to wipe that smile off his face.

That is not the way of the Dao, and I tell myself off.

A voice barks and, having just sat, I leap to my feet at the instruction: "All rise."

The judge walks in, and she immediately makes me think of Eileen. This is double bad news for Adam Wyatt; if the Honourable Judge Jennifer Sydnam gives even the slightest hint that Adam is guilty, he's going down.

Is this how trials work? Am I typical? I hope not.

There is a bit more chatter. To be honest, and I know it's wrong, I'm not paying all the attention I should. Seeing the judge, looking so like Eileen, just brought back to mind what's going on.

Then, then, when I hear what the charge is, it all gets a lot more interesting. We were given notebooks when we were in the jury room, and I reach for mine.

The prosecutor, who I now see is the slightly younger of the two 'been there done that in this courtroom' T-shirt wearers, doesn't seem to have a great deal to do.

Mr Adam Wyatt was doing such and such, on the

day in question. My ears prick up; suddenly this is more interesting than I had expected, way more interesting. What he was doing was in contravention of a specific statute, and the evidence is as presented.

Forget the details. What is really happening here is that the universe is playing games with me, and I can't help but join in, and start making notes.

The prosecutor calls a police officer to the stand, Constable Adrian Sewell. Adrian is a young crew-cut smart example of the Suffolk Constabulary, who looks competent and confident, though possibly slightly bored.

Maybe I would wonder about him, that being a perfectly reasonable bias against police officers, but I've already got my suspicions about Adam Wyatt, and it will take a little more than a policeman who looks 'young-professional and smart-arse' to shake my trust in the law.

They go over the evidence, and it all sounds pretty convincing, and I really can't see why this has even come to a jury.

Now the defence lawyer stands, and there is something about him that catches my attention.

As he rises, he takes some glasses from his top pocket. These have deep black frames and remind me a little of 1960s TVs. He rubs his chin as though thinking, and looks at the police officer.

"Now, could I just trouble you to… elucidate, a little." I get the sense that he's been to the Marianne Tilsley school of pregnant pauses.

He listens to the answer, and I jot it down. Then he nods, his tongue poking under his bottom lip and he adopts a tiny squint, as if he's trying to visualise what has been said.

"Right, good, so, and would you consider—" More questions. I'm not sure where this is going, but it sounds good, and I'm scribbling away.

Then he gets to a point, and asks a more detailed question. He asks it in the way you might ask about the weather. The answer, though, gets me scribbling. Mousey Man has doodled a hangman's noose in his book, and American Lawyer-lady hasn't even opened hers.

Now Mr Uppity Defence Lawyer, from Andin, Justonebound and Hesfree, repeats the answer partly as a question.

PC Adrian Sewell doesn't have a clue, but is getting worried; he repeats the answer.

Mr UDL smiles, pushes his glasses back up his nose, and turns to the judge.

"In that case, Your Honour, I ask for this case to be dismissed."

It was great. I mean, a pin dropping at that point would have been heard like the noise of two bulls flamenco dancing in a china shop.

Her Honour the judge looked at him. "And on what basis would that be?"

"Your Honour, I refer you to the court procedures Update Circular 2015-24a evidence to be accepted in cases relating to—" He then repeated the statute again, but I was busy writing 2014-25a in my notebook.

"I have taken the liberty, Your Honour, of printing out a copy, for you, and for my learned colleague; may I?"

At a nod from the judge, he hands an A4 sheet to her, then a second to the prosecutor.

A prosecutor who now looks not only like the bottom has dropped out of his world, but the world has dropped out of his bottom. The judge looks at the page and raises her eyebrows to the prosecutor. He's read the note twice, then reviewed the answers from PC Sewell, his finger marking a particular point against the Update Circular.

"Your Honour, I… I accept that this ruling is relevant to the Crown's case."

"And?" the judge asks. I can't tell if she's disappointed or if this is just another day at the office.

"In the circumstances, the Crown accepts that the evidence presented should be withdrawn."

"Very well. Then I must instruct the jury." Her Honour turns to us. "Ladies and gentlemen of the jury. What you have just heard is a fairly unusual situation. It is my task in these circumstances to tell you that the Crown has now withdrawn their key evidence. Given that decision, there is no evidence of the crime as stated, and I must instruct you to find the defendant Not Guilty. Will you please retire and return with that decision."

She bangs her gavel, and after a second, we stand, more confused than a bunch of lemmings finding that the law of gravity has been rescinded.

We wander back into the jury room, and I check my watch.

Twelve-thirty.

Twelve-fucking-thirty.

Twelve-amazing-thirty.

We go through our little charade, and fifteen minutes later I'm outside, looking to buy some glasses frames, with no lenses in.

So, amazingly, I'm a lucky little bugger baby, second-chancy bugger baby. I'm sitting outside the magistrates' court not only on time, but fifteen minutes early.

I have my little notebook, and I'm practising pushing my glasses up the bridge of my nose with a single finger, the middle one. I didn't stop for food, and not even a beer. I was too jazzed. So I'm shuffling back and forth a little as I sit here.

There's about six of us, most looking a little defeated, waiting to hear what their future holds; hey, it might be predestined, but you can never know what that destination is.

I check my watch, one-fifty, ten minutes or so.

"Well, Charlie Mellon, you actually turned up, then!"

I jump at the voice, thinking first that I am being called, but no, it's not official enough, and I know it. Terry Deck.

He's standing a fraction off, looking down at me, still with his tan, and still with that supercilious look he seems to make a habit of.

"Terry?" I am surprised, and a few questions come to mind.

"Can't believe it," he says. "I've lost a fiver. Thought you'd just plead by post and suck it up. Didn't see you as someone who fights against the inevitable."

I process that. Little cogs slipping into each other.

"I don't know whether to be flattered or confused that I'm part of your speculation, Terry. Why are you here?"

"Oh, Charlie, the things that you don't know could fill a very large book. But, in answer to your question, I have some papers for Mr Pulbright. Just because he's on the bench today, that doesn't mean his other business interests get neglected." He waves a brown folder at me. If he's making a point, it's a pretty blunt one.

"As for your attendance, or not, it's published in the *East Anglian*, you know – all court attendances are."

"Fame at last," I say.

"I thought you would have had enough of that, after the last few weeks."

He's not wrong there, but Terry's high up on my list of 'people I tend not to get drawn into conversations with', so I ignore that. Part of me would like to follow up on his little jibe, but another part thinks it likely I'd struggle too much with the urge to punch him, so I push it down.

"Think I'll go in." He points at the magistrates' court door. "Watch the show. Going to be a six-pointer, I think, Charlie, and I'm betting that's going to hurt."

As he says this, the door opens and a voice calls, "Mellon, Mr C Mellon."

I leap to my feet, stumble, and bump into Terry Deck.

"Christ, watch out," he shouts, his brown folder scattering papers.

"Oh, I'm sorry, Terry," I say, as I march towards the court door. My foot stamps out on an errant sheet, pinning it to the floor. I pick it up and hand it back to Terry. It has a nice imprint of my size ten shoe on it.

"Here you go. See you inside," I say, leaving him to refill his folder.

The little man who had called my name directs me in, and I stride to the box that is clearly meant for peasants and the accused.

The Magistrates' Court room is not significantly different from the Crown Court this morning, only it doesn't have a place for a jury, and there are three magistrates sitting at one side of the court. There are a few voyeurs in the public gallery, but it is a weird mix of very formal and 'we're just doing our jobs' impartiality.

I'm asked to confirm my name, and if I understand the charges, which I do. Then Pulbright interrupts the proceedings.

"It is necessary that I inform the court that I know the accused."

This doesn't seem to be a big surprise to the fat and bearded chief magistrate to Pulbright's left, nor the thinner grey-haired lady who takes up the third place.

Fat-and-Bearded looks at me.

"Mr Mellon, do you have any objection to Mr Pulbright remaining as part of this panel?"

I think for a moment; well, in for a pound.

"I'm sure Mr Pulbright is a fair and honourable man, Your Honour," I say. "I have no objection."

"Very well, good – thank you – that saves the court time and, Mr Mellon?"

"Yes?"

"We're not judges here; 'Sir' and 'Ma'am' are the customary way of addressing magistrates."

"Oh right, thanks, sir," I say.

From there to start of proceedings is just a few

minutes. Fat-and-Bearded, whose name I find out is Mr Simon Brewster, gets quickly to The Meat.

"Now, Mr Mellon, you are charged with what is usually a fixed-penalty offence, but you have presented yourself to the court. Are we to take it that you are seeking extenuating circumstances? Or have a plea for leniency?"

Pulbright is watching me with a hunger in his eyes that suggests he's feeling as lenient as Judge Jeffreys at the Bloody Assizes, and if you don't know him, Google 'the hanging judge'.

Simon Brewster has hit the nail on the head; he knows exactly why I came today. But it's not why I'm here now. Funny how things can change.

I mean, yes, I had wondered if a deer jumping into your driving seat might count as extenuating, but I had always reckoned that was going to be a hard win. Now, now I have a better idea.

"No, actually, sir." I push my glasses up the bridge of my nose and roll my tongue inside my cheeks. It feels appropriate.

"I came to ask for the case to be dropped."

There aren't really enough people in the room for the whole pin-dropping analogy. In fact, it's the opposite. A certain level of piqued interest rustles in under the door.

"Indeed?" Brewster looks at me. Pulbright smiles, the smile of a snake about to strike. "On what grounds?"

"Can I ask…" I don't quite ignore his question, but deflect it slightly.

"What was the make of the radar gun used on the night in question?"

Pulbright snorts as though suppressing a laugh. As I ask the question, I open my notebook from this morning.

"Mr Clerk? Can you oblige?" Simon Brewster asks a small man sitting at a desk in front of them. His voice sounds a little tired, as though we are about to go through a pointless charade.

"Mr Mellon," he says, as the clerk shuffles the papers, "I trust you are not going to question the service history of this radar gun. That, I have to warn you, is a path that many have tried to wander down, but no one ever returns."

I put my hands up, palms out.

"No, no, I'm sure it was working exactly within its" – I lean forwards, read the notes I made this morning – "operating parameters."

The clerk hands the magistrate what I guess is the police report sheet. He looks at it, confused. The clerk points to one corner of the sheet. I know the answer; Eileen read it to me when I called her.

"Ah, yes, it was an LD 5700, from Polygon Systems. I can even give you the serial number and link to the calibration records if you wish."

I nod, push my glasses back up my nose and roll my tongue under my lip.

Inside, I'm dancing, I'm jigging up and down, I'm laughing. But outside I'm as cool as any local green vegetable you can name.

"Your— sir, a second question, exactly where did the offence occur?"

Pulbright raises his eyes. "Oh do we really have to go through this charade?" He looks at the charge sheet.

"As you know, the A11, just south of Cretingham. Your point, Mr Mellon? We don't have time to waste."

I ignore his annoyance; in fact, I'm enjoying it.

"That's a nice part of the county, isn't it?" I say. "Very wooded, lots of deer around there."

"Yes." Even Brewster is getting testy now. "But please, if you have something you wish to raise, then do it."

I look at my notes again, my finger running down the page looking for, and finding, what I want. Court procedures Update Circular 2015-24a.

"Sir, can I refer you to…" Oh I'm loving this. It's real fun. I should have been a lawyer in a different life. "Court procedure update two oh one five, twenty-four a?" Just as well American Lawyer-lady had corrected my writing.

Pulbright raises his head as though he's just sat on something sharp.

"That procedure update states that the…" Again I look at what Mr UDL said this morning in *his* speeding case. "The LD 5700 and other Lidar-based radar speed determination systems cannot be relied upon in situations with 'significant arboreal density', which, I submit, means lots of trees."

Someone in the back of the court laughs, and I swear I hear a thigh being slapped, but I can't turn around just then.

The two other magistrates are looking at each other. Pulbright has gone red and then purple; I've never seen him looking so good.

"Mr… Mr Clerk, do you have that update?" Brewster asks, but the clerk is already shuffling a big green ring binder with CPU on the spine. Me, I don't care; I've already seen this play out this morning.

I know exactly what's going to happen.

The universe, the universe had set me on this course, made sure that I could hear that first case, and still have time to present my defence. Yeah, go universe.

The clerk, Brewster, Pulbright and the nice grey-haired lady are chatting. The door behind me closes and I resist the desire to bow and raise my hands in triumph.

Simon Brewster looks at me; his hand rubs across his brow.

"Well, Mr Mellon, you seem remarkably au fait" – I have never been called au fait anything before – "with this aspect of the law. It would appear that we must dismiss your case."

I'm a lucky bastard, switched-on lucky bastard, and I'm out of the court before you can say 'what the fuck just happened?'

As I step into the foyer, dancing to the music in my head, I hear slow handclapping.

"Very good, Charlie. You might have dodged that bullet, but I think you are still deep in the shit."

I look up, focus.

Terry Tilsley and his pet ape are standing in front of me.

THIRTEEN

You see, I mean, this is what I need right now, to keep things in perspective.

Because why?

Because while not getting six points on my driving licence definitely goes in the 'good things' column, it's not like it actually solved any of my problems. In the great snakes and ladders board of life, I'm still at the bottom, still facing having to move and, well okay, let's face it, become a more reliable, consistent, and conforming citizen. God help me.

So, in that sense only, in the sense that it is important that I face up to the real world, it is a great thing that Terry and his ape are here.

"Charlie," he says, and I have to admit his smile seems genuine. "That was fun. It was good to see that pompous twat Pulbright get put in his place. How is it that you know him?"

Terry must have been in there. I recall the thigh slap and stifled laughter. He's still thrown me, though, and I'm not sure how to react.

I glance over his shoulder, wondering if I can duck past him and make a break for the door, but somehow that feels overly dramatic. Tilsley seems to recognise my uncertainty.

"Look, Charlie, all I want to do is have a chat about our situation, and actually more about *your* situation."

I remember the blood-splattered business card, and wonder if I'm going to get an offer I can't refuse.

"I had hoped you'd give me a call, not let that Lance Tyler slimeball keep running interference," he continues.

That's a bit annoying really, as though I'm somehow at fault. It pisses me off a bit, and I've still got some of the testosterone from my court appearance bubbling away inside me.

"Well, what did you expect, what with the blood, not very... welcoming, was it?"

He looks at me, his eyes close slightly and his face twists into thought.

"Blood?" He turns to the ape.

"Cedric." *Cedric?* Who has a heavy called Cedric? "When we dropped that card off with Charlie, was that when you hammered your thumb, putting the kids' pictures up?"

Cedric now tries to imitate Terry in the thinking department, but his face goes slightly pale with the effort.

"Yeah, yeah, I think it was."

Tilsley turns to me.

"What? Did you think it was like, what, the Ipswich builder's version of a horse head in the bed?"

I don't know what to say, and Terry laughs. I mean he really laughs, lets it go, and I like him for that. Never trust anyone who laughs only with their lips; all in, that's what I want to see.

"Look, Charlie, honest, I think, think we might be able to help each other. Can we chat?"

I remember the last time a Tilsley invited me for a chat, and that ended up with me owing the bank sixty thousand pounds. Still, maybe I'm on a roll.

"How about a drink?" I say. "I feel like celebrating."

Tilsley nods.

"Well, I'm not usually a lunchtime drinker, but hey, it's nearly 4pm, and anyway, I want to know how you knew about that radar gun thing."

"Okay," I say, and we make for the doors.

On the way to the Cricketers, I explain about the diary mess up, and the gift from the universe, of the case that could get me off. Terry shakes his head and laughs again.

"Remind me not to play poker with you, Charlie," he says, "you looked like you knew all that stuff off pat."

We enter the pub, not too busy, and we find a table to sit at.

"Look," he says. "Cards on the table. I've been asking around about you, especially after that bloody Give Me a Break thing. Classic, classic." Cedric has brought three pints over and we 'cheers'.

"Actually." Now he gives a light chuckle. "I heard one story, that, look… did you play with Snow Patrol?"

He really must have been digging, but then he surprises me even more.

"And what was the stuff about Guatemala, stowing away aboard a banana boat?"

This time it's my turn to laugh.

"No, I didn't stow. I paid. It was the only way I could afford to get back to England. You should try it – it's very relaxing. To be honest, having just avoided getting in trouble with my US visa, I *would* have worked if I had to."

So that got us into the whole thing, meeting Snow Patrol down on the docks, the job, the gig and the fallout. Terry is a good listener, asks the right questions, laughs at the right moments, and doesn't try to top my story.

I am painfully aware that my car is again racking up a national-debt level of car-parking fees, but you know what? I don't care. That bloody ticket has been hanging over me like some sword of Damocles; now it is gone, I just want to relax.

So, I'm soon three pints in, and trying to remember train times from Ipswich to Stowmarket, and we still aren't at Terry's reason for suggesting we go for a drink.

As if sensing my thoughts, Tilsley straightens up slightly.

"Charlie, do you have any idea what my dear wife did for me in the business? Before she decided to fleece me."

I think back to what Rob told me, but my goldfish thoughts are swimming in a sea of bitter, so holding on to them isn't easy.

"The accounts?" I guess, though somehow, I can't imagine her keying invoices into a computer system.

"No, and you know what, I might have been better off if she had been doing that. No, she was, well, I guess you could say she was my chief plotter." He gives a slight laugh. "Which given how much plotting she's been doing recently is apt."

"A plotter?" I ask.

"Yeah. You see, I bet you think that building houses is all about bricks and mortar and bricklayers with hairy arses. Right?"

"Well, I've never really thought about it, but yes, actually building houses does strike me as, like, one of the key things you do," I reply, though I know I'm wrong.

"You see, Charlie, any bloody fool can build a house. The trick—" He sways slightly, and I can see that this is a speech he has made more than a few times. "The trick is having somewhere to build the bloody things. Getting the plots in the first place."

"And that was what Marianne did?"

"Yeah, and she was great at it. She could talk a punter with land to sell into giving us first option better than anyone I know. She—" He stops and looks me straight in the eyes. "She put the Martlesham site together."

I let that run through my head a bit.

"She, what, found the land for you?" I ask.

"Oh no, Charlie. On that site, she did much more." He nods, as though helping me shuffle the thoughts into place.

"She worked very closely with the architect in laying the site out, very closely and heavy on the laying, if you get my drift," he says.

"So, are you saying that she should have known there was something wrong with that plot, the one I'm buying, selling, buying?"

Terry doesn't say anything, just looks at me, eyebrows raised.

"No," I say.

"Yes," he replies, nodding slowly.

"She not only knew, she—" I stop, then it comes to me. "She owns that other bit of land, doesn't she?"

"Bingo," he says, shaking his head.

"But why? I don't get it," I admit.

"How much is a six-hundred-thousand-pound house with the kitchen on land you don't own worth, Charlie?"

I try to think that through.

"I'm guessing, not six hundred thousand pounds," I say.

"Yes, or more accurately, the tiny bit of land she owns is worth a chunk of money. We call it a ransom strip in the business."

It feels a bit like I'm joining dots, and something is coming into view.

"And she did this, deliberately?" I can't see her being quite so scheming.

"Oh, yes." He pauses, suddenly a little more serious. "Don't be fooled, Marianne is a very smart cookie." Now he sighs. "And, well, perhaps I did give her a lot of reasons to be motivated. I'm not entirely blameless, Charlie." He shrugs. "I like women, Charlie, bit of a weak spot."

Suddenly the dots form a much clearer picture, with me just where the middle is.

"Another?" I say, raising my glass.

"Think we're going to need it. Cedric, do the honours please, my man!"

"So," Terry asks as he raises his glass to me when Cedric brings them back. "What was that, with you and Pulbright?"

"What do you mean?" I ask, thinking for a minute, then, "Oh about him knowing me?"

"Yeah."

So, I tell him a little bit about my hate-hate relationship with Pulbright, and he's nodding a bit.

"Yeah, he's one of the, well, you know *The Godfather*?" he suddenly asks.

"Sure, who doesn't?"

"So, you see, well, me I'm what they call part of the Ipswich Mafia. No, not gangsters like that, but there's a group of us, Ricky the Torch, Saunders, Mike the Man. If you know, you know. We're just businessmen, but one way or the other, we've got our fingers in most of the pies."

I get it; I sort of know the names, not that I've ever moved in that arena before.

"Well," Terry continues, "Pulbright, he's like the real old money, sort of looks down on us, you know, but it's—" Now he stops.

"What?" I ask.

"Marianne, she likes that hunt set. I mean, she could run rings around most of them." Again he stops. This time it's as though he is trying to add up a long column of figures in his head.

"How, how did you actually get, you know, started with

Marianne? Sure, you're sort of dark and a little swarthy, but not exactly her type."

"No," I say. "We, I, never, honestly." I'm not sure if he's accusing me.

"Don't worry, Charlie. Marianne and me, those boats sailed in two different directions a long time ago." He's still thinking, teasing something out.

"Didn't you go on holiday with her recently?" I'm still not sure about Terry.

"Me? No, not for ages."

"She said 'Terry' was with her…"

It's like we both see the light at the same time.

"Deck? Terry Deck? She was on holiday with him."

Terry Tilsley slaps his head, then, like he's still building a picture, says, "So Marianne, she, let me guess, she rang you—" He stops. Then: "Oh no, that's… See, she is just… what an amazing woman." He shakes his head.

"Have…" He's still thinking things through. "Have you had an offer to buy your cottages?" It's like a light has come on in his head.

I think about Terry Deck and our little meeting in the woods.

"How the fuck did you know?" I ask, though, although I'm a little way behind, I'm getting there.

"You," he says, "are being played, Charlie, and, maybe, maybe some of that's my fault. You're… you're sort of like collateral damage."

The Cricketers sways a little.

The beer, what Terry is saying, the beer, the last few days, they all start to blur things a bit. Also, I have in the back of my mind that there is something I haven't done, and should have. I should have told Eileen the result of the case, even let her know where the hell I am.

I pat my jacket absently; my phone is in my top pocket. I should call her, but I don't want to lose where Terry is taking me.

He is watching me, nodding.

"Tell me, why wouldn't you accept my offer to cancel our contract to sell, twenty k's not much, I know, but Lance…" His head goes back and he blows out his cheeks. He points at me.

"You never knew. Lance never fucking told you, did he?"

This is all shooting forwards faster than me avoiding a suicidal deer.

FOURTEEN

The key thing is, like the big, big thing, with Chinese food, in the tubs, and the bags, is to not let them tip over. You've got to hold them upright, especially if you're in a flash motor like Tezzer's.

But. And here's the other good thing. Another good thing, there's loads and loads of good things, but Chinese food is *always* welcome, especially if, if, when you are a little late getting home and have been remiss in the communication department.

Not really remiss, as such, more incancancapacitated, which is when your phone leads you a merry dance and the battery dies, or died while you had it on mute.

Of course, they do get hot, if you have a lot of them. The takeaway tubs. But when you are not able to check in with the love of your life and ask what she'd like, you have to get a bit more than you might need, in case. Just in case.

Terry's gone, up off the road. I didn't want him to risk

his Roller on the drive. He would have come, good man, Terry, but I said no, because, well, it is maybe still a bit late to turn up, and though Eileen is always the perfect hostess, Charlie Mellon is no idiot.

Eileen would usually like some chance to set things right and, and you knows, know, it's just possible she's not ready for visitors at, at... Can't look at my watch because the plastic bag is cutting into my hand a little. It is probably half-eleven though, not midnight though, probably.

Keys are... jacket pocket. But the kitchen light is on, and, and that's a good thing. My wife is waiting for me. I love her; have I mentioned that?

Deep breath, big news, and I have to get it all straight, and big Chinese meal in celebration.

"Hi, honey, I'm home," I say as I push the door open with my shoulder, lifting the big, I mean like banquet size, Chinese meal bag in front of me, maybe a bit like a shield.

A memory blossoms in my mind, like black ink from a squid in the sea. A previous time I said that. That time, it did not go well.

This time, I'll play it better.

I look at Eileen. Her hair is tousled, she's a bit more pale than usual, and she's wearing her 'ready to sleep' clothes. This means something, but maybe I'm not reading the signals.

I hold up the bag of Chinese food. Inside, yes, only inside, there is a smear of bright vermillion, from the sweet and sour, I think. Luckily, sweet and sour is not her favourite. I think for a moment, but she does like Chinese, I'm sure.

"Surprise!" I say. It comes out with an extra L, or in fact, when I concentrate, I realise there shouldn't be *any* L, capital or otherwise, but I shrug that off.

Eileen sways slightly, or it might well be me. On balance most likely me, it was probably the effort of working out whether I should or should not include an— Where was I?

"Chinese!" I say again, though actually that was the first time out loud. Previously it was only in my head.

"Charlie," she says, and I melt. It's bad enough when she says Charlie like that when I'm sobe— sobe— when I've not been drinking, but after I have had, like, a *few*, *phew*, then I'm just putty in her hands.

"I was worried," she says. And of course she would have been, and I should have known, but, big things, big deals have been done this night.

"I'm sorry," I say, and I know my face shows how I feel. There is a smile there, that's the one I can't help but have when I'm with her, but I really am sorry, and she knows it.

She comes towards me. I reach for a hug, but somehow miss as she skilfully collects the bag from me. She sighs and shakes her head, mutters, "And when do the other four thousand nine hundred and ninety-eight get here?"

That sort of scoots over my head and, out of force of habit, I plug my phone into the socket next to the dishwasher. It chirps into life as Eileen digs out two plates, one big, one small.

"Good evening?" she asks. "I'm assuming from... I assume you've been celebrating?" Now I might be, I am, more than a little bit not sober, drunk, right, okay drunk.

But I know – what's the word about eggs? – reproach, that's it, reproach in her voice. Most probably—

My phone, suddenly gifted with electricity, bursts into life.

There's a banner on the front of the screen, then another, then another. I have missed a lot of calls.

"Sorry," I say again. "It's been a weird day. I always said, didn't I say, right at the start, that 'unusual' was going to be a good way to describe today?" Had I said that out loud? The first time, I mean.

Eileen spoons a little rice onto her plate and rescues some of the beef – beef, that's her favourite – from one of the tubs. She looks at me, glancing down at the bountiful array of white tubs now laid out in front of us. I reach for a spoon, but she beats me to it with a meaningful look, the meaning being something like 'I don't trust you not to drop food everywhere other than the plate'.

"So?" She tries again. "What are we celebrating?"

"Well," I say, leaning back in the chair and spooning a little rice onto the kitchen floor.

"First, we're not selling the cottages!" I say in triumph.

The effect is lost. She looks at me, confused. Maybe, maybe I... no, I hadn't told her.

"Well, of course not, what do you mean?"

"Details, details, BUT," I say, and she blinks a little at the capitals.

"BUT Terry Tilsley, he—"

"Terry Tilsley – what do you mean, Charlie? Who have you been with? I asked Van. He said you were with him."

That is confusing news. "But," she continues, "so did

Mike, Ivan and Pat. Your mates, good friends, but not entirely helpful."

"No," I say. "I was with Terry, definitely Terry, and…" Did he? He did; he really said it. A moment of clarity comes. The two of us in the Cricketers, good friends, him leaning forwards and looking into my eyes, both of us a bit bleary.

"Look," he'd said. "Marianne, and me, well, I've got to pay her out for the divorce. But she's dragged you into this, Charlie. Because it helped her with Pulbright, so…"

Yes, I've got it clear. I turn to Eileen.

"Terry, he's going to buy me out of the house contract!"

"I thought, thought you were stuck, had to sell to Marianne?"

"So did I. But, that, that Lance… I should never had had him as my solicitor and hers."

Eileen looks at me with her 'I'm sure I said that' look, but doesn't push it.

"And Terry reckons he can either pay money to Marianne, in the settletsettllement." Tough word to say sometimes, settlement.

"Or buy me out, and have a little less for her!"

"But Terry Tilsley, can you trust him, really?"

That gives me a pause, but I reckon I can.

"I think so, yes, I'm sure."

I lean forwards, pull out the cheque he gave me.

"Look." The cheque is nicely folded and has only a tiny amount of sweet and sour on it.

Eileen looks at it.

"Charlie!"

"Yes, fifty thousand pounds. He said it will be worth twenty-five thousand pounds just to see Marianne's face when she finds out."

Fifty thousand pounds, fifty thousand reasons why I don't have to get a job, fifty thousand cushion in the bank. Goodbye overdraft; hello wheeling-dealing pounds.

I'm a lucky bastard, shifty lucky bastard.

As long as Terry doesn't cancel the cheque when he wakes up in the morning. He wouldn't, I'm sure. Surely he wouldn't change his mind?

My phone rings.

I lean over and look at the screen. It says 'TerrrryTi'.

Shit.

I click the phone and scoop it up.

"Charlie." I hear Terry's voice, louder than I expect – no speaker on, so I guess he must be shouting.

"Did you tell Eileen, Charlie?" He's a little bit slurred, but I can interpret, probably because I'm in the same state.

"Yes I did," I say.

"Was she happy, Charlie?" It's a stupid question really, so I nod.

"Charlie?" He says, "I've been thinking."

Shit, shit.

"You know what I do Charlie?"

"Erm, wheel and deal, I reckon, Terry."

He laughs.

"Yes, fair enough, but, you know, how I started."

"Building houses?" I hazard a guess. Eileen is looking at me, confused.

"That's right!" He quietens down. "And," he continues,

"I was thinking. I mean. Look, Charlie, I don't want to be rude, but that kitchen of yours."

"Yes?"

"Well, I've seen rustic, Charlie, but yours is—" The phone breaks up for a second, then comes back.

"So, yeah. I'm going to have to rip out that kitchen in Martlesham, to rework the plot. But—" Again the phone breaks up, to return moments later.

"So, I'll get it installed at yours, fully fitted, top-end gear, cupboards, counters, washing machine, fridge, the lot. What do you think?"

ACKNOWLEDGEMENTS

I would like to thank David Bell and Jill Taylor, my official beta readers, and Claudine Fiche, for her running commentary. Thanks too to my editor, Hannah McCall, who (amongst other skills) could deduce where I had planned to put my commas, even when I'd put them somewhere else. Also, I must acknowledge my wife, Glyn, who never complains when I am sweating over a hot keyboard rather than helping around the house.

ABOUT THE AUTHOR

After successful careers as a bank manager and scientific analysis company owner, Ian Siragher retired to pursue creative ventures. Now, he spends his days writing, running, and crafting ceramics. Based in Cambridge, he shares his home with an understanding wife, a flock of goldfinches, and the odd squirrel.